DATE DUE

AUG 1 5 2015 RF	
SEP 2 1 2015	
DEC 3 0 2016	

BRODART, CO.   Cat. No. 23-221

CLATTERING HOOFS

Center Point
Large Print

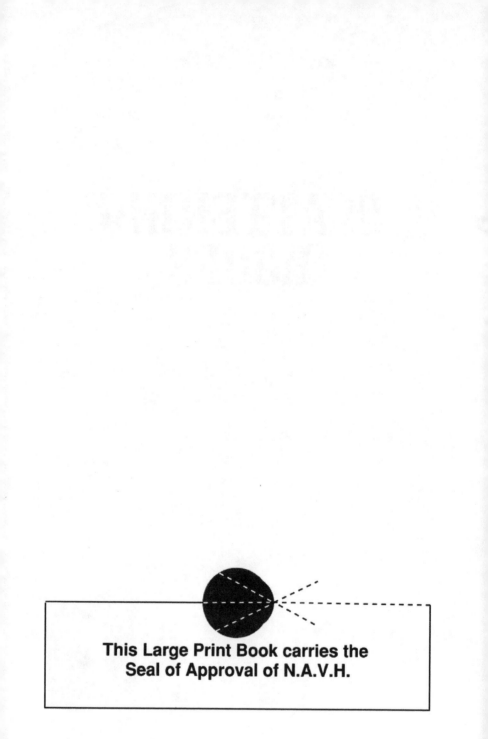

**This Large Print Book carries the
Seal of Approval of N.A.V.H.**

CLATTERING HOOFS

William MacLeod Raine

CENTER POINT LARGE PRINT
THORNDIKE, MAINE

This Center Point Large Print edition
is published in the year 2015 by arrangement with
Golden West Literary Agency.

First US Edition: Houghton Mifflin
First UK Edition: Hodder & Stoughton

The text of this Large Print edition is unabridged.
In other aspects, this book may vary
from the original edition.
Printed in the United States of America
on permanent paper.
Set in 16-point Times New Roman type.

ISBN: 978-1-62899-563-3 (hardcover)
ISBN: 978-1-62899-568-8 (paperback)

Library of Congress Cataloging-in-Publication Data

Raine, William MacLeod, 1871–1954.
  Clattering hoofs / William MacLeod Raine. — Center Point Large Print
edition.
    pages cm
  ISBN 978-1-62899-563-3 (hardcover : alk. paper)
  ISBN 978-1-62899-568-8 (pbk. : alk. paper)
  1. Large type books. I. Title.
PS3535.A385C57 2015
813′.52—dc23
                                                          2015007853

Contents

CLATTERING HOOFS

1 A HOSTAGE FOR PABLO

Sandra sat at the table making out a list of groceries to be bought for the ranch. Later in the day she and her brother Nelson would drive over to the cross-road store and get them.

"The sugar is plumb out too, Miss Sandra, an' in two-three days I'll be scrapin' the bottom of the flour barrel," Jim Budd said. "Beats all what a lot of eatin' is done on this here ranch."

"When the wagon goes tomorrow it can pick up the flour," Sandra decided. "We can bring the other supplies. You haven't forgotten anything?"

"I disremember havin' forgot a thing," Jim replied, and flashed a set of shining teeth in a face black as the ace of spades. The huge cook found it easy to grin at his young mistress. He thought her the loveliest human under heaven, and he adored her. In his warped life few people had been kind to him. At the Circle J R ranch he had found a home.

Into the kitchen burst a redheaded boy, eyes popping with excitement. "You know what, sis?" he cried. "They've just brought in Rod Spillman. He's been shot."

Sandra stared at her brother, the grocery list banished from her mind. After a moment of shocked silence she asked a question. "Who shot him?"

Nelson shook his head. "I dunno. They're taking him into the bunkhouse. Wouldn't let me see him. Told me to scat."

The girl ran out to the porch. She moved with the light grace of youth and perfect health. From the bunkhouse a man walked toward the stable. Sandra intercepted him.

"Buck, is it true about Rod?" she asked.

The cowpuncher stopped. "Yes'm. They sure enough got him."

"You mean he's . . . dead?"

"That's right. We found him near the mouth of French Gulch."

"Who did it?"

"Rustlers. We dunno who for certain. They run off a bunch of our beef stuff. Looks like Rod must of bumped into them while they were making the gather."

John Ranger stepped from his office to the porch. He carried a rifle in his hand. "Hustle up the mounts, Buck," he ordered. "We want to get started."

"You are taking out after the men who killed Rod?" his daughter asked after she had joined him.

"Yes. The boys are notifying the neighbors. We're meeting at Blunt's."

"Buck says you don't know who did it."

"We think it was Scarface and his gang. They were seen last night in the valley."

"You'll be careful, Father."

Ranger was a large hard-muscled man who

looked able to take care of himself. "Don't worry about me," he said. "Those scoundrels aren't fighting. They are running."

"Is there anything I can do, Father?"

"Not a thing, honey. It's a bad business. They must have shot Rod so he couldn't tell who they were."

Five minutes later the owner of the J R and three of his men cantered down the road, leaving a cloud of dust in their wake.

Though still under nineteen, Sandra had managed the house since the death of her mother two years before. Her slim body looked slight, but there was in her a toughness of fiber given by life on the frontier and the responsibilities it had thrust upon her. The death of Rod shocked her, yet she did not let it interfere with the work of the house. By the time she had changed the bed linen and swept the rooms Jim Budd had dinner ready.

"When do we start for the store?" Nelson asked her as he finished a second helping of rice pudding.

"As soon as you have hitched up Chance to the buggy," she told him. "I promised to stop and see Elvira on my way back."

"Good. Mebbe we'll hear at Blunt's whether they have caught the rustlers."

They took the short cut through the brush, following a trail just wide enough for the buggy. Shoots of mesquite and cactus slapped at the wheels. The girl had chosen this road to escape the clouds of yellow dust that travel on the main highway would stir up.

Chance was a short-coupled, round-bellied buckskin with no ambition to break records. He preferred to walk, but when Nelson tickled his flank with the whip he would reluctantly break into a slow trot.

At Bitter Wells they met a horseman, Miguel Torres, a middle-aged Mexican who owned a ranch in the vicinity. He had been their neighbor ever since they could remember, and Nelson pulled up to exchange news of the pursuit of the rustlers.

The road dipped to the flats, and for the next mile they moved along a jungle of cholla, prickly pear, and occasional huisaches. Cattle runs cut through here and there. Once they crossed a dry wash of burning sand over which heat shimmered.

Four Mexicans rode out of the brush and drew up on the road in front of them, evidently to discuss the direction they wanted to follow. They wore the tight trousers, sombreros, and short decorated vests of vaqueros in their native land. One of them caught sight of the buggy and raised a shout.

Sandra did not know the men, but at first she was not at all alarmed. She had been brought up in a land where there were many Mexicans, and she knew them for a gentle friendly race. These riders were armed with rifles. It occurred to her they might be a detachment looking for the rustlers.

They pounded toward the buggy at a gallop and dragged their mounts to a halt.

"Oho!" one of them cried in Spanish. "We have flushed a plump little quail in the desert."

Both Sandra and her brother were frightened. These men were a villainous-looking lot, and their mocking laughter was not reassuring.

"What do you want?" Nelson demanded. "John Ranger is our father. Please get out of the road and let us go on."

"So you are children of the great John Ranger," a bearded ruffian said. "That is good. Pablo will like that. He will keep you for hostages."

It came to Sandra that he meant Pablo Lopez, the notorious bandit whose name was a terror to the border. He lived in Sonora, but several times his band had swept into Arizona to burn and pillage ranches and to drive cattle across the line.

"If you will let us go my father will pay you anything you ask," Sandra promised.

"Si, señorita, he will pay, but we will not let you go."

Nelson let out a cry for help. Fear choked up in his throat. Pablo Lopez was a villain without conscience, and it was a pleasure to him to kill gringos. He recruited his band from the riff-raff of the border, and he preyed on his own race too.

"Come, little quail," the bearded ruffian jeered, still in Spanish. "Come to the loving arms of Pedro."

He reached forward, and his hands closed around the waist of the girl. Nelson struck at him with the whip. Another outlaw brought the barrel of a forty-five down on the boy's head. Though Sandra struggled, she was dragged across the wheel of the buggy. Her fingers clawed at the dirty brown face of her captor.

"Que diablo!" he cried, pinioning her wrists with the fingers of one hand. "This is no quail, but a hawk. Be still, chiquita, or Pedro will slap that pretty face."

She screamed, with no real hope that any friend might hear. Miles of desert lay between her and any who might come to the rescue.

Sandra was held close to the thick body of the bearded outlaw, face toward him. Vainly she tried to wriggle out of his encircling arm, then with unexpected suddenness stopped fighting. Over the man's shoulder she had seen a horseman at the top of the rise from which the buggy had just descended.

For an instant the newcomer sat there, silhouetted against the horizon, a lean long-bodied fellow with a rifle in his hands. His horse jumped to a gallop, and he charged down the slope. Sandra had no time to guess who he was or why he was coming. She was too absorbed to breathe. It was afterward that she likened that headlong rush to the flight of an avenging angel.

2 A Tough Hombre Trapped

Out of a gash in the hills two men rode warily to the edge of the mesa and searched with their eyes the torn valley below. Seen from above, its floor was as wrinkled as a crumpled sheet of brown wrapping paper. The surface was scarred by lomas, washes, and arroyos running down from the bench back of it.

A brazen sun beat down on baked terrain sown with cactus and greasewood. In this harsh desiccated region the struggle to live was continuous. Vegetation was tough, with clutching claws. Reptiles carried their defensive poison. The animals that at rare moments flitted through the brush were fierce and furtive.

But no more savage than the men whose gaze squinted up and down the basin at their feet. The skin of the cholla was less tough than theirs. When cornered they could strike with the swift deadliness of the sidewinder. Across their saddles rifles lay ready for instant use. The butts of revolvers projected from the pockets attached to the shiny leather chaps they wore. Into every fold and wrinkle of their clothes the dust of long travel had filtered.

"Filled with absentees, looks like," one of them drawled.

His companion added dryly, "I hope."

The first speaker, a long dark man with a scar across his left cheek from ear to chin, lifted a hand in signal. Cattle dribbled out of the cut through which they had just come, pushed forward by a heavy-set squat man bringing up the drag. The animals moved wearily. It was plain they had been driven far and hard. The bawling of the beasts for water was almost incessant.

Anxiously the scarfaced man slanted a look at the westering sun. "Come dark we'll be in the clear—if night ever gets here. Once we reach the pass they'll never find us."

"Likely we had a long head start." The squat man's glance swept the valley slowly. In the tangled panorama below him he could see no sign of human life. "No use gettin' goosey, I reckon. Loan me a chaw, Sim."

Sim was the oldest of the three and the smallest, with a face as seamed as a dried-up winter apple. He drew a plug of tobacco from his hip pocket and threw it across to the other and watched the sharp teeth at work. "You don't have to eat the whole plug," he remonstrated. "If I was you, Chunk, I'd buy me two bits worth of chewing some time and see how my own tobacco tasted."

They turned the leaders into a draw that dropped down to the valley and presently the herd was in motion again. A cloud of fine dust, stirred by the tramping feet, rose into the air and marked their progress. The cattle smelled water and began to hurry. Scarface tried to check them, fearing a stampede, but the cattle pounded past him on a run. They tore down to the creek, which was dry except for half a dozen large pools, and crowded into the water. Those in the rear fought to get forward, while the leaders held stubbornly to the water until they had drunk their fill. The herders had their hands full moving the watered stock out of the way to make place for the thirsty steers.

They were getting the last of the cattle out of the bed of the creek when Chunk looked up and gave a shout of warning. Four armed men had just topped a knoll two hundred yards away and were coming up the valley toward them. The heavy-set man whirled his cowpony and jumped it to a gallop. Scarface took his dust not a dozen yards in the rear. It took Sim a moment to understand what was spurring his companions to flight. He was on the side of the herd nearest the approaching riders, and he lost more time circling the closely packed cattle.

A voice called to him to halt, but Sim had urgent business elsewhere. He stooped low in the saddle, his quirt flogging the buckskin he rode. The crack of a Winchester sounded, then another. The body of the little man sank lower. He clutched at the horn of the saddle. His head slid along the shoulder of his mount toward the ground. As he plunged downward, the fingers of his hand relaxed their grip on the horn.

Three of the pursuers went past him without stopping, the fourth pulled up and swung from the saddle. The body of the little man lay face down in the sand. He turned it over. Though the lips of the rustler were bloodless and his face grey, he was still alive. He recognized John Ranger, the man at his side.

"Who got you into this mess, Sim?" the cattleman asked.

The outlaw shook his head. His voice was low and faint. "You've killed me. Ain't that enough?" he murmured.

They were his last words. He shut his eyes. A moment later his body relaxed and seemed to sink into itself.

Rustlers and cowmen had disappeared over a rise, but to Ranger had come the sound of shots, four or five of them, the last one fainter as the distance increased. He remounted and rode after his friends. The reason why the thieves had fled without a fight was clear to him. They were not so much afraid of a battle as of having their identity discovered. A rustler caught in the act had either to get out of the country or be killed. Since these fellows were not ready to leave they had to avoid recognition.

Near the end of the valley Ranger pulled up, uncertain whether the riders had ridden to the right or the left of the great rock which rose like a giant flatiron to separate the two cañons running out of the flats to the hills beyond. A rifle boomed again, far above him to the left. The explosion told him which gulch to follow. Before he reached the scene of action he heard other shots.

The cañon opened into a small park hemmed in by a rock wall, at the foot of which was a boulder field. In one swift glance Ranger's eyes picked up his companions. Two of them were crouched behind cottonwoods and the third back of a fallen log, all watching the rock pile lying close to the cliff.

"Got a coon treed, Pete?" Ranger asked.

"Y'betcha. He's skulking in the rocks." The voice of the speaker was flat and venomous, his foxlike face sour and bitter. Peter McNulty was his name. He ran a small spread up by Double Fork. "Darned fool hasn't anything but a six-gun. We'll smoke him out soon."

The man behind another cottonwood had a suggestion. "Can't get at him from here, John. How about you riding up the gully and potting him from the bluff? He'll have to throw in his hand then."

"All right, Russ. The fellow you knocked off his horse down below has cashed in. He was old Sim Jones."

Russell Hart frowned. He was a quiet and responsible cattleman. It gave him no pleasure to know that he had killed a man, and particularly as inoffensive a man as Sim Jones. Wryly, by inference at least, he justified himself. "That's what bad company does for a man," he said. "If he hadn't thrown in with Scarface he would have gone straight enough. Sim was trifling, but there was no harm in him."

Ranger swung his horse round and guided it into a sunken channel that had been cut by floods from the ridge above to the park. At the summit he dismounted and tied the pony, then moved forward cautiously to the edge of the precipice. The trapped man was kneeling back of a boulder, revolver in hand. Other rocks protected his flanks.

The cattleman took careful aim and fired at the flat plane of one of the rocks. Startled at this attack from the air, the man below looked up. The face turned toward Ranger was bearded but young.

"Throw up your hands and walk out of there," ordered Ranger.

The man with the revolver knew he was beaten. His forty-five would not carry accurately to any of his foes. Ranger was quite safe on the bluff, but from where he stood he could send bullets tearing into the body of the other.

"What's all the shooting about?" demanded the stranger. "Why should you fellows jump me when I'm riding peaceably about my business?"

"Don't talk. Drop that gun and get going."

"All right. Call off yore wolves and I'll go out."

Ranger shouted to the others that the fellow in the rocks was surrendering. Hands up, the man walked out from the boulder field. Two rifles covered him as he moved forward. When he was eight or ten paces from the men carrying them he dropped his arms. He was a slim young fellow, coffee brown, in cowboy boots, levis, and well-worn Stetson. His blue-grey eyes were hard and frosty. In his motions there was a catlike litheness. The muscles of his legs and shoulders rippled like those of a panther.

"I'll listen to yore apologies," he drawled.

Pete McNulty tittered, his small eyes gloating. "He's gettin' fixed to saw off a whopper on us. I'll bet it's good."

"What is this—a sheriff's posse?" the prisoner snapped.

"If any questions are necessary, we'll ask them," Hart answered harshly. He did not like the job they had agreed to do, and he was hardening his heart to it.

The man in levis was a stranger to them, but that meant nothing. Drifters came and went. That Scarface had picked up some scalawag on the dodge to help on the raid was very likely.

"I think we finish this now." The man who had been behind the log shuffled around the end of it and joined the others. He moved ponderously, his short heavy legs supporting an enormous torso. Leathery folds hung loose on cheek and jaw. His

21

deepset, peering little eyes looked shortsighted. Altogether, he resembled a rhinoceros. Though his name was Hans Uhlmann, his intimates called him Rhino. "Nice and quick, then get started with the cattle."

The cornered man tightened his stomach muscles. He braced himself to meet what might be coming, deep-set eyes fierce as those of a trapped wolf. For he knew Uhlmann of old, and that knowledge set a passionate hatred churning in his heart. He owed the man a deep and lasting grudge, one he had waited long years to satisfy. That the ranchman did not recognize him was understand-able. The big man had seen him last a pink-cheeked boy of nineteen, smooth-faced, thin as a rail. Now he was bearded. His body had filled out. The bitter intervening years had etched harsh lines in his face, given it an edge of lean sternness. Even a casual observer could not have missed the steely hardness, the defiant challenge of one at war with the world.

"You've made a mistake," he said. "I'm not the man you want."

Uhlmann showed bad teeth in a cruel grin. "You're the man we'll hang. Right now. Do the job and get on our way."

The brutal ruthlessness of the man's words angered the captive. They had made up their minds. They were not going to pay any attention to his story.

"What am I supposed to have done?" he asked.

Hart spoke, ignoring the question. "I reckon Scarface met up with you recently. You're a stranger here."

"Right. My name is Cape Sloan. Never heard of this Scarface."

McNulty laughed, with heavy sarcasm. "He doesn't know Scarface—wasn't rustling stock with him. He was just riding along peaceable when we went gunning for him."

"Get your rope, Pete," Uhlmann said.

Sloan could read in the faces of McNulty and Uhlmann nothing that gave him hope. That of the former was full of cruel mirth. The German's was set as an iron mask. Toward Hart and Ranger he pointed his appeal.

"You haven't told me yet what my crime is," he said quietly.

"You know damned well what it is," McNulty broke out. "No sense in talking more. Let's get this business done."

"I started this morning from Redrock," the stranger said. "Last night I stayed at the road house there. That I can prove. All day I have traveled alone."

McNulty showed his yellow teeth in an ugly grin. "Didn't I tell you boys he would spread the mustard good?"

"I stopped at a Chink restaurant on Congress Street in Tucson for breakfast. A deputy sheriff

23

named Mosely sat opposite me at the table. We talked about the Apache Kid."

"So *you* say," jeered McNulty. "Why don't you claim you sat opposite John L. Sullivan?"

Sloan kept his eyes on Ranger and Hart. McNulty he ignored completely. "If you write to the road house at Redrock or to Mosely you'll find that what I say is true."

"We ain't gonna write anywhere. We're gonna string you to a tree."

"Don't push on the reins, Pete," Hart counseled quietly. "We'll listen to what this man has to say."

"Where do you hail from?" Ranger asked.

For a half a second Sloan hesitated. "From Holbrook, I drifted west from Vegas."

"Cowboy?"

"Yes."

"With what outfits have you ridden?"

"I've worked for the Bar B B near Holbrook and for the A T O in New Mexico."

"When did you work for the A T O?" Ranger inquired.

"Couple of years ago."

"The A T O has been out of business for four years," McNulty shouted jubilantly. "That cooks his goose."

The stranger knotted his brows in thought. "That's right. Time jumps away so fast you can't keep up with it. I drew my last pay check from Tidwell 'most five years ago."

"What does Tidwell look like?" Hart queried.

"He's a fat bald man with only one good eye—wears a patch over the other."

"What's that got to do with the question? This guy might be Tidwell's brother for all we care. Point is, he's a rustler caught stealing cows. That's enough." McNulty tossed the loop of the rope in his hand over the head of the suspect, who promptly released himself from it.

"What are you doing in this country?" Ranger demanded.

Again there was a little pause before the young man opened his lips to answer. Before he could speak McNulty slid in an answer. "Why, that's an easy one, John. He's stealing our stock."

"I asked him, not you, Pete," mentioned Ranger.

"Just seeing what's over the next hill," Sloan answered. "You know how punchers move around. Thought I'd pick up a job riding for some outfit."

Uhlmann took the rope from McNulty and shuffled a step or two closer to the victim. "What's the use of talk? We caught him stealing our stuff. No use wasting time."

The cowboy choked down the dread rising in him. "I tell you I'm the wrong man," he said evenly. "Let me prove it."

3   Pablo Lopez Takes a Hand

"Fellow, this case is closed," McNulty retorted. "You been tried and convicted. By facts. Like Rhino says, we caught you in the act."

Cape Sloan talked, for his life. But he didn't let his desperation sweep him away. His voice was quiet and steady.

"If I was driving off your stuff, where are the other fellows that were with me? They didn't come up this gulch."

"You say Scarface didn't come up here?" Ranger asked.

"Nobody passed me between here and the foot of the hill—neither this Scarface you are talking about nor anybody else."

Ranger put a question to Hart. "You saw Scarface take this turn at the Flatiron, didn't you?"

"Not exactly," Hart admitted. "Someone on a horse was moving up the gulch ahead of us. Naturally we thought it was one of the birds we wanted."

"It was, too," cut in McNulty. "It was this fellow."

"There must be some other trail they could have taken," Sloan protested. "They didn't come up here."

"There was the other fork," Ranger agreed.

"Looky here, boys," McNulty urged. "We got

the dead wood on this man. They weren't out of our sight hardly a minute—just when they dipped down into the bend before the Flatiron. Then we see him again, riding hell-for-leather up the cañon. Only by that time he ain't the one we want, by his way of it. Me, I don't believe in fairy tales. This vanishing stuff don't go with Pete."

"There must be tracks where they took the other fork," Sloan said.

"Might be," Hart nodded. "Though there was a lot of loose rubble on the ground there."

"I don't want to make a mistake about this," Ranger said. "We'll take a look."

"There's a cottonwood over there handy," Uhlmann grumbled. "No trees at the foot of the hill. We're wasting time."

John Ranger stood six feet two, a man in the prime of life. He wore a short thick beard, and the eyes above it were strong and steady. No man in the neighborhood was more respected.

"I can afford to waste a quarter of an hour to make sure I am not hanging an innocent man," he replied curtly, and turned his horse down the cañon.

At the fork Uhlmann guarded the prisoner while the others examined the ground for the tracks of horses. There were marks where hoofs had slipped an inch or two on the loose rubble, but since there had been no rain for weeks there was no way of telling how recent they were. The three men moved up the hill looking for tracks that might tell a more convincing story, but when they returned ten minutes later none of them was sure.

"All bunk what he claims," McNulty shouted to Uhlmann. "They didn't come this way."

"We don't know that," Hart differed. "Horses have been up this cañon, but we can't tell when."

"I say hang him right damn now," the foxfaced man voted. "Rustling is one disease you can't cure a fellow of except with a rope."

The blue-grey eyes of Sloan flamed hot with anger. "You're tough as bull neck rawhide when you're talking to an unarmed man with a gun in yore hand and two-three other men to back yore play," he said scornfully.

"You can't talk that way to me," blustered McNulty angrily.

"I am talking that way to you. I'm telling you that you're a yellow-bellied coyote, or you wouldn't want to hang an innocent man who can prove he wasn't in this raid if you give him time."

Before he could be stopped McNulty slammed the barrel of his rifle against the side of the stranger's head. Sloan swayed on his feet and would have fallen if Hart had not supported him.

"Proving what I've just said," he told McNulty hardily.

"Exactly that," Ranger agreed. "If you lay a hand to this man again, Pete, I'll wear you out with my quirt. We may have to hang him, but I'm not going to have him abused first."

"I reckon he's guilty," Hart said, after he had tied his bandanna around the bleeding head of their prisoner. "But I don't want to live regretting today all the rest of my life. I think we ought to go back to Blunt's place and let the other fellows have a say in this."

"You're shouting when you say we've got to hang him, Russ," Uhlmann replied roughly. "But what's the sense of taking him back to Blunt's? We're the fellows who caught him and we're the ones that ought to have the say-so. What more do you want? We caught him in the act."

"I wouldn't be riding on a raid without a rifle, would I?" Sloan asked.

"You threw it away to help your alibi," McNulty chipped in sourly.

"I've seen this guy before somewhere," the German scowled. "Wish I could remember where. Maybe with Scarface some time. He ain't so much a stranger as he claims he is."

"You can hold me till you find out whether my story is true," Sloan told them.

"No," Uhlmann growled. "What's the sense of being soft? Before we started we agreed to hang any of them we caught. They shot up Spillman, didn't they?"

"He'd likely bust out of any place we put him," McNulty grumbled. "Thing to do is to finish this while we've got him."

"Even though I'm innocent," their prisoner added.

"You're guilty as the devil," the German flung out bluntly. "All right. Let's go back to Blunt's. There are no trees there, but we can prop up a wagon tongue for him."

Near the sandy bed of the Creek they drew up beside the body of Sim Jones.

"I wish it hadn't been Sim I got," Hart said, looking down at the weak, rather kindly, face of the dead rustler. "He had no business running with Scarface. I reckon if I had worked hard enough I could have won him away from that crowd. We all treated him as if he was unimportant and kinda laughed at him. So when Scarface buttered him up it flattered him."

"Sim got what he asked for," Uhlmann spoke up coldly. "When he started running off other men's stock he might have known he had this coming. Anyhow, he didn't amount to a hill of beans. I'll say though"—he glanced across at the prisoner callously—"that I'm glad we caught another waddy to keep company with Sim and help him from feeling lonesome where he's gone."

They roped the body to the mount of McNulty back of the saddle and continued down the valley. Uhlmann kept guard over the captured cowboy while the others drove the recovered cattle.

Sloan's thoughts were somber. His reckless feet had carried him along dangerous trails and they had brought him at last to this. He would be lucky if he escaped from the plight in which he was.

Cowmen intent on setting an example to warn other rustlers did not usually take two or three days to investigate the story of a man caught on the spot.

While they were passing through a cut in the hills that jammed them close together he overheard a few words that passed between Ranger and Hart.

"He isn't much more than a boy," the former said. "Though he has the look of a man who has lived in hell."

"Nits make lice if you leave them be," Hart answered.

The pressure of the cattle brought Sloan knee to knee with Ranger for a few moments.

He said, stiffly: "I'm not asking mercy because I'm young, Mr. Ranger. For eight years I've been a grown man. I don't want pity but justice. I wasn't trying to steal yore cattle. I don't know any of the men who were. All I ask is decent fair play. Wire to Mosely at Tucson. Describe me. Ask if he didn't eat breakfast with me today. I'll pay for the message."

"There's no place within thirty miles from which to send a telegram."

"What's thirty miles when a life is at stake?"

"Nothing. I'll do my best for you, but the feeling is intense. There has been a lot of night raiding and we have lost many cattle. This time they killed a cowboy named Spillman who saw them making the gather. You can't blame the boys for being excited."

"How can I?" Sloan flung back bitterly. "If they are excited, it would be unreasonable for me to object to their hanging me even if I am innocent."

Ranger had no answer to that. It was not quite just, he reflected, to expect a man whose life was at stake to make allowances for those judging him.

From a hogback they looked down on an undulating brush country of greasewood, mesquite, and cactus. To reach it they passed through a grove of sahuaros struggling up the hill, their trunks pitted with holes made by woodpeckers.

Ranger's gaze rested on their captive, a worried frown on his face. Whatever else might be said about him, the fellow was a cool customer. He had a hard tough look, in his eyes a reckless, almost arrogant challenge, the defiance of one with plenty of fighting tallow. The cattleman half believed his story, but he had a feeling that Sloan was holding something back. It was not wander-lust that had sent him into this part of the country. He was no footloose puncher moved only by restlessness. A definite reason had brought him here. The man rode at loose ease in the saddle, but there was in him a banked explosive force that differentiated him from the average drifting cowboy.

Moving to the top of a loma, Sloan caught sight

of windmill blades flashing in the sun. McNulty made it a point to ride close to him.

"Blunt's," he explained, pointing to the windmill, his mean eyes exulting. "Its cross-bars will be better than a wagon tongue."

Sloan did not answer. He did not want to give him the satisfaction of a reply. Uhlmann, he noticed, did not appear to be guarding him closely. This was an invitation for him to attempt escape. He knew that if he tried it the German would shoot him down before he had covered forty yards. This was a hopeful sign. The fellow would not be tempting him to make a break for liberty if he was quite sure the conference at Blunt's would vote for an immediate hanging without waiting for his story to be verified or disproved.

The voice of Hart rang out. "Look!" he cried.

Out of an arroyo a rider appeared. He was flogging his mount with a quirt. They could see that he was swaying in the saddle. With one hand he clung to the horn.

"It's Bill Hays," McNulty announced. "What's the matter with him?"

The man headed straight for them. They could hear him shouting, but could not make out what he was saying. He skirted the edge of the herd and pulled up not a yard from Sloan. Uhlmann caught him as he slid from the saddle.

"Pablo Lopez' raiders," he gasped before sinking into unconsciousness.

There was a stain of blood on the front of his shirt still wet and soggy.

"By Moses, here they come!" McNulty shouted. "I'm lighting outa here."

"No," Ranger snapped. "They'll get you sure. We'll move back into the wash we just crossed. They may take the stock and not attack us."

McNulty was close to panic. His frightened eyes clung to the dozen riders charging toward them. Bullets whistled past him.

"They'll murder us," he yelped.

Uhlmann pushed into his hand a rifle and the reins of the horse he had been riding.

"Git a-holt of yoreself, fellow," he snarled. "This is a fight you're in." The German stooped and picked up Hays, then strode toward the wash.

McNulty reached there long before any of the others. He was in a panic of terror. In his haste he had dropped the rifle of the German and released his horse. Back of the two-foot bank he lay trembling. The reputation of Pablo Lopez was well-known. On raids across the line from Mexico his bandits killed gringos right and left.

Hart and Ranger stayed to protect Uhlmann by covering his retreat. Their Winchesters flung back an answer to the shots of the outlaws. All of them came safely to the bed of the dry stream.

Uhlmann put the wounded man in the sand and turned to McNulty. "Where's my rifle?" he demanded.

"I . . . slipped . . . and it dropped," the poor wretch quavered.

The German caught him by the coat collar and dragged him to his knees. His hard horny hand slapped the colorless face.

"Fight, damn you, or I'll put a bullet through your belly now," he said savagely.

The big man did not wait for an answer. He went lumbering back through the brush to get the rifle. Bullets whipped past him, but he paid no attention to them. The Mexicans were riding fast and could fire with no accuracy. A few seconds later he was back in the wash with his weapon.

"What's become of the rustler?" he asked.

"I saw him fork Bill Hays' horse," Hart said. "Thought he was bringing it here."

"He must either have lit out or got shot," Ranger guessed.

"Cut his stick? That's what he's done. Bill's bronc is faster than his." There was shrill complaint in the high voice of McNulty. "Left us here to be killed while he slips away. I knew we'd ought to have hanged him right away."

"We're not going to be killed." Ranger's voice was cool and resolute. "We're going to get a few of these murderous devils. They never could shoot straight."

The sound of Ranger's rifle echoed back and forth between the banks of the wash loud as the roar of a cannon. One of the Mexicans pitched headlong from his horse. Those behind him pulled up hurriedly and broke for cover to right and left.

"Good work, John," encouraged Hart. "Number one rubbed out. We'll be all right yet. They'll hear the firing at Blunt's and some of the boys will come moseying this way to help us." He caught a glimpse of a head peering above a hummock and blazed away at it.

4   SLOAN INTERRUPTS

The intervention of Lopez' raiders came to Cape Sloan as a chance for escape to be seized at once. A man hard and resolute, under other circumstances he would have stayed with the cattlemen to help stand off the attack of the bandits. But he saw no percentage in remaining, since if he survived the battle there would still be the likelihood of being hanged later.

He swung to the saddle from which the wounded man had fallen and made off at a right angle through the brush. His captors were too busy looking after their own safety to pay any attention to him. Though he put the horse to a gallop, he rode crouched, his body close to the back of his mount, in the hope of using the mesquite as a screen between him and the outlaws. It was a comfort to see Hays' rifle close at hand in the scabbard beside his leg.

Life on the frontier, lived recklessly, had made of Sloan a hard-bitten realist. If possible, he meant to make a clean getaway. First, he had to avoid being shot down by the raiders, and afterward to make a wide detour of the Blunt ranch in order not to be stopped by any of those hunting the Scarface depredators. In spite of his keen watchfulness against the immediate danger, he felt a sardonic amusement at the development of the situation. The foray of one band of rustlers had imperiled him; that of a much more malignant one had brought him rescue.

A stranger to the chaparral would have found difficulty in picking a way through the dense growth, but Sloan wound in and out without once pulling to a walk the cowpony he was astride. The yucca struck at his legs with points of steel. Strong spines of the cholla and the prickly pear seemed to be clutching for him. But he was so expert a brush rider that he could miss the needles by a hair's breadth without slackening his pace.

Back of him he heard the firing of the guns drumming defiance. They told him that the first charge had been broken and that for the time at least the battle had settled down to a siege. Later Lopez' men would probably get tired of that and try another attack in force unless a rescue party from the ranch interfered with them.

The noise of the explosions sounded fainter as the distance between him and the wash increased. He had been traveling back into a hill country, but after a time he pulled up to decide on a course. By now he must be well south of the Blunt place and could swing around it if he kept to the brush. There was no longer any danger of pursuit by the Mexicans. Whether they had seen him at all he did not know. If so, they had let him go and concentrated on the men in the wash. He guessed

that after finding that they could not rub out
Ranger's party without loss they might drive the
cattle away, not stopping to exterminate the
owners. Sloan had heard that though Lopez was
ruthless he liked to run as little risk as possible.

There was no longer any need of haste. The
young man moved down into the flats, holding
the buckskin to a walk. Technically he had become
a horse thief, but that did not seem important at
the moment. When he did not need the animal
any longer he could turn it loose and it would
return to the home ranch. The rifle he would keep,
at least until he had reached a place of safety.

The sun had slid down close to the jagged
horizon line. Inside of two hours darkness would
sift down over the land. After that he would be in
little danger. During the night he could get forty
miles away from here. His plan had been to stay,
for reasons he did not yet want to make public.
But until he had cleared up this matter of the
rustling that would be madness. Even before this
mischance, he had known that every hour he spent
here would be perilous.

He came to a road that cut through the mesquite,
not a main-traveled one. It was narrow, and in
places young brush had grown up in it. The wheel
tracks were faint. Upon it the wilderness brush
was encroaching. Greasewood and ocatillo reached
out across it and whipped at the flanks of his
horse.

As he came into the road he heard the creaking of wheels and at once drew back into the chaparral where he would not be seen. A buggy came around the bend, driven by a boy of about fourteen. There was a hole in the lad's straw hat and through it a tuft of red hair had pushed into the open. Beside him sat a girl several years older.

Cape Sloan had read of golden girls, but he had never before seen one that fitted the mental picture he had formed. This one had honey-colored hair twisted around her head in strands. Her eyes were deep sky blue, and her cheeks had a soft peach bloom. A slant of sunlight was pouring straight at her, as if a stage had been set to throw her young beauty into relief. She was laughing, and he glimpsed a double row of shiny ivory teeth. Though slenderly modeled, there was promise of strength in her straightbacked supple body.

The buggy dipped into a draw and after it had disappeared Sloan took the road again and followed. Before he had gone fifty yards he heard a jangle of voices, a whoop of jeering laughter, and a boyish treble raised in frightened protest. Trouble of some sort, he decided, and was sure of it when the scream of a girl reached him.

Swiftly he rode to the top of the rise and looked down. He saw four men surrounding the buggy. The girl was in the arms of one of them, flung across the saddle in front of him.

"We take you to Pablo, señorita," one of them

called to her. "Maybe he hold you for a nice fat ransom. Or maybe—"

He finished the sentence with a ribald laugh. There was cruel gloating in the sound of it. Sloan knew that these men were not of the kindly smiling Mexicans who made a picturesque background to this desert land. They were members of the band of Pablo Lopez, the dregs of the wild turbulent borderland.

Sloan touched his mount with the spur and charged down the slope. He knew it was a mad business, but gave that no thought. During the two or three seconds while the horse pounded down the slope his mind moved in swift stabbing flashes. The boy's head lay against the back of the seat. He had probably been pistol-whipped. That was a game two could play—if he ever got the chance.

One of the bandits turned, shouted a startled warning, and fired wildly at the man on the galloping horse. Another bullet whistled past the ears of Sloan. A third outlaw fired just as Sloan dragged his mount to a halt.

The rifle in Sloan's hands swung up and crashed down on the head of the man who had first seen him. The rider went out of the saddle as slack as a pole-axed bullock. A second raider spurred his pony against the cyclonic stranger. A knife flashed in the sun. The head and body of Sloan swerved, but too late to escape entirely. A red hot flame ripped through his shoulder. He drew back the Winchester and fired it from his hip.

An agonized expression distorted the face of the attacker and the knife dropped from his hand to the sand. Wide-stretched fingers caught at his stomach. The muscles of his back collapsed and he slid head first to the ground.

Cape Sloan lifted his voice in shout. "Come on, fellows. We've got 'em."

The remaining two bandits wanted no more of this. One flung a hurried shot at Sloan and dragged his horse around to escape. The other dropped the girl and raced down the road at the heels of his fellow.

Sloan swung from the saddle, grounded the reins, and stepped forward to see how badly the boy was hurt. Groggily the lad stared at him.

"He hit me with a gun," the boy explained, the world still swimming before his eyes.

The girl climbed into the buggy and put an arm around him. "Are you all right, Nels? I mean—are you much hurt, dear?"

Her brother felt his head gently. "Gee, I'll say I am."

Sloan examined the lump above the temple. It had been a fairly light tap. The skin was not broken and there was no blood. If there was no concussion Nelson had got off easily.

"He'll have a headache, but I don't think he is much hurt," Sloan decided.

Cape had kept an eye on both of the prostrate bandits. Now he examined their wounds. The one he had shot was dead. His companion showed signs of life. Sloan stripped both of them of their weapons.

"Where are the other men—the ones you called?" the girl asked.

"There are no others." Cape smiled. "Thought I'd encourage these scoundrels to light out before they had massacred me."

"I haven't seen you before, have I?" she said. "You don't live around here."

"My name is Cape Sloan." He added, "I'm a stranger in these parts."

The horse of one of the raiders was grazing close to the trace. No sign of the second one could be seen. The animal had probably run down the road after the departing outlaws.

Sloan unhitched the horse from the buggy and removed the harness. The girl's eyes followed him as he moved.

"My name is Alexandra Ranger," she said. "This is my brother Nelson. We live at the Circle J R ranch."

"If your father is John Ranger I think I've met him," Sloan answered, his eyes grim.

She looked down at the dead man and shuddered. "It's . . . dreadful, isn't it? Who can they be? What did they want?" Her voice was low and held a moving huskiness. It stirred in him a queer emotion he did not understand. Except for diversion women had not meant much in his young life. It had been many years since he had exchanged a smile with one.

"They belong to Pablo Lopez' gang. A mess of them are raiding this district today." He did not mention that he had last seen a dozen of them trying to kill her father. If there was bad news waiting for her she would learn it in time without his help. "We've got to get out of here *pronto*. I don't know how far away the rest of the gang are. Your brother can ride this horse. You'll have to take that one." He indicated the one the dead man had been riding.

"Yes," she replied, taking orders from him without comment. The color had washed out of her cheeks, but she gave no evidence of hysteria. "Can you help Nels up?"

He lifted the boy to the back of the buggy horse.

"You're all right, aren't you?" he asked. "Not lightheaded?"

"Sure, I'm all right. Where are we going?"

"I don't know yet. Just now into the brush." He turned to Alexandra. "You'll have to ride astride."

"Yes. Will you help me up, please? It's such a high horse."

He put a hand under one foot and lifted. She swung into the seat and tried to pull her skirts down, but a long stretch of slender shapely leg showed.

For anything that his wooden face registered

she might have been a wrinkled Indian squaw. His eyes apparently took no note of the small firm breasts or of the long curves of her gracious figure. His job was to save them and himself. He wasted no time on amenities. He whipped up his left arm and said curtly, "This way."

Though fear was still knocking at her heart, she was full of curiosity about him. The horse he was riding bore a brand. What was he doing with one of her father's mounts? Why had he stiffened at mention of her name? He was a man who unconsciously invited the eyes of women, not less because of his obvious indifference to them. There was strength in the bone conformation of his face and a sardonic recklessness in the expression. The motions of his body showed an easy grace, due to the poised co-ordination of mind and long flowing muscles. She had never seen one more sure of himself.

They cut into the chaparral, Sloan bringing up the rear. In silence they traveled for at least a mile before he halted the little procession.

"How far is the nearest ranch?" he inquired.

"About three miles, maybe," Nelson answered. "The Blunt place. Wouldn't you say about three miles, Sandra?"

Sandra thought that might be right.

The men hunting the rustlers were to rendezvous at Blunt's. Cape guessed that would be the safest point for which to strike.

45

"Let's go," he said.

"Wait," Sandra cried, pointing to a red stain on his shirt. "You're wounded. Where the knife cut you."

Sloan brushed aside her concern impatiently. "A scratch. It will wait."

5 A REUNION AT BLUNT'S

The battle of the wash had developed into a snipers' contest. This suited the defenders. Time was running in their favor. Lopez had to get the stock across the line before his retreat was cut off. Soon he would decide that was more important than killing two or three gringos. Moreover, there was always the chance that cowmen riding to the rendezvous at Blunt's would hear the firing and come to the rescue.

"All we have to do is sit tight and hold the fort," Ranger said. "I've been in a lot worse holes than this."

"What I'd like is to get a bead on old Lopez himself and watch him kick," growled Uhlmann.

"What I'd rather see is the whole caboodle of them high-tailin' it away from here," McNulty differed. Though he did not feel comfortable he had settled down and was behaving better.

The words were hardly out of his mouth before the attackers began to evacuate their positions. Those in the wash could see the dust of moving cattle. There were still occasional shots from the brush, but it was an easy guess that a few men were posted to hold them until the stock could be pushed a mile or two toward the line.

It was half an hour later before the cattlemen

dared leave their cover. Very cautiously they moved, fearing an ambuscade. But the raiders had cleared out.

There was no thought at present of attempting to recover the cattle. Bill Hays had to be got to a place where his wound could be properly dressed. Blunt's ranch was the nearest.

Ranger thought the wounded man could not get that far on horseback. "One of us could go get a buckboard," he suggested. "The rest of us could carry him out to the cow trail that runs up to Coyote Creek."

Uhlmann offered to ride to Blunt's.

"Keep away off to the north," Hart advised. "I figure Lopez is skedaddlin' for the line fast as he can push the cattle. But keep yore eyes skinned every foot of the way."

"Better take my horse," McNulty said. "He's fast."

The others waited for some minutes after Uhlmann had gone before starting with Hays. They half expected to hear the sound of shots and were relieved that none broke the stillness. By this time the German must be safely well on his way.

Two of them carried Hays, taking turns. The third walked forty yards in advance, his eyes searching the bushes, a rifle in his hands. Pablo might have left a couple of sharpshooters to pick them off when they were not expecting an ambush.

At Coyote Creek Hart and McNulty waited while Ranger went back to the wash to bring up the horses. He had not rejoined them more than a few minutes when they heard the sound of wheels and presently of voices.

Hart shouted a challenge and Uhlmann answered. Three armed men and the driver of the buckboard were with him. One of them was Joe Blunt. He drew Ranger aside.

"I don't want to frighten you, John," he said. "But just before I left the house I heard something that worries me. Miguel Torres met yore boy and girl in a buggy about two hours ago near Bitter Wells. They were headed toward our place, to see Elvira, likely. But they haven't got there, or hadn't when we left."

Ranger's heart died within him. Lopez would probably pass Bitter Wells on his way back to the border. Two years earlier he had been condemned to death for the murder of a settler's family and had broken prison a few days before the execution hour. Other charges were piled against him. If he met the young people neither fear nor pity would have any weight with him.

"Did you send anyone out to—to make inquiries?" the father asked.

"Soon as we heard Pablo was on the loose Torres gathered a posse and started back toward Bitter Wells. He's a good man, John, both game and smart. He'll do his best."

"Yes," Ranger agreed. But there was no confidence in his assent. Darkness was falling over the land, and there would be small chance of finding the raiders in the night. Even Torres, good trailer though he was, could not cut sign without light.

"Chances are Pablo's men haven't run into Sandra and Nels at all," Blunt continued.

Again Ranger said "Yes" without conviction. If they had not been stopped his children would have reached the Blunt ranch long ago. "I'll take Uhlmann and Hart and Sid Russell with me. We'll pass by the ranch to make sure the children haven't been heard from, and from there we'll strike south."

"They may have learned Lopez was raiding and turned back to yore ranch."

"I'll check on that."

Heavy-hearted, Ranger rode into the night. With any luck either his posse or that of Torres might strike the cattle drive before it reached the line. But there would be danger to Sandra and Nelson in a fight. Lopez was a merciless devil. Rather than give them up he might in sheer malice shoot them down. The best way would be to bargain with him, if that was possible.

They traveled fast. Ahead of them they could see the lights of the ranchhouse. They struck the main road, and after about a mile deflected from it to the private one running up to the white ranchhouse.

A sentry challenged them. Ranger's answer was

a sharp question. "Anything heard of the children yet?"

"Not yet, Mr. Ranger."

"Blunt will be back in half an hour. How many men have you here that you can spare me?"

"Lemme see. Tom Lundy could go. I can. And Buck Ferguson."

"Slap on yore saddles. We can't wait. Join us at Bitter Wells. Bring all the men you can."

"If Lopez is driving a herd we can beat him to the line."

To them there came a sound of a horse hoof striking a stone.

Ranger's body stiffened. He stared into the gathering darkness, shifting the rifle in his hands to be ready for instant action. "Who's there?" he demanded sharply.

The vague bulk of riders came out of the night.

"Halt where you are," Ranger ordered.

The high boyish voice of Nelson Ranger rang out. "That's my father." He slid from the back of his mount and ran forward.

John Ranger took the boy in his arms. "Your sister?" he cried.

"I'm all right," Sandra shouted. She was already out of the saddle and flying toward him.

One of her father's arms went around her shoulders. "Thank God!" he murmured shakily. To the boy he said a moment later: "You've been hurt."

"You bet." The youngster was half laughing, half crying. He was excited and a little hysterical. The dangerous adventure had shaken him, but he was proud of his wound, though only an inch of skin had been scalped from his head. "One of Pablo Lopez' men did that. We left him lying in the road."

A third rider had moved forward out of the shadows. Uhlmann shuffled toward him and gave a triumphant yelp. "By jimminy, it's the rustler. Don't move, fellow, or I'll pump a slug into you."

"I'm a statue of patience on a monument," Sloan jeered.

Sandra's relaxed muscles grew taut. She broke from her father's embrace. "Put that gun down," she ordered Uhlmann. "He saved us from Lopez. He's wounded."

The German's heavy jaw dropped, but his gaze clung to Sloan and his rifle still covered the young man. "He's a cow thief just the same."

Ranger strode swiftly after his daughter. "You hard of hearing, Hans?" he snapped. His hand closed on the barrel of the rifle and pushed it down.

Sloan swung out of the saddle hull heavily. The fingers of one hand held tightly to the horn to steady himself. His head felt strangely light, and the earth tilted up to meet the moonlit sky. For the first time in his life he felt as if he were going to faint.

But white teeth flashed in a smile defiant and derisive. "Thought I'd better drop in at the rendezvous," he said. "McNulty and the Dutchman can't have their hanging without a hangee."

6 A CHIP ON HIS SHOULDER

Ranger took first things first. "Let's get into the house and look at your wound," he said. "Can you walk?"

"Learned twenty-six years ago come Christmas," Sloan replied, a thin grin on his sardonic face.

He gave up the support of the saddle horn and moved forward jauntily. But his step faltered.

Sandra slipped an arm around his waist. "Lean on me," she told him.

Her father took the other side. "Don't walk. We'll carry you."

He would not have it that way. "Just a li'l' knife rip in the shoulder. Nothing to make a fuss about."

But he let them steady and help him to the steps, up them, and to the lounge in the parlor, where he promptly fainted from the loss of blood. Life in this rough brush country developed many accidents. John Ranger had doctored broken limbs, gunshot wounds, and knife gashes. Now he gave competent first aid to Sloan.

"Will he be all right?" Sandra asked him while he was washing his hands in the tin basin outside the house.

"Ought to be good as new in a few days," her father said. "A fine clean muscular specimen like he is builds blood fast." He dried his hands on a none too clean towel. "Now I'll listen to your story, honey."

Nelson had joined them. The two saw that the tale lost nothing in the telling. The stark fact stood out that Sloan had charged four desperadoes, killed one, slammed another unconscious, and driven the other two away.

"He's got sand in his craw," the cattleman admitted. "All the time Pete and Hans were wanting to hang him he was as cool as if they were talking about another fellow."

"Hang him!" Sandra cried aghast. "What for?"

"We trapped him up a cañon where we had driven Scarface. He claims he isn't one of the gang. I'm beginning to believe it. I hope he is telling the truth."

"Of course he is," his daughter cried in hot indignation. "He's wonderful, Father. He came down the hill like a tornado. It was all over in ten seconds. I was terribly frightened, but I needn't have been."

"He just banged one of 'em over the head and shot another through the belly quicker 'n scat. The others lit out like the heel flies were after them." The eyes of the boy were big with reminiscent excitement. "Gee! He could of licked a regiment."

"You aren't going to let anybody harm him, are you?" Sandra asked. "After what he did for us."

"No." John Ranger spoke with crisp decision.

"I'll have a talk with the boys. There won't be any trouble."

"He isn't a thief," Sandra announced loyally. "And if he was I wouldn't care."

The cattleman wished he was as sure Sloan was innocent. But innocent or guilty it was not going to make any difference with him.

Blunt and his party reached the ranch. Bill Hays was put to bed and his wound dressed. One of Ranger's riders started on the fifty-mile ride to bring a doctor. After supper John gathered the men around him at the corral.

He told the story of how this man Sloan had saved his children from the raiders. There was a long silence after he had finished.

Blunt spoke first. "He has guts. That's sure."

"But he's a cow thief just the same," McNulty added.

Ranger looked at him with contempt in his steady eyes. "I don't think it. We'll know in a couple of days whether his story is true. But right now I'm serving notice that whether it is or isn't nobody is going to harm this man."

Uhlmann protested sourly. "Now look here, John. We can't turn a cow thief loose because he's game. He would be a menace to the community. Take Scarface. They don't make them any gamer than he is, but by jiminy, if I get my gun sights on him he's going to die."

Ranger said, spacing his words deliberately:

"We're not talking about Scarface, but about a man who has just saved my children at great risk to himself, a man who had got away scot free and came back because he had to make sure that they would get home safe. I'm talking about the man lying wounded in that room."

"But if he's a rustler—" began Blunt unhappily.

"If he is a rustler we'll drive him out of the district. But that will be all." Ranger did not lift his voice, but there was an icy threat in his words. "Anybody who lifts a hand against him will have to settle with me."

Blunt shifted ground. "John is right, boys. I'd feel the same as he does if it had been my Elvira. Guilty or not guilty, we'll have to take a chance on this young fellow."

Uhlmann grumbled that he had cattle in the bunch taken by the rustlers. They were on their way to Mexico now. If he lost them, he'd be damned if he was going to let anybody be generous at his expense.

"When you know how many you have lost, make a bill and send it to me," Ranger told him scornfully. "I'll pay it unless it is shown that Sloan was not one of Scarface's men."

"Don't think I won't send it to you," Uhlmann retorted. "Get soft with cow thieves if you like. I won't."

Within twenty-four hours the truth of Sloan's story was confirmed. He had spent the night of the

57

raid at a roadhouse in Redrock. The following morning, while the raiders must have been chousing the stolen stock across the flats to the hills, he had eaten breakfast at a Chinese restaurant in Tucson, just off the old plaza. He had sat opposite the deputy sheriff Mosely while they ate their flapjacks and steak and had discussed the depredations of the Apache Kid a dozen years earlier.

Some days later Sloan was sitting on the porch of the Blunt house in the warm sunshine waiting for a wagon that was to take him to the Circle J R. Two men rode up the lane to the house and swung from their saddles. They were McNulty and Uhlmann. Blunt was shoeing a horse and they stopped for a minute to talk with him. While they were still talking, a wagon driven by Ranger rolled into the yard.

The owner of the Circle J R pulled up in front of the porch. The bed of the wagon was filled with hay to make the riding easier.

"Ready to go?" Ranger asked Sloan.

"Yes, sir. But there's no need of my bothering you. I'm doing all right here. In a couple of days I'll move on."

"You won't bother us. We all want you to make a long visit at the ranch. The children won't let me rest until I get you."

McNulty and Uhlmann clumped forward from the outdoor blacksmith shop with the awkward gait of men who wear tight high-heeled cowboy boots. Pete went up the porch steps to Sloan, an ingratiating smile on his face. He held out a hand.

"Put her there, pardner," he said. "Looks like the joke is on we'uns. You can't hardly blame us, of course. The story you pulled was the thinnest darned one I ever did hear. But, as the old sayin' is, all's well that ends well."

Sloan did not seem to see the hand. He looked coldly at McNulty. When he spoke his voice was icy, without a trace of passion. "What I said about you the other day still goes. I wouldn't want to live in the same township with a mean-hearted scoundrel willing to hang a man without giving him a chance to prove his innocence."

An angry flush swept McNulty's face. Blunt had come from the forge and was standing beside Ranger, a pleased smile in his eyes. He did not object to hearing the little scamp told off. But Pete resented public castigation.

"If that's the way you want it, suits me," he blustered. "Since you're askin for it, I'll say I'm not satisfied yet. By my way of it, you're still a cow thief."

"For that, next time we meet I'll flog you within an inch of yore life," Sloan promised, a silken threat in his low voice.

"You can talk tough now, because you claim you're a sick man," Uhlmann said sourly. "But when you're well don't try to ride me, unless you want to come with your gun a-smokin'.' "

"Enough of that, boys," Ranger interrupted hurriedly. "Mr. Sloan has a right to be annoyed. If you two had got your way, we would have hanged an innocent man. You ought to be mighty pleased he's living. It's a lesson to all of us not to go off half-cocked. If you're ready, we'll go now, Sloan."

Cape Sloan rose, a wiry brown man with a dynamic force in him that was arresting. His gaze traveled with leisurely contempt over McNulty and rested on the pachydermous face of Uhlmann. He stood apparently at careless ease, a thumb hooked in his sagging belt.

"In a moment, Mr. Ranger." His steady narrowed eyes were still on Uhlmann. "It was my left shoulder the greaser cut," he mentioned, slurring the words gently. "My right arm is good as ever, if anybody wants to find out."

Ranger stepped swiftly between the German and Sloan. "Cut out that kind of talk, both of you," he ordered sternly. "You're grown men, not kids. You fellows let each other alone. The difficulty is settled now."

Sloan's smile was grim. "You in particular stay away from me, McNulty," he said. "My promise still stands. You can't call me a rustler and get off scot-free. If we meet again I'll wear a quirt on you."

He turned his back on Pete and climbed into the wagon.

7 JIM BUDD AND SLOAN AGREE TO BURY THE PAST

The Circle J R ranchhouse was a long low rambling building that had been constructed bit by bit, new wings being added as the owner grew more prosperous. Deep porches ran around the front and sides, with vines climbing trellises to give protection from the broiling heat of midday. The house was furnished comfortably and with taste. There was a piano in the sitting room, and along the walls were well-filled bookcases. The tawdry bric-a-brac one usually found in parlors was notably absent. In the bedroom to which Nelson took the guest cheerful chintz curtains had been hung. The armchair beside the window was deep and built to give the body rest.

As soon as Sloan had washed away the dust of the journey he was called to supper. He was starting to sit down when a huge black man in an apron came in from the kitchen carrying a platter of fried chicken. The Negro's staring eyes goggled at him. It was a bad moment for Cape Sloan. His stomach muscles tightened. For a second or two he missed what Ranger was saying, but he picked up the sequence and answered before the cattleman noticed. During the rest of the meal he gave his surface mind to the conversation at the table. His deeper thoughts were concerned with Jim Budd and the consequences of this unfortunate meeting.

Since he was a convalescent, Sandra insisted that he retire early. He protested only formally, for he was tired from the jolting journey in the wagon. While he was undressing a knock came on the door of his room. It was Jim Budd who tiptoed in after his invitation to enter. He had expected Jim would make him a visit.

Sloan looked up at him from the bed where he was sitting. He wondered what winds of mischance had blown the Negro here.

"And to think I had to bump into you," he said, with obvious distaste.

"Yassuh," Jim agreed. "We sure done come a long way to meet up."

"Do they know who you are?"

"They don' know where I wuz."

"How do you happen to be working at the Circle J R?"

"Why, when they turn me loose I kinda jes' started driftin' east, as you might say. Mister Ranger was looking for a cook. Me, I was workin' in a restaurant at Benson where he come in, an' we fix up for me to do the cookin' here."

"If they knew you had been in the pen they wouldn't keep you a day."

"I reckon that's c'rect. But I wouldn't know. Mister Ranger sure a fine man, an' the little missis sho the finest lady in de land. Mebbe they might keep me." His face took on a look of humble pleading. "You wouldn't go for to tell them, Mister Webb."

"The name is Sloan." He frowned at the honest dish face of the cook. "I don't know. I'll have to think about that."

"I ain't any bad man. I never wuz. That fellow Candish I gouge was a mighty bad killer. He jump me, jes' because I was a colored man."

Sloan knew that was true. Budd had been railroaded to prison. He had wounded Candish in self-defense. The chances were that he would live peaceably the rest of his life. No doubt he was devoted to the family for whom he was now working. The ranch guest felt a wry sense of sardonic amusement at the way he had inverted their roles. He was the one who would be in danger if the truth were known. For he had escaped before his sentence was finished and if discovered would be dragged back, flogged, and lose his time for good conduct.

"Mister Webb—"

"Sloan," interrupted the ranch guest.

"All right, Sloan then. You wuz Webb when you wuz in the pen at Yuma with me, but if you say Sloan that all right with me. What I wanna say is that I done served my time in prison for wounding Candish. I hadn't ought to of been in there a day. When they turned me loose I came 'way out here to make a fresh start. I'm doing fine. I'm with good folks I would do a heap for. I never done you any harm. Whyfor do you want to stir things up and get me flung out on my ear?"

"I don't want to throw you out of a good job where you are giving satisfaction, Jim. But I want to play fair with the Rangers too."

There was a faint gleam of grinning irony in Jim's reply. "I reckon then you'll want to tell them all about yo'self too, Mister We—Sloan."

"No, Jim, I don't want to do that. I'm here just for a short visit. I don't want them or anybody else to know about my stay in the pen at Yuma." Sloan came back to Jim's case. "We all knew there that you aren't a bad man, Jim. You ought never to have been convicted. I don't see how it can hurt the Rangers for you to stay here. You really like them?"

"I ain't got any folks of my own—never did have. My wife run away with a yaller nigger, and that busted up what li'l' home I had. Here's where I wan' to stay the rest of my life. They good to me. Never was any people I like as well. I feel like they're mine, kind of, if you understand me."

"That is fine, Jim. We'll call bygones bygones. What about me? Can you keep that big grinning mouth shut and not let anybody know you've ever seen me before?"

"Sure I can. Listen, Mister Webb-Sloan."

"Sloan," corrected the other. "Be sure to get that right."

"Yessir. Well, I think a powerful lot of Miss Sandra. When you rode in hell-for-leather and saved her from a whole passel of bandits you ce'tainly made me feel a powerful lot of respect, Mr. Sloan. My big mouth is done already padlocked."

8   Sandra Speaks Out

At the Circle J R the guest took life easier than he had done for many a day. Sandra did not let him get up with the family, but saw that Jim prepared a breakfast for him long after the others had eaten. He lounged about the place and let the sunny hours slip away in pleasant indolence. Sometimes he strolled down to the bunkhouse and chatted with a rider who had broken an ankle when his horse stepped into a gopher hole; or he sat on the corral fence and watched the cowboys top young horses they were breaking to the saddle. Occasionally he sat in a rocking chair on the porch of the big house and read a book called *The Three Musketeers*, dealing with the remarkable and improbable adventures of an amazing chap called D'Artagnan.

Nelson hovered around him a good deal. The boy was passing through an attack of hero-worship and was drawn to Sloan as a moth to the lamp. The young man had what it takes to win a boy—a touch of recklessness, cool courage, an easy indifferent grace, and back of him a life lived dangerously. Moreover, he knew exactly how to treat a boy. He never talked down to him, and he had a flair for "joshing" the youngster without making him conscious of the inferiority of the teens.

Of the Golden Girl he caught only glimpses during the day as she went to and fro about her work. Having been since her mother's death sole mistress of the ranch, she had charge of buying supplies not only for the main house but for the boys at the bunkhouse as well. Sloan was surprised at the efficiency with which she did her job. He did not at all wonder at the deep liking and respect, amounting almost to reverence, she won from the tough, tanned young men working for her father. In the case of Jim Budd the devotion he showed was almost pathetic. If it would have helped her he would have chopped the fingers from his hand.

After supper Sandra always joined her father and Sloan on the porch. During the past hour cool shadows from the hills had blanketed stretches of the valley and lifted the heat from its dusty floor. The stark bare mountains glowed with jewels, their brilliancy softening to violet and purple lakes in the crotches between the peaks, filling them with mysterious dark pools. After the sun had set, magic began to fill the desert night.

Cape Sloan was very much aware of the girl sitting near him, though she spoke seldom. The young man was inclined to let Ranger carry the conversation, but the cattleman drew him out and forced him to take a share. Sandra observed that their guest was no ignorant cowboy. He could talk well, on many subjects. He had traveled a good deal, not only in the West but as far as Rio de Janeiro and the cattle country of Brazil. But she noticed that his wary and reticent remarks covered a good many elisions about his life. His youth he told about when questioned, and he did not avoid the wanderings of the past two months. But before that there was a gap of five or six years concerning which he said nothing.

Also, there was some secret understanding between him and Jim Budd. She had seen Jim's startled astonishment at their first meeting and the momentary discomposure of Sloan. When she had talked with Jim about it he denied ever having met their guest before—and she did not believe him. There had been something in the past that both of them wanted to conceal, some dark and unhappy memory rising to plague them now. An evil ghost from Cape Sloan's wild and turbulent youth had come to life again.

Sandra felt a hint of wariness about his indolent ease. It seemed to her a mask worn by a man always alert and even suspicious. She found confirmation of this view in an incident that occurred the third day of Sloan's stay at the ranch.

Late in the afternoon a man rode into the yard and dismounted in front of the house. Sandra chanced to be with their guest on the porch. She had just brought out a pitcher of lemonade and a glass for him.

The horseman tied his mount and came up the steps. He was heavy-set, middle-aged, with bleached blue eyes in a deeply tanned face. Scores of tiny wrinkles went out from the outer corners of the eyes like spokes from a hub. His cowboy boots were old and scuffed, his Stetson faded and floppy. Dust had sifted into the creases of the corduroy trousers and coat. The checked shirt had been washed so often that all the life had gone out of the color.

He said, smiling at the girl: "My throat's dry as a lime kiln, Miss Sandra. Does that rate me a drink of yore lemonade?"

She nodded. "It's ice-cold. I'll get a glass for you. This is Mr. Sloan, sheriff." To Cape she said, "Sheriff Norlin."

There was the slightest steely hardening in Sloan's eyes. She would not have noticed it if she had not been watching. The men looked at each other steadily as they shook hands. What they said had nothing to do with what they were thinking.

Norlin mopped his face with a bandanna, after he had murmured "Pleased to meet you," and mentioned that it was nice to get in the shade after being cooked by a blistering sun for four-five hours. The younger man remarked that he didn't ever remember it being hotter at this time of year.

Sandra went in for a glass and when she returned Norlin was telling Sloan that Lopez had been forced to abandon the stolen herd just this side of the line. A troop of cavalry had come on the raiders by chance and sent them scuttling into the brush. That was good, Sloan said. And how about Scarface? Had they heard anything of him?

"No." The sheriff rubbed the palm of his hand across an unshaven face meditatively and slanted a searching look at Sloan. "Looks like he has holed up and pulled the hole in after him. I reckon if anybody could give us information—"

He dropped the sentence there. Sloan was of no help.

"Maybe someone who knows him might give you a line on where his hangouts are," Cape said smoothly.

Norlin admitted to himself that he was unduly suspicious. He had in his pocket a letter from the deputy sheriff Mosely describing the young man who had sat opposite him at breakfast the morning after the raid. It fitted very accurately this youth who called himself Cape Sloan. The fellow could not have been in two different places at the same time. Yet he did not act just like an innocent man. There was a touch of challenge in his manner that was almost insolent, a sort of a "You-be-damned, prove it if you can" air.

"I've brought some sugar," Sandra told the sheriff, "in case you like your lemonade sweet."

He sampled the lemonade and said it was just the way he liked it. "Cooler up in the mountains," he suggested, cocking an eye at the other man.

Sloan recognized this as a trial balloon. "Should think it would be," he agreed.

"Did you say you came by way of Globe?"

"I didn't say." Cape's voice was cool and indifferent. It invited no further discussion of the subject. "I'll throw in with the sheriff about the lemonade, Miss Ranger. Best I ever drank."

"It tastes better because the day is so hot." She looked into the pitcher. "There's a dividend left for you."

"No, no. I've had my share. You drink it."

Sheriff Norlin had an elusive little notion flitting through his mind that he had seen this young man before. There was something faintly familiar about his voice, or was it in his manner of speaking?

"Not yore first visit to this part of the country, Mr. Sloan, I take it," he said.

"You think I don't look like a tenderfoot, sheriff." There was a slight drawling derision in the tone. "I reckon that's a compliment coming from an old-timer."

Sandra was a little annoyed at Cape Sloan. She knew he was taking an impish pleasure in side-stepping the sheriff's questions even though a frank answer would involve him in no trouble. For some reason he had built up a defense so

71

quick to assert itself that it was almost belligerent.

"I had a letter from Mosely today," Norlin said. "You'll be glad to know it clears you, Mr. Sloan."

"Since I knew it would, I won't throw my hat up in the air and cheer about it," the young man answered dryly.

After the sheriff had left, Sandra's guest offered a drawling comment. "If I'd known my *pasear* into your country was going to upset so many citizens, I reckon I would have brought a letter of introduction from the governor."

Sandra's honest eyes met his directly. He had raised the question. She would tell him the truth. "I think you are a good deal to blame yourself. You act like a small boy with a chip on his shoulder. If you were more frank and friendly—"

"Friendly with the fellows who want to hang me for something I didn't do?" he inquired with his sardonic smile.

"Sheriff Norlin isn't trying to hang you," she said sturdily. "I don't want to find out anything you don't want to tell. I'm on your side anyhow. But since I'm not a complete fool I can see you are holding something back." She raised a hand quickly to head off his interruption. "You have a right to your secrets. That's not the point. You were dodging Sheriff Norlin's questions just to irritate him. What difference does it make whether you did or didn't come through Globe?"

"No difference," he admitted. "But Norlin had just one legitimate point of interest in me, my connection with the Scarface gang. When he discovered I hadn't any he ought to have been through. But after he got Mosley's letter he rode twenty miles to see me."

"To make sure you fitted the description Mr. Mosely gave of you. That was his duty."

"After he saw me he still wasn't satisfied."

"Because of your . . . evasions."

He brushed the sheriff out of the picture. "In spite of those . . . evasions . . . you are still for me. Isn't that what you said?"

His cool hard eyes drilled into her. She felt a pulse of excitement begin to beat in her throat. No balanced judgment would ever decide her feelings toward this man. It was not only that he had done her a great service at much risk to himself. Something reached out from that lean body with the whipcord muscles, from the strong reckless face, that drew her irresistibly to him.

She said, in a low voice: "I think you have been wild and lawless and that there is something . . . shocking . . . in your past. But whatever you have done, you are not evil. A man's actions, at some crisis, and what he really is, are two different things. I don't have to be told what is troubling you to know that I am on your side."

Swiftly she turned and walked into the house.

The man's gaze followed her. He was astonished at what she had said, at the insight which had probed through the incriminating facts to the essential truth. She lived on the other side of a gulf he could not cross. None the less a warm glad excitement filled his breast.

He beat it down, almost savagely. His way of life was chosen. It was one that probably would include violence and bloodshed. There was no room in it for a woman like Sandra Ranger, nor for any of the pleasant and kindly friendships that might temper his ruthlessness. He was in a tight spot from which he did not expect to get out alive. But he had set himself to a task. He meant to go through with it unless his enemies destroyed him first.

9 CONCERNING A GENT ON THE MAKE

The name of Jug Packard came up one evening while the Ranger family were sitting with Cape Sloan on the porch facing the shadowy outlines of the Huachucas. The ranch guest had dropped a casual question to which he knew the answer.

"Yes," replied John. "There's right smart ore there. Copper, and some gold."

"In paying values?"

"You must have heard of the Johnny B—near the mouth of Geronimo Gulch."

"Seems to me I have. Is it locally owned?" Cape kept his voice indifferent. Nobody could have guessed by hearing him that he was doing more than making talk to pass time.

"Jug Packard holds a controlling interest."

The young man stilled a yawn with his fore-fingers. The obvious lack of interest was fraudulent. He had not heard the name for years, but the sound of it set a pulse of excitement strumming in him. "Lives in New York, with an office on Wall Street, I reckon," he suggested.

"No, sir. Lives at Tucson, when he isn't at the mine. Mostly he stays right at Jugtown, where the works are. His family put on considerable dog at Tucson, but the old man dresses like he did when

75

he didn't have a nickel. A tramp wouldn't say 'Thank you' for anything Jug wears."

"I see. An old-timer, a diamond in the rough."

"An old-timer all right. He's been here since Baldy was a hole in the ground, but I wouldn't call him exactly a diamond or rave about his heart of gold."

"A millionaire?"

"He's got money enough to burn a wet mule." Ranger added, after a moment: "Jug is a crabbed old tightwad. Hangs on to a dollar so hard he squeezes the eagle off it before he turns it loose."

"But otherwise an estimable citizen," Sloan commented. His sardonic face was in the shadow of the vines and told no tales.

"Hmp! Not unless rumor is a lying jade," returned Ranger. He was a man who spoke his mind, and he did not like the mine owner. "I wouldn't trust him farther than I could throw a bull by the tail. Some nasty stories about Jug have floated around. By the way, your friend Uhlmann used to be a foreman or pit boss or something or other for him."

"Did he mention that he was my friend?" the younger man asked with frosty irony.

Ranger leaned back in his chair, drew on his pipe, and released the smoke slowly. "Jug came in as a mule skinner for a freight outfit," he said. "The pachies ambushed the party on the Oracle road and would have got the whole caboodle if

Bob Webb and two-three of his boys hadn't happened along and drove them off. Jug was wounded, so Bob took him to Tucson and looked after the bills till he got on his feet again. They say Mrs. Webb nursed him. Anyhow, later Bob took him down to the Johnny B and gave him a job."

"Mr. Packard seems to have made good there," Sloan said dryly.

"Jug is one of those fellows born to make money. If he sees a dime around that isn't nailed down he gets it. No doubt he saw right away that there was a fortune in the Johnny B. Jug is mighty competent, the kind that is bound to get to the top. Webb was kinda easy-going. He relied on Jug a lot. In three-four years he was superintendent and had a small interest in the mine. All he needed was that toe-hold." The cattleman stopped talking. He put his boots on the porch railing and relaxed.

His daughter prodded him. She was in the lane of lamplight that streamed from the window of the parlor. "Well, go on," she urged.

It was her eyes, Sloan decided, that quickened a personality interesting and exciting. They were shining now like pools of liquid fire. He did not know that she had divined intuitively that this story somehow concerned him greatly.

"Webb was killed when a charge exploded unexpectedly in one of the drifts," her father continued. "After that Jug took charge, though

Mr. Webb still owned most of the property. He organized it into a stock company, and by that time he held the next biggest interest to Mrs. Webb. The mine ran into a streak of bad luck. They lost the pay vein, and none of the drifts seemed to have much ore. For a couple of years the Johnny B shut down. The stock went down to almost nothing. Jug bought it right and left, a good deal of it from Mrs. Webb, who had to get money to keep herself and her two kids. When the mine opened up again Jug owned nine-tenths of the stock. Almost right away they struck a bonanza."

"Fortunate for Packard," Sloan remarked.

The girl looked at him quickly. He was covering up carefully, but back of his arid reserve she read a deep bitterness. "You think Mr. Packard just happened to hit pay ore?" she asked.

"That's his story. You can take it or leave it." Ranger's resentment at the man exploded into words. "No, I think he pulled off some kind of shenanigan. Maybe he knew the ore was there and shut down to get control."

"Who kept the mine books?" Sloan asked abruptly.

"I don't know. Why?"

"He might have been looting the mine before it shut down—pocketing the profits so as to have enough to buy up the stock later."

"I wouldn't put it past him. Anyhow, he has the Johnny B, however he got it."

"And Mrs. Webb—what did she do about it?" Sandra asked.

"What could she do?" Ranger answered. "Jug had been too slick for her."

"So the story ends there."

"No. After a while young Webb came back and raised a row. He was a wild young coot, I gather. Got off on the wrong foot and killed a fellow named Giles Lemmon, who was one of Jug's men. They gave him twenty years in the penitentiary."

"Which made it nice for Mr. Packard," Sloan drawled. "Showing how all things work together for good to them that love the Lord."

"How dreadful!" Sandra murmured. "For him and his poor mother, if she was still living."

"She was then," Ranger replied. "She isn't now. Two years after he went to prison I read in the paper of her death."

"And the son—he's still in the penitentiary?"

"I reckon so, Sandra. Maybe he deserved what he got. When a man kills he can't kick if he has to pay the price. But one thing is sure. Jug Packard brought about that killing. He was more to blame than the boy."

"Men with as much money as Packard don't go to prison," Sloan said, a cynical bitterness in his face.

"Oh, I hope that isn't true in this country," Sandra cried.

"In the land of the free, where all men are born equal," the ranch guest mocked.

"It isn't true, Sandra," the girl's father said. "Though I'm afraid it is true that a rich man can often buy delays and even avoidance of punishment that a poor one can't afford. In Packard's case there was no evidence that he had committed a crime. I've said too much. I don't know he slickered Mrs. Webb out of her mine. That's only my private opinion."

Sloan rose and said he thought he would be turning in for the night. Sandra was shocked at his face. His mouth was a thin tight slit and there was something wolfish in his tortured eyes.

10 SANDRA GUESSES A SECRET

Jim Budd was transferring a box of grocery supplies from a wagon to the kitchen when Sloan drifted across the yard to meet him. The cook stopped in the doorway, box in front of him, and gave the ranch guest a morning greeting.

"How is you this fine day, Mr.—Sloan?"

"Fine as the wheat, Jim. Go ahead. I'll come into the kitchen."

Budd deposited the groceries on the table and turned to find out what the other wanted to say to him. Sloan wasted no time.

"I understand a colored boy who cooks at the Johnny B mine will probably drop in to see you this afternoon," he said.

"Yessuh, he 'most generally does on his way to town. Miss Sandra tell you Sam wuz cumin'?"

"She said he might. Do you know how long he has worked at the Johnny B?"

"More'n ten years, he tole me."

"I want you to do me a favor, Jim. Find out from him if you can where Stan Fraser is now. Years ago he used to run the engine at the mine. Put it sort of careless. Make out you once knew him. And whatever you do, don't let him know you're asking for me."

"Okay, Mr.—Sloan."

Sandra came into the kitchen and Cape explained his presence with an apologetic laugh. "I've got so little to do that I go around gassing with everybody and interfering with their work. But you'll be rid of me tomorrow. I'll be on my way."

"Where are you going?" she asked.

"I'm not dead sure. Think I'll try to pick up a job on some ranch."

She said nothing more about it, but she made up her mind not to let him ride for any outfit in this part of the territory if she could help it. She believed he was in great danger here. He ought to go away to a place where he was unknown, where he was not surrounded by enemies. It would be madness for him to stay here, especially so since he was brooding over some dark purpose of revenge. That he was the son of Bob Webb she felt sure. Either he had been released from prison or he had escaped. If he got into fresh trouble, even though he might be out on parole, he would be dragged back again without a trial.

The intensity of her feeling was disturbing. When they met, excitement flooded her breast and left her a little breathless. She wondered if this were love, and told herself she hoped not. There could be no happy consummation to such madness. How could one walk through life happily beside a man who strode with such reckless feet along perilous trails? A silly question, she put it to herself severely, about a man who was showing not the least interest in her.

She took to her father the problem of Cape Sloan's future. He was in the room he used as an office, checking a bill from a hardware store. Sandra waited while he finished adding a column.

"Aren't you ashamed, Mr. Ranger, to have an ex-convict here as a guest?" she asked.

He frowned at her. "What nonsense have you in your head?"

"I'm talking about Mr. Sloan, alias Webb. I'm not sure he is a released convict. He may be an escaped one." She added, with a smile: "In which case of course you are an accessory and will have to go back with him."

"You mean that this man is Bob Webb's son?"

"That's what I mean." She gave up abruptly the playful approach she had adopted. She found herself too distressed for foolery. "He says he is going to get work on some ranch near here. I know he is back looking for more trouble. You must make him get out of this part of the country as quick as he can."

"What makes you think he is Webb?"

"I watched him last night while you were telling about how Jug Packard got the Johnny B. He sat back where you could not notice his face. But I saw it—so hard and bitter and savage."

Ranger marshaled stray impressions of his own. "You may be right. Come to think of it, he looks some like Bob Webb did. Or would, without that beard. The same bony structure of face. If he is young Webb, he ought not to be in this neck of the woods. Why would he come back?"

"I don't know. But he didn't come to shake hands with Jug Packard. There's another thing. Do you know whether he might have been turned loose on parole? If not—"

"There was a prison break at Yuma a few months ago," Ranger said. "I read only the head-lines in the paper. Three or four men escaped. Webb might have been one of them." He stroked his short beard reflectively. "I think we'll have to call Sloan in for a show-down."

"What if he admits he is Webb?"

"Nothing to do but urge him to leave Arizona."

"If he has made up his mind to stay he won't go."

"Now that he is smoked out he'll probably go."

Sandra glanced through the window, said quickly, "Here he is."

Sloan stood in the doorway and looked from one to the other. "Excuse me," he said to Ranger. "I didn't know you were busy."

"Come in," his host invited. "We have some-thing to talk over with you."

Again the guest's glance slid from the cattleman to his daughter. "About how to get rid of a guest who outstays his welcome, I reckon," he said. "I'll relieve yore minds. I'm traveling this afternoon.

And since we're together, I'll tell you right now how grateful I am for all the kindness you have shown me."

Ranger flushed with embarrassment. He did not find it easy to broach the subject in his mind.

"We're in your debt more than we can ever repay, Mr. Sloan," he began. "You're welcome to stay here till Christmas if you like. But, the fact is, the way things are with you, if we've guessed right—"

The ranchman bogged down. He could not bluntly tell this man they thought he was a convict and a murderer.

"Just how are things with me?" Sloan asked, his voice murmurously ironic.

"We are wondering if you aren't Bob Webb's son," Ranger gulped out.

Sloan smiled, after an instant's pause. "Miss Ranger has quite an imagination, hasn't she?"

Color crept into the cheeks of the girl. "You're right to blame me," she admitted. "My father would never have thought of it."

"She mentioned it to me because she was afraid you are stacking up trouble for yourself," Ranger corrected.

"For argument's sake, let us say I am Bob Webb's son." The steely eyes of the young man held fast to those of the girl. "And an escaped convict. What do you propose to do about it?"

"We think this is the most dangerous spot in the

world for you," she answered, her words low and husky. "Whatever purpose has brought you here can bring only trouble, unless you give it up. They'll discover who you are, just as we have done. You must go far away from here at once."

"My brother has a cattle ranch on the White River in Colorado. It's a fine country, but thinly settled. He would find a job for you if we asked it." Ranger finished with direct advice. "I would go tonight. Any delay might be disastrous."

"I'll go part way at least tonight," Sloan promised with a sardonic grin. "Whatever happens, you'll have done yore full duty by me—and some more. I'll never forget yore kindness to me."

"You don't mean to leave Arizona at all," Sandra charged. "You mean to stay and—and—"

There was the beginning of panic in her eyes. She did not know the conclusion of her sentence, only that it would be something dreadful.

"I'll leave as soon as I've finished my business."

"What business?" she demanded.

"Personal and private." His cynical smile denied her any knowledge of it or any part in it.

The repulse was a slap in the face. But she cared nothing for that. Her mind was too intent on saving him.

"Stay around here and you'll leave with handcuffs on your wrists!" she cried.

"Sandra!" her father warned sternly.

The young man disregarded Ranger and spoke

to the girl. In his eyes she saw again the reckless defiance of consequences. "I don't think so. One place I'm not going to is Yuma."

From a white miserable face she stared at him. He meant that he would be killed rather than go back to prison. All his thinking was warped by the horrible experience he had endured. When he first went to the penitentiary he must have been just a boy. She had read stories written by released prisoners who had been shut up by society like wild beasts. It had twisted and embittered their lives. That was how it was with Cape Sloan. Existence had narrowed down with him to a determination to get revenge. And there was no way to show him that he was making a fatal mistake, that today might mark the beginning of a new life if he could escape the mental miasma in which he moved.

When he rode away next morning Sandra watched him from the window of her bedroom. She had already said a smiling good-bye to him at breakfast, but there was no smile in her eyes or on her lips now. She was convinced that he was going to his death—perhaps not today or this week, but soon—and she believed he knew it. Yet he rode flatbacked and lightly, a sardonic recklessness in the grey-blue eyes set so challengingly in the coffee-brown face. It was dreadful to fear that all the virile strength of him might in a moment be stricken from that superb body.

This morning Cape Sloan was not thinking about anything so grim as death. The warm sun was shining. A gentle breeze from the Huachucas stirred the mistletoe in the live oaks. It was the kind of day to make a man glad he was alive. Sloan's thoughts were of the girl he was leaving behind him, though he did not let these deflect him from giving wary attention to the country through which he was traveling. He had been for months a man on the dodge. More than once he had shaved capture by a hair's breadth. Since the hour of his prison break there had been scarcely a day when he had not walked with danger at his side. But meeting Sandra had set the sap of hope stirring in him again. He would beat it down savagely later, but for the time he let its sweet madness flow through him.

There were ranches in the valley, but he circled them carefully, to meet as few people as he could. The morning was old when he struck the San Pedro river and followed it to the little village of Charleston drowsing in the sun. The river swept half way round the town, a row of fine cottonwood trees on the bank.

Cape loosened the revolver in its holster, to make sure of free action in case he had to draw. The chances were he would not be molested, but a man who rode as wild a trail as he did could not take any chances.

11 STAN FRASER BUYS CHIPS

It was high noon when Cape Sloan rode into the little town of Charleston and tied up at the hitch rack in front of the Rawhide Corral. He strolled through the big gate and stopped beside a small man in jeans who was greasing a wagon.

"Mr. Stan Fraser?" asked Sloan.

"Yes, sir," the owner of the name answered crisply.

He had a lean sun-tanned face much wrinkled around the eyes, which were steel-blue and looked at his questioner very steadily. Fraser was nearer fifty than forty, but the years had not tamed a certain youthful jauntiness in him. His pinched-in Stetson was tilted to one side and the bandanna around his leathery throat was as colorful as an Arizona sunset.

The muscles of Sloan's face stiffened. He spoke slowly, choosing his words carefully. "You cussed old cow thief, I might have known I'd find you in this rustler's town where honest men are as scarce as hens' teeth. I'm sure surprised the law hasn't caught up with you yet in spite of all the deviltry you've done."

Fraser's eyes grew frosty. "A man who talks like you are doing has come to pick a fight. Before you start smokin' mebbe you'll tell me what the trouble is about. After that I'll accommodate you if you'll give me time to get a gun."

The features of the younger man relaxed to a smile. "Not fighting talk if I grin when I say it," he denied. "Don't you know who I am, you old one-gallus brushpopper?"

Astonishment rubbed the anger from the face of Fraser. Recognition came slowly, after a long half-minute of eye searching. "By criminy, you're young Bob Webb," he cried. His gaze swept over the corral fence, and up and down the street. "What in heck you doing here, boy? You'd ought to be holed up in Mexico."

"Thought I'd drop in and shake hands with an old friend. But you don't need to shout about it. There might be someone here with the idea that I ought to be holed up in Yuma and the two hundred dollars reward money jingling in his pocket."

The owner of the corral lowered his voice. "You're dead right about that. This place is infested by lowdown scalawags who would sell their brothers for a dollar Mex. They claim that in Curly Bill's time there was some honor among thieves. If a fellow was a crook he was safe here or at Galeyville or anywhere in this corner of Cochise County, safe from the law anyhow. But not now. Plenty of rustlers and bad men drop in here to get corned up. They are particular though to keep a saddled bronc in the alley to fork for a quick getaway."

"Since I rate as a crook I'd better do that too," Sloan said.

Fraser flushed. "Quit talkin' foolishness, boy. You're the son of my old boss, who was the whitest, straightest man who ever threw a saddle on a horse. You've had bad luck. I know thirty fellows walking the streets today who have killed for one reason or another. None of 'em ever served a day for it. You were just a kid, and they socked you twenty years. The scoundrels railroaded you. Everybody knows you got a raw deal."

"And do nothing about it," Sloan added cynically.

"What can we do, boy? We got up a petition to the governor for a pardon. Jug Packard blocked it. He's a political power in the territory now. If I was you, I'd lie low with me till night and then ride hell-for-leather till you had crossed the line into mañana-land."

"Don't worry about me," the young man advised carelessly. "Nobody is going to drag me back to Yuma, not while I'm alive. I came to have a talk with you, Stan. After that I'll vamoose."

Stan Fraser looked at the hard bony bearded face, lips close shut, eyes cold and steely, at the smoothly-muscled shoulders and the poised confidence of the man's carriage, and he realized that it would be hard to recognize in him the loose-jointed gangling boy who had been convicted of killing Giles Lemmon more than seven years ago.

He shrugged his shoulders. "You're just like yore father. No use telling him anything. He'd go his own way. When I said Jug Packard was a cold-blooded traitor without an ounce of decency or gratitude in him, Bob wouldn't listen to me. He got hot under the collar." The boss of the wagon yard hesitated a moment before blurting out what was in his mind. "I can't prove it, but it's my opinion yore father was killed by foul play. When we brought his body out of the drift I saw Hans Uhlmann and Jug whispering together. Hans was the only fellow except Bob down on that level at the time of the explosion."

"You think Uhlmann was paid by Packard to get rid of my father?"

"I've told you all I know," Fraser replied. "You do the thinking."

Sloan nodded. "I know that talk like that is dangerous. As for its going any further, you can be sure nobody else will ever know you said it." Recalling subsequent events the eyes of the convict grew bitter and the muscles of his jaw stood out like ropes. "I don't suppose you ever heard that after my father's death Packard proposed to divorce his wife and marry my mother. She was terribly angry and put him in his place. Then he decided to take the Johnny B lock, stock, and barrel. That way he got my share too."

"And there's not a thing you could do about it."

"Not then."

The older man slanted a sharp look at Sloan. "Or now. Don't you start getting any crazy ideas in your head, boy. You tried it once and it ruined yore life."

"Yes," the escaped prisoner agreed. "I didn't know enough then to fight a man like Packard. I blundered in like a fool and was framed. The story I told at my trial was true. Both Packard and Uhlmann gave false testimony. When the firing began I was near the middle of the room, with Uhlmann on one side of me and Lemmon on the other. I ducked under the desk, and by chance Uhlmann's bullet caught Lemmon in the throat. Packard made Uhlmann stop shooting. He figured it would look better not to kill me, but to send me to the penitentiary."

"I knew it was some kind of frame-up, but I thought they deviled you into killing Lemmon." The mind of Fraser picked up something else the young man had said. "You didn't know enough then, and now they have the cards stacked against you. No use trying to fight Packard. Even if the law wasn't waiting to drag you to Yuma you couldn't do a thing. He's had time to get everything fixed. The way it is now you haven't a dead man's chance. First move you make, they throw you back into a cell. Be reasonable, son. You're young yet. Get out of this country and make a new start. Forget Packard. One of these days he'll get his."

Sloan ignored that. "Uhlmann didn't have a nickel when he was working at the Johnny B. They say he has a pretty good ranch now. How did he get it?"

"I've got quite a bump of curiosity myself, and I once looked into that. He claimed an uncle died and left him fifteen thousand dollars. That's not true. Jug set him up in business, took a mortgage on the place, and a year or so later released it. I'll bet Rhino never paid a dime of it. He knew too much, and Jug had to square him."

"Of course that was the way of it," Cape Sloan assented. "They'll stand together. I couldn't get anything on them that way."

"Nor any other way."

"A fellow named Newman used to do the bookkeeping for the mine. Is he still there, do you know?"

"No. He quit long ago. Works in the Southern Pacific railroad offices at Tucson." Fraser added further information. "Funny thing about that. I met him soon after he had quit Packard and asked him why he had left the Johnny B. He gave me a quick look and shut up talking right then. Looked to me as if he was scared to say anything."

"Think I'll drift over to Tucson," Sloan mentioned.

Fraser slapped down on the tire of the nearest wheel the dabbler with which he had been scraping grease on the axle. "I can see you are lookin' for trouble, Bob," he yelped excitedly. "Haven't you got a lick of sense? Jug Packard is in the saddle. He'll rub you outa his way soon as he finds out you're around. If you don't pull yore freight he'll pull you in a wooden box or have you slapped back in jail. Jug is the cock-a-doodle-do around here."

A fiery wave seemed to pass through the younger man. He might make wreckage of his life, if there was any of it left that had not already been shattered, but he would stand up and fight to a finish.

"You think this man murdered my father. So do I. He robbed my mother and broke her heart when his lies put me in the penitentiary. With me locked up, he left my little sister alone in the world. What kind of a weak-kneed quitter do you think I am?"

His friend gave up trying to dissuade this bitter reckless man. Bob Webb's son would walk unafraid into desperate peril if need be, as his father had more than once done before him. He was as tough as ironwood and as unrelenting as a wolf. It flashed across the mind of Fraser that he would not like to be in the shoes of Jug Packard as long as this enemy was alive.

"All right," the little man said quietly. "I'll side you. The best friend I ever had was yore father."

The convict shook his head. "No, Stan. I'm

playing a lone hand. They'll probably get me. I'll not drag you down too."

Fraser flared up angrily. "Hell! Do you think you're the only darn fool in the world? I've got no wife or kids. You can't make up my mind for me. I'll ride the river with you, fellow."

"Whether I want you to or not?" Sloan asked.

"Y'betcha! This is a free country. You can't stop me from going where you do any more than I can prevent you from doing what you've a mind to do."

"But this is my job, Stan," the younger man explained. "It's not yours. I have a right to risk my own life. The way I'm fixed it's not worth anything anyhow. But I can't lead you into trouble."

"Who's leading me?" The old-timer bristled up to Sloan. "Not a young squirt like you. I'm trailin' along to dry-nurse you."

Cape Sloan knew that his friend was game as a bulldog. He had been brought up in the outdoor school of the frontier which kept in session twelve months of every year. It was a rough and tumble school where there was no law to protect a man except the Colt strapped to his side. Stan was a small wiry bundle of energy. There was an old saying in the West that all men are the same size behind a six-gun. Cape could guess by the quick excitement in the eyes of the corral keeper that he was eager to escape from his present humdrum existence and turn back the clock to face the perils of a renewed youth.

"There may be trouble," Stan reminded him.

"Sure there'll be trouble. Ain't that what I keep tellin' you?"

"My idea is to move lawfully, getting evidence against Packard that will stand up in court."

"That's fine with me."

"But it won't be with Packard. If it looks like I'm getting anywhere it's a cinch that guy will start to smoke."

Fraser opened his eyes with mock astonishment. "You don't think that good old mealy-mouthed Jug would start anything like that?" he demurred with obvious sarcasm.

"How would I feel if one of their bullets got you instead of me?" Sloan wanted to know.

"They have not molded the bullet yet that will get me," the little gamecock retorted. "I'm sittin' in, boy. Done bought chips. Where do we go from here?"

"We go and have dinner first if there's a restaurant in this burg."

"Best place is Ma Skelton's. I eat there. Let's go."

They strolled across the street to an adobe house that had been plastered once on the outside but was beginning to scale.

"Remember that my name is Cape Sloan," the man who claimed it warned the other.

97

A few moments later Fraser introduced the stranger to Ma Skelton. She was a large angular woman in the late forties with a hard leathery face and brusque manner behind which was concealed a warm and generous heart open to all in distress. More than one cowboy with a broken leg had convalesced at her home in spite of the fact that he had not saved a nickel to pay for food, lodging, and rough nursing. No matter how tough an *hombre* the invalid might be, that was always one debt he paid later if his span of life was not cut short. In case he was inclined to be forgetful, Ma's other guests prodded his memory forcibly.

12 SLOAN RENEWS A PROMISE

"Dinner's ready," Ma Skelton said. "Sit down. Any place."

Sloan and Fraser stepped across a bench that ran along the table close to a wall and sat down. Several others joined them at the table.

A long dark man came into the room and closed the door behind him. He stood there for a moment, poised and wary, his gaze sweeping the place in a check-up of those present. Cape Sloan understood that look. It was both furtive and searching. He had himself acquired one much like it from months on the dodge. The man had a livid scar across the left cheek, stretching almost from ear to chin.

The newcomer circled the table and sat down with his back to the wall beside Cape. From where he was he could see instantly anybody who came in either from the outside or the kitchen. The forty-four at his side pressed against Sloan's thigh. Without a word of greeting to those present he reached for the platter of steak the waitress had just brought, chose the largest portion, slid a half dish of fried potatoes to his plate, and began to eat voraciously.

"Anything new up San Simon way, Scarface?" Fraser inquired amiably.

The disfigured man slanted a resentful look at the corral owner. When he came to town he did not care to have his name bandied about. For though the local residents knew him there might be law officers around who had never met him. He growled out that nothing ever happened in his locale.

Since Sloan had half guessed that this man was Scarface, his poker face betrayed no least interest in the rustler. The business of eating appeared to absorb his full interest. Under other circumstances he might have felt it his duty to help arrest the fellow, but he was himself a fugitive and had been for years wholly on the side of the hunted lawbreaker rather than the pursuing officer.

Dinner was nearly over when the door opened to let in four men who quite evidently had been lined up in front of a bar prior to adjournment for eating. The one in the van was a big redfaced man in the clothes of a town dweller. He gave the hostess a placatory smile.

"I reckon we're a few minutes late, Ma," he said airily.

She stared at him with a wooden uncompromising face. "At this house dinner is served at ten minutes past twelve, as you very well know."

"Now, Ma, we had a little business to finish and couldn't get here any sooner," he protested. "You wouldn't deny food to hungry men?"

"Yore business was at O'Brien's saloon," she told him bluntly. "This is the third time in ten days you've pulled this on me, Rip Morris. You know my rule, and I've warned you before. Get here on time—or stay away."

"Two cowboys got in here after one o'clock yesterday and you fed them," Morris reminded her.

"So I did. They had been on a cattle drive since five in the morning and not idling before a bar. That was an exception. This isn't."

One of the others who had just come in spoke up sourly. He was a mean-looking fellow with a face that would have curdled cream. "So we don't get dinner," he snapped. "Is that it?"

"Not here you don't."

A snarling oath slid out of the corner of his thin lips. "We'll take our trade where it's wanted, Rip," he sneered. "There are other places to eat beside this."

"Then go to them, Pete McNulty," Ma Skelton snapped. "And never show yore face in this house again if you don't want to stop a flatiron with yore ugly mouth."

Uhlmann was another of the four. At sight of him and McNulty the escaped convict had become at once watchful. He observed that both of them had nodded a greeting to Scarface with no evidence of animosity. This was surprising. A few days ago they had been clamoring for his

101

blood. He had stolen their stock and killed the rider of a neighboring cattleman.

As McNulty turned sullenly to go, Scarface murmured out of the corner of his mouth. "Be seeing you later."

Uhlmann's glassy eyes fell on Sloan. "Look who's here, Pete," he snorted.

McNulty glared at the young man. "Blast my eyes, Rhino," he cried, "if it ain't our friend the rustler again."

The hard gaze of the convict bored into the man. "Wrong on both counts," he said very quietly. "Not yore friend and not a rustler. This makes twice you've called me a thief."

"Caught you in the act, didn't we?" shrilled McNulty.

Scarface looked suspiciously from the little ranchman to Sloan and back again. "What's eatin' you, Pete?" he wanted to know. "You got anything against rustlers? Or is it just this one that annoys you?"

"He claims I was helping you run off a bunch of stolen stock the day of the Lopez raid," Sloan explained.

"I never saw you before," Scarface retorted. "I don't get what this is all about."

"We trapped him in Two-Fork Cañon with our stuff and he tried to play he was innocent and you guilty," McNulty explained. His frown was meant to warn Scarface that he would tell him all about it later. "Course Rhino and I knew better than that."

Sloan said, still without raising his voice, "When I meet you in the street later, McNulty, if I do, I'll wear you to a frazzle with my quirt."

Ma Skelton addressed herself sharply to Sloan. "Young man, we won't hear any more out of *you*. Nobody can bring quarrels to this house and unload them here. I won't have it."

"I've said all I'm going to say, ma'am," Cape promised, and busied himself with his pie.

"If you fool with me, fellow, I'll let daylight through you," McNulty warned.

He retreated hurriedly, for Ma Skelton was striding toward him. Two of his companions clumped out of the boardinghouse at his heels. Uhlmann lingered a moment, the little eyes in his leathery face fastened on Sloan.

"I've seen you some place before that time we met in the gulch," he said, a puzzled frown on his forehead.

"Maybe at Delmonico's in New York," Cape suggested ironically.

"One of these days I'll remember when and where, fellow."

"Then we'll sing about auld acquaintance."

"Don't get funny with me," Uhlmann snarled.

Sloan looked up at Ma Skelton, a grin on his face. "No comment to make. All I'll talk about is the weather."

An angry animal growl rumbled from Uhlmann's throat as he lumbered out of the room.

"A nice pleasant gent to keep away from," Fraser commented lightly.

Nobody else had any remark to add. As the corral owner had suggested, Uhlmann was a good person to let alone. Presently Scarface rose, paid for his dinner, and departed.

Fraser and Sloan walked out into the dusty unpaved street and stood on the wooden sidewalk the planks of which were falling into decay. The buildings were of adobe and frame, the latter all with false fronts upon which the lettering was faded. In the days of John Ringo and Curly Bill, Charleston had been a riotous little town, but its hour of glory was now in the past.

13 McNulty Has a Bad Five Minutes

"What the Sam Hill is this about you being a rustler?" Fraser asked.

His friend smiled grimly. "Mr. McNulty had a rope around my neck the other day. They were set on hanging me to the nearest tree. Their story was that I belonged to the Scarface gang, which had just raided a bunch of cattle and killed one of John Ranger's cowboys."

"I heard something about that, but I didn't know you were the man they caught. John was with them when they caught you, I was told."

"Yes. He and Russell Hart. All four of them thought I was one of the rustlers, but Ranger and Hart were willing to wait and make sure. Uhlmann and McNulty wanted me hanged right then. At the time I thought they were just a pair of cold-blooded ruffians, but I'm not so sure now. They claimed they wanted to get Scarface and were full of threats against him. It doesn't look now as if they are so crazy to get him. In the dining room they acted as if they had some kind of under-standing. Scarface told them he would be seeing them later. Why, if they are honest cattlemen and he is stealing their stock?"

"Doesn't look too good, does it? Ten-fifteen

years ago Pete McNulty had a bad name. His neighbors thought he was stealing their stuff but couldn't prove it. Maybe he is up to his old tricks."

"There were one or two of his and of Uhlmann's animals in the drive," Sloan said. "But that might be a blind. These fellows might be along with the hunters to make sure they didn't get the thieves. And when they caught me that suited them fine. They could hang me and go home, leaving Scarface to slip away. I'll bet that's how it was."

"You certainly get around where the trouble is," the old-timer commented with a grin. "It ain't enough for you to have a reward out for you as an escaped convict. You've got to get into a jam for rustling too and escape the noose by a miracle. On top of that you build up a nice little feud with McNulty and Uhlmann. For a guy who is supposed to be not lookin' for notice you sure gather a lot of attention. You don't really aim to quirt this bird, do you?"

"Not if I don't meet him."

"There ain't two hundred people in town. If one of you don't light out *pronto* you're bound to meet. Try to give this fellow leather, and he'll plug a hole in you."

"I don't think so. He's yellow."

"That makes him more dangerous. He's liable to get scared and let you have it."

"Well, it's too late to help that now."

"With yore past you're in no shape to go around

with a chip on yore shoulder. The thing to do is sing small. My idea is to light out of here this evening. I'll get Mose Tarwater to look after the corral while I'm gone."

"Why go at all?" Sloan asked. "You're under no obligation to go butting into my grief."

"That's done settled," Fraser told the younger man irritably. "We'll go sit in my office where you won't be noticed."

"All right. In just a minute. I want to get some Bull Durham."

Sloan stepped across the road to the store on the corner. He passed two saddled horses tied to a hitch rack. They were drowsing in the sun. A quirt hung looped over the horn of the saddle nearest him.

Out of the store McNulty came. He stood lounging against the door jamb, his head turned over the left shoulder. He was talking with somebody in the store.

Sloan stepped back and flicked the quirt from the horn. A moment later McNulty caught sight of him. The rancher jerked a Colt forty-five from its pocket in his leather chaps.

"Don't you come any nearer me," he yelped, his voice shrill with alarm. "Not a step, or I'll plug you."

Cape's stride did not falter. It brought him forward evenly and deliberately. "Not you, McNulty," he said quietly. "Not while I'm looking at you." On his lips was a contemptuous smile, but the man in the doorway found no comfort in it. The implacable blue-grey eyes shook his nerve, told him with dreadful certainty that he was delivered into the hands of his enemy. That his own boasting had brought punishment home to him made it no easier to face. The hand holding the gun trembled. Under his ribs the heart died within him. He could not send a message from his flaccid will to the finger crooked around the trigger.

"Rip—Rhino!" he shrieked. "Here's that Sloan lookin' for you. Hurry!"

Uhlmann's huge shapeless body appeared back of his companion. Sloan was not five feet from the wavering revolver. He said, still with no excitement in his steady voice, "A private matter to settle between me and McNulty, one you're not in, Uhlmann."

Cape plucked his victim from the doorway with his left hand as the lash whipped round the wrist holding the weapon. McNulty let out a cry of pain, and the forty-five clattered to the sidewalk.

The German put his hands in his pockets and grinned. This was no fuss of his. He did not like this stranger who had come into his life, and he knew that if they continued to meet there would be trouble some day. But he lived by the code of the outdoor West, at least when he was in the public eye.

"Hop to it, Pete," he encouraged. "Knock hell out of him. Whale the stuffing outa the brash fool."

The quirt in Sloan's hand wound itself with a whish around the thighs of McNulty. It rose and fell again and again. The tortured man cursed, threatened, screamed. He tried to fling himself to the ground to escape, but Cape dragged him back to his feet. The lash encircled Pete's legs like a rope of fire. He howled for help from Uhlmann and begged for mercy.

Sloan flung the writhing wretch from him and dropped the whip. He looked around, to find himself the focus of a score of eyes. They were watching him from doors and window, from the road and the sidewalk. Uhlmann's big body still filled the doorway, one thumb hitched in the sagging belt at his side.

Fraser put a hand on his friend's arm. "Come on, boy," he said. "Show's over."

"What was it all about?" somebody asked.

Rip Morris laughed. He shared the opinion of many others about Pete McNulty, that the fellow was a rat, and he had enjoyed seeing him brought low. "Pete said this fellow Sloan was a cow thief, and I reckon he objected."

The breast of the thrashed man was still racked by sobs he could not control, but he made a feeble attempt to save face. "He had a quirt—and I slipped."

"That's right," Uhlmann retorted scornfully. "All you had was a gun, except yore fists. You certainly showed up good, Pete."

"You're a fine friend, Rhino," whined McNulty. "Stood there and let him use a whip on me, when I was kinda stunned and couldn't fight back."

Uhlmann's beady eyes were cold and expressionless. "You're a grown man, ain't you? Toting a forty-five in your hand. Whyfor would I interfere? If you can't back yore play, don't call a man a thief." The German turned to the owner of the corral. "You a friend of this bird who goes around hunting trouble?" he demanded.

"No, I don't reckon Pete would call me a friend of his," Fraser answered.

"I'm not talking about Pete, but this bird Sloan here."

"Why, yes, I've known Bob some time."

"Bob? Thought his first name was Cape."

Fraser hastened to cover his error. "So it is. But when he was a kid some of us called him Bob. Kind of a nickname."

"Well, whatever you call him, tell him from me that I don't like the color of his hair, nor his face, nor anything about him. Tell him if he wants to stay healthy to keep outa my sight."

Sloan said his little piece. "And tell Mr. Uhlmann from me, Stan, that he's got me plumb scared to death. If I could find a hole handy I would certainly crawl into it."

Fraser grinned cheerfully. "Now, boys, let's not start a rookus. A pleasant time has been had by all, except Pete. Why spoil it now? Come along, Bob."

Sloan turned and walked across the street with Fraser. They picked their way along the sidewalk, in order not to tread on broken boards. Stan slid a look compound of irritation and admiration at Bob Webb's son.

"I've sure enough tied myself up with a wampus cat," he said reproachfully. "I wonder how near that yellow wolf came to filling you with lead. Don't you know better than to walk up to a forty-five pointed at you?"

"It wasn't pointed at me most of the time," Sloan defended apologetically. "The point of the gun was wandering all over Cochise County."

"Yeah, in the hands of a man scared stiff. That kind is most dangerous. I looked to hear his gun tear loose any moment. If that's the way you expect to fight Jug Packard and his gunmen you won't last longer than a snowball in hell."

"This fellow wasn't Packard or one of his warriors. He was just a rabbit."

"You're the luckiest fighting fool I ever saw. If McNulty didn't happen to be a guy everyone despises you would never have got away with it. I could see that Rhino was half a mind to butt in, but he wanted to see Pete get what was coming to him. When he got nasty later I wasn't surprised."

"Nor I. But I figured him out right—guessed he

would decide, the way we all do out here, that a grown man has to fight his own battles."

"Hmp!" grunted Fraser, "Uhlmann has plenty of sand in his craw, but he hasn't any code you would dare bank on. The fellow would just as soon shoot you in the back as not, if nobody saw him."

"He didn't recognize me anyhow."

"No, but he's edging close. One of these days he will. You have some of your dad's ways, and it will come over him all of a sudden that you are young Webb. I didn't help any when I called you Bob twice."

"I'll try to keep out of his sight after this."

They had reached the Rawhide Corral. In one of the stalls they found a big bay horse that had not been there when they left.

"That is Scarface Brown's horse," Fraser said. "When he is in town he usually leaves it here. He's coming over from the store now."

The rustler had shiny leather chaps over his jeans. He wore a faded hickory shirt and a big white sombrero that drooped down on his face. Though his brows were knotted in a scowl, there was a reluctant good will in the eyes turned on Sloan.

"Fellow, you ain't got sense enough to pound sand in a rat hole, or you wouldn't of been crazy enough to walk up to Pete's gun thataway." A gleam of mirth twitched at his dark face. "You sure gave him the leather a-plenty. He's a mean little polecat. Nobody likes him. You ought to be popular with the boys." After a slight hesitation he added: "But you're not with some of them. Take Uhlmann now."

"I gathered that he is a little annoyed at me," Sloan replied dryly.

"Annoyed is not the word. He has figured out who you are. Something about the way you walk told him."

"And who am I?"

"You're Bob Webb, he claims. Rhino is fixin' to do something about it."

"What does he mean to do?"

"He didn't exactly say. But I reckon it will be sudden. Don't make any mistake. You can't monkey with him the way you did with Pete."

Sloan nodded. His cool appraising eyes rested on the rustler. "I'm much obliged, sir. But I don't quite see where you stand. I notice things. The other day Uhlmann and McNulty thought hanging was too good for you. They did considerable talking. They don't seem to be so eager now."

The rustler's frown carried a warning. "Strictly their business and mine. Don't make it yours."

The smile on Sloan's sardonic face was friendly. "I can wonder why you are telling me this if you are tied up with Uhlmann, can't I?"

"Hell, I don't have to give reasons," Scarface growled irritably. "Just because a man does business with another doesn't mean he has to back every play he makes. You did me a favor the other day without meaning to when I was being crowded some. That'll do for you, won't it?"

"If I nearly shoved my neck into a rope loop it wasn't out of kindness to you," Sloan said. "You've got a better reason than that. It sticks in yore craw to see a man murdered without a chance for his life."

"Uhlmann played you a rotten trick once, I've heard. I never did like the brute. If you can slip across the line into Mexico that will be all right with me." Scarface turned to Fraser. "I'll be hittin' the trail now, Stan. I'm headin' south a ways. Maybe yore friend will join me till our trails divide."

"I appreciate the offer," Sloan told the outlaw. "But I'm riding in another direction."

"If I was in yore shoes it would be south," Scarface reiterated. "But you're playin' the hand."

He rode away with a wave of the hand, a dangerous sinister scoundrel, but one Cape much preferred to his associates Uhlmann and McNulty.

Sloan remained at the corral while Fraser hunted up Mose Tarwater to take over for him during his absence. Cape was not happy about what he had done. He recognized ruefully the liabilities of his temperament. What if McNulty had called him a thief? Hard names break no bones. He might have let the little sneak go. To use a whip on a man was degrading to both parties. After Cape had flung down the quirt he had felt for a time physically sick. One had no right to treat another human being with such contempt. Wasn't there something in the Bible about a man being made in the image of God? Already he had paid bitterly for his hot temper. If he had any sense at all by this time he would have learned to curb and control his anger.

Though still a boy when he was taken to the penitentiary, he had already become embittered at the injustice of a social system that permitted the innocent to be robbed by a smoot scoundrel using the law to cover his theft and to ruin the life of a lad framed for a killing he had not committed. The endless days in prison, every minute regulated by armed guards who treated him like a chained wild beast, had intensified the sour resentment churning in him.

A clean fastidious streak in his character had saved him from the underground vileness propagated by some of his fellow convicts. He lived within himself, apart from the prison politics, too proud to cater to those in authority or to join in the plots of those in his cell block. It had been only by sheer chance that an opportunity had come for him to join in the jail break organized by others.

During the days that followed he had lived like a hunted wolf, ready to kill or be killed at a moment's notice. Then Sandra had come into his life. The friendliness and the kindly consideration with which she and her family had treated him had gone to his heart as water does to the roots of a thirsty plant. He had fought against the softness beginning to undermine his hatred. In Sandra's way of life he had no part, he told himself.

14 THE HALF-PINT SQUIRT SAYS HIS PIECE

Fraser came hurrying back almost on a run. "Slap yore saddle on, son. We're gettin' outa here quick. Something cooking over at O'Brien's. Uhlmann has three-four of the boys in a huddle, and that spells nothing good for you."

They left by the back gate of the corral to avoid notice. More than once they looked back, half expecting to see men mounting in pursuit. Except for a few horses tied to hitch racks the street was as deserted as one in a Mexican village during the hours of siesta.

Sloan laughed. "I'm not so important as you thought I was," he said. "Nobody cares whether I go or stay."

"Don't fool yoreself," the little man barked. "This country is gonna be plenty hot for you. Rhino will see to that."

They did not follow the road to Tombstone but cut across the hills. Below them they could see a wagon moving along the winding road to the quartz mill of the Tough Nut Mining company, but nowhere was there visible on it a body of riders who might be looking for an escaped convict with a reward on his head.

Fraser noticed that though young Webb, or Sloan

as he now called himself, gave evidence in his actions and bearing of a desperate recklessness, born of the assurance that he would some day pass out to the sound of crashing guns as slugs tore into his body, he none the less scrutinized vigilantly the terrain they traveled, just as his wary eyes an hour ago had probed into the enemies he was facing. He had set himself a task, and until he had finished it he meant if possible to stay alive.

"We'd better not reach Tombstone till after dark," Fraser suggested. "There's a reward notice for you posted at the post office and at Hatch's saloon. We'll slip in kinda inconspicuous and put up at a rooming-house I know on Allen Street."

They unsaddled in a hill pocket and lay down beneath a live oak which protected them from the heat of the sun. Cape fell asleep within five minutes. He had been hunted so long that he had learned to snatch rest whenever he could do so with safety. The sun had set when Fraser awakened him by throwing a chunk of dead wood at his legs.

Sloan came to life suddenly, gun in hand. He glared at his friend a moment, then grinned at him sheepishly.

"Force of habit," he apologized.

"That's why I threw the chunk at you," Fraser explained. "I reckoned you might be jumpy if you were roused by hand, and I'd hate to have you sorry about puncturing me."

It was after dark when they slipped into Tombstone and left their horses at the O.K. Corral, which a few years earlier had been the scene of the famous gun battle between the Earp brothers and the McLowry-Clanton faction. They walked up Fremont Street to Fourth and ate in a small Mexican restaurant. There was better food at the Can-Can, but they decided against going there on account of its popularity. Best to meet as few people as possible. Before sun-up they expected to be on the road for Tucson.

For the same reason they avoided the Grand Hotel and put up at a cheap rooming-house just outside the business district.

"You stay put right here, son," Fraser ordered. "I'll drift uptown and look around. Maybe Uhlmann has sent word that you may be in town tonight. If there's any news floating about, I'll pick it up."

He sauntered up Allen Street and dropped in at the Crystal Palace. Back of the bar, near one end of it, was a blackboard on an easel upon which were tacked notices of an ice-cream social at the Methodist church, of a school entertainment, and of the new bill at the Birdcage Theater. Beside them was a poster offering two hundred dollars reward for the arrest of Robert Webb, who had escaped from the penitentiary at Yuma on the night of June 22, together with Chub Leavitt and Oscar Holton, both of whom had since been recaptured.

He was described as a man of twenty-six years of age, weight one hundred and sixty pounds, wiry and athletic, not likely to be captured without a struggle. Blue eyes. Thick brown hair. Height, five feet ten. Disposition, morose. Was clean-shaven at the time of the prison break.

Fraser put a foot on the rail and ordered a drink. After supplying him, the bartender nodded toward the easel.

"Saw you reading that poster," he said. "Funny about that. I hear he was in Charleston today, but I don't believe it. If you ask me, he's probably in Mexico. Say, somewheres around Mazatlan or Monterrey. He's had plenty of time to light out. He wouldn't be fool enough to stick around here."

With that opinion Fraser agreed. "Sure, unless he's a plumb idjit. Who says he was at Charleston?"

"Fellow by the name of Uhlmann. Claims to have recognized him. He was in here a while ago. Uhlmann, I mean. With some of his cronies. He was lookin' for Webb."

"Well, I haven't lost him," Fraser drawled. "I'll say this. I knew Giles Lemmon, the fellow he was sent to the pen for killing. Anybody who has served seven years for bumping off that curly wolf has done paid the account with a hell of a lot of surplusage."

The man with the apron put his hairy forearms on the bar and leaned forward. "I was in Prescott when young Webb was tried," he said. "Never saw him. But I've met Jug Packard, and I've heard plenty about how he robbed the Webbs and fixed it so this boy had to go to the pen. Just between you and me and the gate post, brother, they sometimes put the wrong man behind the bars."

"You've talked a mouthful." Fraser finished his drink and turned to go.

Before he reached the swing doors several men pushed through them and came into the room. A wry twisted little smile showed on the face of the corral owner. He knew that there would be trouble ahead unless he lied convincingly. For the first man through the door was Uhlmann. Behind him trooped Morris, McNulty, and a big fellow from the San Simon Valley who called himself Cole Hawkins.

"'Lo, boys," Fraser invited. "Have one on me."

"Where is yore friend Webb?" demanded Uhlmann.

Stan's wide hat was tilted jauntily. He put an elbow on the bar and looked at the huge man with affected surprise.

"Why, I wouldn't know exactly. He went south with Scarface. My guess is that he ought to be crossing the line about now."

"That's a lie. Scarface left Charleston alone—before you and Webb did."

"That's right. About fifteen minutes before us.

121

Webb and I separated outside of town. He went south, to catch up with Scarface."

"I don't believe it," Uhlmann growled angrily. "He's here in town somewhere."

"What makes you think that?" Fraser asked. "He's not a plumb jackass. When Scarface came to the corral he told us you had recognized Webb. Bob figured that spelled trouble, so soon as I had fixed him up with some grub he hit the trail for mañana-land."

Uhlmann mulled that over in sullen silence. It seemed altogether likely. Scarface had told him bluntly he ought to let young Webb alone. Nothing was more probable than that he had warned the man in danger, and if so the only sane thing for Webb to do was to get to the safety of Mexico as fast as a horse could carry him.

But this was not a satisfactory solution for Uhlmann. He wanted to believe that the man he had injured was within reach so that he could strike again.

"If he was going with Scarface, why didn't they start together?" McNulty asked suspiciously.

Fraser gave the man his studied attention. "I've mentioned the reason. Webb stayed while I rustled him some grub. You interested in meeting him—again?"

"One for you, Pete," Hawkins said, grinning.

Uhlmann pushed to the forefront of the talk. "*I'm* interested in meeting him, if you want to know, Fraser. Seems you're a friend of this jailbird. That's yore business, since you want to run with trash like that. But—"

"You've done said it, Rhino," interrupted the little man. "I pick my own company without advice from anybody else."

"Yeah, then listen, fellow." Uhlmann's voice rumbled anger. "I don't let any half-pint squirt pull any shenanigan on me. Get between me and Webb, and I'll tromp you down like I would a beetle."

There was a clean strain of fighting tallow in Fraser. He had ridden the Texas brush country when those who dwelt there fought the raiding Kiowas and Comanches. He had followed the cattle trails to Dodge and Ellsworth regardless of stampedes, blizzards, and bank-full rivers. It was a chief article in his creed to back down for no man.

"Interesting," he murmured, as if to himself. "I've read that the bigger they are the harder they fall—and they are sure easier to hit."

Hawkins slammed a heavy fist joyously on the top of the bar. "The li'l' bantam rooster crows fine. Damfidon't take him up on his offer. Line up, boys. Mr. Fraser's treat."

Reluctantly Uhlmann accepted the drink. There was no percentage in quarreling with Fraser. The owner of the Rawhide Corral was a privileged character. He was an honest man in a community where rogues abounded. He did not interfere with them, and they in turn let him go his own own way. Perhaps it was his blunt fearlessness that made him popular.

"Just the same, if you know what's good for you, Fraser, you'd better cut out siding with Webb," the German grumbled.

"That's what I say," agreed McNulty.

"I reckon Rhino is mighty glad to have yore backing, Pete," Fraser said gently. Since he was not looking for a quarrel with the big ruffian he ignored his threat.

McNulty looked at him angrily, started to speak, and changed his mind. Every time his trousers rubbed against the thighs beneath them he was given a painful reminder of the possible penalty on free speech.

15   THE RANGERS MAKE A CALL

When Sandra drove with her father to Tucson by the old mission road, the day after their hunted guest had ridden from the ranch, it was ostensibly to get material for a new dress. But there was another more urgent reason for the trip. This she broached to John Ranger at the end of her shopping spree. They were eating supper at a Chinese restaurant on Commerce Street.

"Jim Budd told me that Mr. Sloan's sister lives in Tucson," she said, as her father lit his post-prandial cigar. "I'm not very happy about him. He risked his life to save Nels and me. We were able to do so little for him. I'm wondering if we couldn't meet his sister and maybe help him in some way."

Ranger shook the light from his match and considered this. "It's not our fault that we didn't do more, Sandra. He has his neck bowed to go his own way."

She sighed. "Yes, I know. But it wouldn't do any harm to get in touch with his sister. She's married, Jim says."

"How does Jim know so much about her?"

The girl decided to speak out the suspicion in her mind. "I think he was in the penitentiary with Cape Sloan."

"What makes you think that?"

She gave her reasons. They were not convincing, but they might very well be true, the cattleman reflected.

"If you're right about this, I suppose I'll have to let Jim go," he said regretfully.

"Why will you?" she flared up. "Jim is one of the nicest colored men I ever knew. He is devoted to us. I know he is. Just because he has been in prison—"

John smiled indulgently at the cook's champion. "I won't be hasty about it. We'll find out why he was in, and all about his record. Maybe he is entitled to another chance. I like him too. And about Webb—"

"We'd better call him Sloan," she suggested. "Or we'll make a mistake and call him Webb when somebody else is around."

"All right, Sloan. I'm willing to look his sister up. Do you know her married name?"

"No. Jim had never heard it."

"We'll have to move carefully, so as not to get anybody wondering why we are looking for her." He took three or four puffs at his cigar while Sandra waited. "I'll speak to Phil Davis. He's on the *Star* staff and knows everybody in town, more or less. He and I are good friends. He'll keep his mouth shut."

Ranger walked to the office of the *Star* to have a talk with Davis, recently promoted to managing

126

editor. The newspaper man was rotund, middle-aged, and very deaf. At sight of the caller his eyes lit. A good many years earlier they had been in a small party that had stood off a bunch of Apaches for two days.

He jumped up and slapped the ranchman on the back. "You blamed old skeezicks! Where have you been all these years? You come to town and never look me up. Why not?"

"I'm looking you up now," Ranger shouted in his ear. "It was just three months ago I saw you."

They sat down at the desk. The owner of the Circle J R drew a paper pad toward him and scribbled a line. Davis read, "My business is private. Mind if I write it?"

The editor nodded. "Hop to it, John."

Ranger wrote: "I want to find the sister of Bob Webb, the man who was sent to the pen for killing Giles Lemmon. She has been married since, I've been told."

"Young Webb broke jail two-three months ago," Davis murmured.

The cattleman used the pad again. "I know that. It's his sister I'm interested in just now. Thought you might help me locate her."

Davis moved over to a long table with a *Star* file of the previous year. After leafing the bound volume for five minutes he found what he was seeking. It was a story half a stick long telling of the marriage of Joan Webb to Henry Mitchell. He turned to the town directory and ran down a column of names beginning with M.

"They live at 423 Fourth Street, or did when this was got out," he said. "Fortunate you didn't ask for the address of her brother. I'd have had to tell you, somewhere in Mexico."

"Much obliged," Ranger scrawled. "I'll be pleased if you'll forget I asked you."

"Sure. If there's a story in it, let me know when it can be published."

"There isn't, Phil." Ranger crumpled up the sheet of paper he had used and put it in his pocket.

They talked of other things for a few minutes. When a printer in his shirt sleeves brought in a galley of proof John departed.

He was a little troubled in mind by a feeling that his daughter was emotionally involved in the fate of Bob Webb. If so, she was bound to be unhappy until the fancy had spent itself. He thought of taking this up with her but decided it was better not to do so. Her good sense would tell her that there could be no possible future for her with this man, and he did not want to embarrass either himself or her.

The heat of the day still hung over the town as they walked to the address given in the directory. The man who came to the door was a blond good-looking young fellow with a frank open countenance. He identified himself as Henry Mitchell and said that his wife was at home. As he ushered them into the parlor he was plainly a bit puzzled. He had never seen these strangers before. The girl was one of the loveliest he had ever met, and her father—if the man was her father—was evidently a solid cattleman of importance.

Joan Mitchell was a very pretty dark-eyed young woman not very long out of her teens. When Ranger mentioned her brother's name she showed instant signals of alarm. He reassured her at once. They were friends, he explained, and told her the whole story, as far as he knew it, of Bob Webb's adventures since their first meeting.

"So you see we are very much in his debt," Ranger concluded. "We want to put ourselves at your service to help in any way we can."

"But I don't know where he is," Joan said. "I wish I did. Since he escaped I have had one letter from him. He did not tell me his plans. I want so much to see him."

Her husband added an explanation. "Joan understands that Bob could not come here. The place is watched. I think the letter that reached her had been opened and sealed again. Fortunately there was nothing but the postmark to give away Bob's whereabouts, and of course he had left there long before word could be wired to find and arrest him."

"Bob did not kill Giles Lemmon, though if he had it would have been self-defense," Joan cried.

"He told me so before he was tried and again after he was convicted. It was a crazy idea for him to try to talk Mr. Packard into doing justice to mother. I expect Bob got excited. Lemmon and another man named Uhlmann started shooting at him and by accident Uhlmann killed Lemmon. So they got rid of Bob by lying him into the penitentiary." Her voice broke to a sob. "And now they are hunting him like a wild beast. I suppose they will kill him."

Sandra moved to Joan's side and put an arm around her. "I don't think so. He isn't a boy now, but a strong and clever man."

"Why doesn't he get out of the country?" Joan asked piteously. "He can't dodge around Arizona forever."

John Ranger and his daughter were of that opinion too, but they did not voice it. Some day Webb would ride into a town to buy provisions and he would be arrested or shot down while trying to escape.

"He is hoping to get evidence that Packard got the Johnny B crookedly," Ranger told her. "I don't think he can do it. Jug must have covered his tracks long ago."

"I haven't seen Bob for over a year," his sister said. "I suppose he is still very hard and bitter."

"He lives in a shell," Sandra answered. "Beneath that he is as kind and gentle as any of us, though he doesn't want anybody to know it."

As the Rangers walked back to their hotel, Sandra said hopelessly, "There's nothing we can do for him—nothing at all."

"Not just now," her father agreed. "There may come a day when we can help him."

They passed the dark entrance of a store in which a man was lurking. Neither of them glanced at him, though they were near enough to have reached out and touched him. He was the man who called himself Cape Sloan.

16   CHANDLER NEWMAN TALKS

An hour after the Rangers got back to their hotel the son of the proprietor came up to announce that a man in the lobby was inquiring for them.

"Says his name is Fraser. I was to mention Guaymas to you."

The eyes of the cattleman warmed. "Must be Stan Fraser," he told his daughter. "Before you were born I got in a jam at a fandango at Guaymas. It looked like kingdom come for me when a young fellow I had never seen before threw in with me. We went outa that hall side by side with our guns smoking, and quick as we could fork our broncs pulled our freight to hide out in the brush. For several days soldiers hunted us, but we made it back across the line finally."

Sandra's eyes were wide. "Did you kill anybody?"

"No. We winged a couple. I didn't start the trouble. A big Mexican crowded me." John turned to the boy. "Tell Mr. Fraser to come up."

After the greetings were over Fraser explained his presence. "Henry Mitchell told me you were in town and staying here. He said you hadn't been gone ten minutes when I dropped in."

"You know Mr. Mitchell?" Ranger asked.

"Never met him before. I took a message from Bob Webb to his sister."

"He isn't here—in Tucson?" Sandra questioned.

Stan smiled at her. "Maybe you'd better not ask where he is. It's supposed to be a secret. Bob does not want to implicate his friends."

"Then he's here," she cried quickly.

"I didn't say so. But I know how friendly you feel toward him. Mitchell said you would do anything for Bob you could. There's a way you could help, if it wouldn't embarrass you."

"Of course we'll do whatever it is," Sandra promised.

"A man named Chandler Newman lives here— works in the Southern Pacific offices. He used to be bookkeeper for Jug Packard at the Johnny B mine. I'm pretty sure he knows something about the dirty work Packard pulled off in getting control of the mine and freezing out the Webbs. If he does, he has kept his mouth padlocked. Afraid of Jug, my guess is. The point is, could you get him to talk, John?"

"My opinion is that Webb—we'd better call him Sloan even among ourselves—must give up this idea of getting even with Packard if he hopes to escape," the cattleman said.

"That would be any sane man's opinion," Fraser agreed. "But Sloan won't have it that way. He's got his neck bowed and means to go through. He figures not only that Packard has ruined his life but is responsible for the death of his mother. I think if he could pull Packard down he would be content to pay with his life."

"We'd better see this Newman," Sandra decided. "Maybe if he has nothing to tell us Mr. Sloan will give up this crazy idea."

"I'd go see Newman myself, but if I was seen talking with him they might track me back to Bob," Fraser told them. "We don't want Packard to get the idea that anything is stirring."

"If you have his address we'll call on Newman tonight," Sandra cried.

John Ranger did not want to take his daughter with him, but she insisted so strongly on it that he gave way. The ranchman could see that she wished to have a part in anything that might help Sloan.

Chandler Newman was a thin colorless individual, pale and narrow-chested. He was not mentally equipped to stand up to as ruthless a villain as Jug Packard. But he had in him a clean core of honesty. He had broken with Packard because he would not have anything to do with so flagrant a steal as his employer was putting across on the widow of the man who had befriended him. But farther than that he did not intend to go. Knowing Packard, he was going to do nothing that would invite his anger. He had the obstinacy of a weak man, and Ranger faced that barrier at once when he mentioned why he had come.

"Nothing to say," the bookkeeper insisted, and

repeated the words when Ranger refused to accept that as final.

Not until Sandra saw that her father was going to fail did she have any part in the talk. They were sitting in a small parlor with their host and his wife. Mrs. Newman was younger than her husband, plump, with bright beady eyes and quick birdlike motions. As they talked, her gaze shifted from one to another quickly.

"I want to tell you something, Mr. Newman," Sandra began. "You've heard about the raid of the Lopez gang not long ago. Maybe you don't know that four of the ruffians captured me and my young brother. One of them wounded him and another dragged me from a buggy to his horse. I knew something dreadful was in store for me. Just then a man topped a rise in the road and saw us. He came at a gallop, slammed one of the bandits down with the barrel of his rifle, shot another dead, and drove the others away. I never saw anything so daring. It's a wonder he escaped alive."

"We read something about it," Mrs. Newman said, her shining eyes fixed on this eager lovely girl.

"That man was Bob Webb," Sandra explained. "So you see we have got to save him."

Mary Newman saw more than that. This golden girl was in love with the escaped convict. Nothing less could account for the rapt look in her blue eyes. "Yes," she agreed. "If you can."

"Bob Webb did not kill Giles Lemmon. He says so, and we are sure he is telling the truth. It suited Jug Packard to have him sent to prison, and he fixed the testimony so that the boy was convicted."

Mrs. Newman looked at her husband. You've always thought that, Chan."

"You keep out of this, Mary," Newman snapped.

"But why?" Sandra cried. "If he isn't guilty we ought to find out and try to get him freed. You wouldn't want an innocent man to spend half his life in prison to satisfy a scoundrel's grudge?"

"What I think doesn't matter," Newman replied doggedly. "All I've heard is rumors. Why come to me?"

"We came to you to find out something you do know," the girl said, her husky voice tremulous with emotion. "You kept the books for the Johnny B. All the time Packard was engineering his steal of the mine from Mrs. Webb you were right there. You must know how he did it. Was he robbing her of the ore? He closed down for two years to make the stock worth nothing. Had he struck a rich vein before he did that?"

Mrs. Newman did not speak, but she looked steadily at her husband, compulsion in her eyes.

"All that is a closed book," the man blurted out. He was unhappy at the position in which he was placed. He knew that his wife had never been wholly satisfied at his silence, but she had

136

persuaded herself that to speak would do no good and would surely endanger Chandler. "No use trying to reopen it. Jug has the mine now, and nobody can do a thing about it."

"Bob Webb doesn't think so," Ranger answered. "It is the one chance he has of saving what is left of his life. For Heaven's sake, speak out if you have any proof of Packard's chicanery."

"There was a fire at the mine," Newman said. "The books were burned."

"Go on, Chan," his wife insisted in a low voice.

"It wouldn't do Webb any good for me to speak, but one of Jug's gunmen would get me sure." The words seemed to be dragged out of Newman's mouth.

"It isn't for us to say whether it would do Mr. Webb any good," Mary differed. "Perhaps it might. Anyhow, now the question has come up again I think you ought to tell what you know."

"You know what will happen to me if I do," Newman protested. "I wouldn't live long enough to tell the story in court."

"You're overestimating Packard's power," Ranger told him. "I've been threatened several times in my life, once by a notorious killer and another time by a bad outlaw gang. I'm here. They have gone. The dangers we foresee rarely harm us. If we walk up to them, they usually aren't there."

"This is different. I'm no gunfighter. You are an outdoor man, used to weapons, and known to be game. And you are a prominent citizen, with a bunch of cowboys back of you, whereas I am nobody. There wouldn't be much of a fuss made if I was shot down."

"Couldn't we get protection for Mr. Newman?" Sandra asked her father.

"If he tells his story to the district attorney and swears to it before a notary it would not do Packard any good to hurt him," the cattleman said. "In fact, it would greatly prejudice his chances in court."

"That would do me a lot of good if I was dead," Newman retorted, with a bitter laugh.

Sandra realized that the man would have to be given some assurance of safety. It was all very well for her father to talk about walking through danger and seeing it vanish like mist before the sun. But John Ranger had always trod the way of the strong, whereas Chandler Newman was a bookish timid man with too much imagination, one who had never taken a risk that could be avoided. A plan sprang to her mind that might be feasible. Ranger did a lot of shipping over the Southern Pacific and was on friendly terms with the manager of the western division.

"You have been talking about getting a bookkeeper to bring your books down to date and to clean up a lot of back correspondence," the girl suggested. "Maybe Mr. Compton would give Mr. Newman a leave of absence for three or four months to come to the ranch. He and Mrs. Newman could live in our old adobe house. It's very comfortable. They would be quite safe there."

"I could certainly use you to advantage," Ranger admitted, speaking to the clerk. "You could stay with us until this whole thing is settled one way or another. If Packard wins out I'm sure Compton would place you in Los Angeles or San Diego."

A flush of pleasure came into the face of Mary Newman. "We've talked so often of moving to California," she reminded her husband.

Before yielding he felt it necessary to defend his past inaction. "When I saw what Packard was doing I wrote an unsigned letter to Mrs. Webb," he said. "As soon as I could do it I gave up my job at the Johnny B."

"Right," commented the cattleman. "You felt you could not work for a scoundrel."

"Packard did not want me to leave. He made it plain that if I did any talking he would settle with me. Twice since I left him he has sent for me to come to his house here. Each time he gave me a quarter of beef, but I felt the threat back of his interest in me."

"His threats can't harm you if you are at the Circle J R," Ranger promised.

Newman was nervous as a caged wildcat, but he made a start in his story at last. "I discovered he had struck a rich vein when I saw by chance two sets of smelter returns from the same shipment. One was very rich; the other didn't pay the expenses of smelting. Packard must have given the manager of the smelter a percentage to help him in his crookedness. My idea is that before he shut down he made enough to buy up the stock when it went off to a low price. I kept copies of the duplicate returns and have them yet." In answer to questions Newman gave the name of the smelter. The manager had been discharged a year later for robbing the company. Newman had heard he was now living in Phoenix.

"Someone else must have known what was going on," Ranger hazarded. "There must have been at least one bookkeeper in with the super-intendent to falsify the returns."

Newman agreed that must have been the case.

"If we can find out who it was we may be able to bring pressure on him to talk," the ranchman said. "At any rate we can try."

He arranged with the Newmans to see Compton at once to get a leave of absence. As soon as it was granted the bookkeeper and his wife had better move to the ranch. On that last point Newman was heartily in accord with him. He wanted to be in a safe shelter when Packard discovered what was afoot.

17 IN A LADY'S BEDROOM

Henry Mitchell came back into the dark hall and reported that all was clear. Joan clung to her brother with clenched fingers, as though her physical grip on him could hold him from the danger pressing close.

"If you would only forget what has happened and ride out of the country," she cried. "Leave us to clear all this mess up. You have good friends now who will help."

Bob Webb, alias Cape Sloan, gently opened her fists and freed himself from her. "Everything will be all right now," he promised. "I'll not throw down on myself. *Adios, muchacha.*"

As he kissed her good-bye he tasted the salt tears on her cheek. To his mind there jumped a picture of a small girl with pigtails sitting on their father's lap listening to a good-night story of a mired calf rescued from a quicksand. Memories of the old days flooded him. He was moved and took care not to show it. She belonged to that vanished chapter of his life when he had thought the future was his to shape as he wished.

Stan Fraser came out of the darkness to meet him.

"Everything dandy out here," the little old-timer said. "Long as nobody knows you are in Tucson and you keep under cover you'd ought to be all right. What I'm worried about is Uhlmann and his crowd. McNulty talked like they might drift over this way. My idea is for us to get out now and camp on the mesa, then soon as it is day be on our way."

Webb agreed that might be a good idea.

They walked back through the business section along empty streets. Except for the gambling houses and their patrons the town seemed sunk in sleep. Inside the Legal Tender and the Silver Dollar they could hear the rattle of chips and the voices of the players. Fraser tilted his head toward the former.

"Many's the time I've bucked the wheel in there with yore dad. He was sure a wild colt when he was young."

"I've watched the little ball spin there myself some," Webb admitted.

Out of the Legal Tender poured a jet of men.

"Told you I'd take the bank to a cleaning," one of them boasted.

The huge graceless figure beside him let out a yelp of triumph. His gaze had fallen on the escaped convict. He opened his mouth to shout recognition. Instead, he gave a groan and sagged against the wall. The long barrel of Stan Fraser's pistol had crashed down on his cranium. Uhlmann for the moment had lost interest.

"Burn the wind, boy," Fraser cried, and he dived

into the stairway leading to the private poker rooms in the second story.

Webb took the treads after his friend, racing up them two at a time. The roar of a forty-five from the entrance below filled the well with a noise like the blasting of dynamite. Stan flung open a door of a room where five men in their shirt-sleeves sat around a table with chips in front of them and cards in their hands.

The players stared at the two men charging through the room to the small stairway in the far corner.

"What in hell—?" one of them began to protest.

Bob Webb's arm swept the chimney from the bracket lamp attached to the wall and plunged the room in darkness. He followed his friend up the dark closed way to the trap-door above. Through it they went to the roof.

"Where now?" he asked.

Fraser did not know. He hoped there was another opening to permit descent into an adjoining building. If not, they were out of luck. As they moved forward to look for a road of escape they heard the noisy clamor of many voices below. Men were milling around in the poker room confused by the lack of light.

"Found one," Fraser called to his companion.

Fortunately the trap-door was not bolted inside. Bob went down into the dark pit after Stan, stopping only to close and latch the heavy framework of the vent. The ladder led them to a store room from which they stepped into a passage with rooms on both sides.

"Must be the Tucson Hotel we're in," whispered Fraser.

They had no time to waste. Already they could hear the stamping feet on the roof and the shouts of the searchers.

"We've walked into a rat trap, looks like," Bob mentioned. "Nothing to do but go on down and fight our way out."

A gleam of wintry humor lit the little man's eyes. "We might take a room for the night."

Bob did not answer in words. But Fraser had given him an idea. There would be small chance now of breaking through below to safety. The gambling houses had emptied into the street to join the chase. Why not invite themselves to share the room of one of the hotel guests? Under compulsion he might be induced to hide them. It would at least give them a breathing space during which they could decide what was best to do.

Very few of the rooms were locked. The habit of the country was to forget keys. Bob opened a door, looked in, and discovered through the darkness two children asleep in a bed. He withdrew and closed the door gently.

"Kids in there," he told his companion.

They softfooted down the hall and tried again. From the doorway Bob's glance swept the room.

The bed had been slept in but was at the moment unoccupied.

"Filled with absentees," Webb murmured.

There was a rustle at the window. A shadow bulked close to it from which stood out a white face.

"What do you want?" a woman's voice asked sharply.

"Sorry, ma'am," Bob apologized. "Mistake. Wrong room."

Before he could leave she flung out a protest, her voice fined down almost to a whisper. "Wait. You're Cape Sloan. They are attacking you."

Bob would have known that voice among a thousand. Its low throaty cadence set the excitement strumming in his blood. He guessed that Sandra had been wakened and drawn to the window by the sound of the firing.

The shuffling of many feet on the roof above came plainly to them. Somebody was hammering on the trap-door. In another minute searching men would fill the corridor.

"We're lookin' for a port in storm," Fraser said.

"But not this one," Webb added quickly. "We'll be on our way, Miss Sandra."

"No," the girl objected. "You're safer here. They won't come in without knocking, and when they knock I'll meet them at the door."

"That will be fine," Fraser replied. "We'll stand back out of sight."

But Webb was not so sure. If it was ever dis-covered that she had hidden them gossip about her would fill the countryside.

"We'll find another room," he insisted.

She was at the door before him, her arms stretched wide across it. "Don't be foolish. They are on their way down now. It's all right. Father is in the next room."

Already boots were clattering down the ladder. It was almost too late to go. If they left the chance of escape was not one in ten.

"Much obliged, Miss Sandra," Fraser spoke softly, to make sure of not being heard. "We're in a tight spot sure enough."

"Get back of the bed and crouch down," she ordered. "Hurry, please. They'll be here in no time."

A man was knocking on a door farther down the hall demanding admittance. Reluctantly Bob joined his friend back of the bed.

Urgent shouts beat through the wall to them. "They didn't go downstairs . . . Must be somewhere here if they came down through the trap-door . . . Search the rooms, boys." And then the angry snarl of Uhlmann: "It was that little cuss Fraser busted me on the head."

A fist beat on the door panel of the room. "Hey! Open up here. We're searching the hotel."

Sandra flung a glance behind her to make sure her guests were concealed. The thumping of her heart was so loud that she was afraid it would be heard. As she opened the door her fingers drew the nightgown closer around her throat.

"W-what do you want?" she quavered.

She was manifestly frightened, and her fear was no disservice. The men in the corridor were rough customers, some of them scoundrels. But they had the frontier respect for good women, at least the outward semblance of it. Sandra recognized one, a man who dealt in cattle, by name Rip Morris.

He lifted his hat. "Sorry, miss. Don't be scared. We're lookin' for an escaped convict. We think he's in the hotel here somewhere."

The door was open six or eight inches. She clung to the knob. "You don't mean—in my room?"

"No need to be afraid, miss," he assured her. "If he is, we won't let him hurt you. Point is, he might have slipped in here while you were asleep."

"But he couldn't have!" she cried, panic in her voice. "I haven't been asleep. At the first shots I got up. Nobody could have come in without me seeing him."

John Ranger came into the room through a connecting door. "What's all this?" he demanded sternly.

"We're huntin' for that escaped murderer Webb," Morris explained apologetically. "He's around somewhere—probably in the hotel."

"Not in my daughter's room, Rip," retorted Ranger's warning voice. "You don't mean that."

"He might of slipped in to hide without her noticin' him," Uhlmann growled.

"But I told them I was awake and got up when the shooting started," Sandra explained to her father.

"That's settled then," Ranger snapped. "Get going, boys."

"Sure, Mr. Ranger," a man in the background said. "Sorry we disturbed the young lady. Might have been an empty room far as we knew. Let's go, Rip."

Ranger closed the door without ceremony. He stood there a long minute listening to the hunters troop down the hall and try the next room. When he turned at last, it was to say in a low voice, "Come out from behind that bed."

The crouching men stood up.

"We butted in, not knowing this was Miss Sandra's room," Fraser mentioned. "They were crowdin' us, and we had to go somewhere."

"I made them stay and hide," Sandra added.

Without glancing at her, Ranger said sharply, "Get back of that bed and put some clothes on."

Sandra drew back in shocked embarrassment. She had been so entirely concerned with the safety of Bob Webb that she had forgotten she was barefoot and wore only a nightgown over her slender body. From the back of a chair she snatched a garment and held it in front of her.

The intruding fugitives walked to the window

and looked out. They heard the rustle of clothes and the stir of swift feet. Presently a small distressed voice said, "All right."

Fraser said gently, "We're sure obliged to Miss Sandra for helping us out of a mighty hot spot, John."

"I'll never forget it," Webb added. The thought of her young loveliness, startled fear for him stamped so vividly on her face, still quickened the blood in his veins.

"It came so sudden," the girl explained shyly. "I didn't think about—clothes."

Ranger did not discuss that point. The situation explained itself. "You're a hard man to help, Webb," he told the convict bluntly. "In your circumstances nobody but a fool would be in Tucson—or in Arizona at all."

"How often I've told him that," Fraser agreed.

All of them were speaking in voices so low that they were almost whispers.

"We were just leaving when we ran across Uhlmann coming out of the Legal Tender." Webb attempted no justification. "I know I'm a nuisance. Sorry it has to be that way. Better give up trying to help me. I don't want to get you into trouble—or Stan either for that matter."

"It's you we're worried about," Sandra reminded him.

"Better let us carry on, Webb," the cattleman urged. "We are taking the Newmans to the Circle

J R to protect the husband. He will testify that Packard falsified the smelter returns. The superintendent of the smelter must have been in on the deal. I understand he now lives at Phoenix. I am going to check on the thing from that end too. It looks as if we have got something on Jug that might bust him wide open, providing we can drive our wedge in and prove a conspiracy. Frankly, you can't be of any help in this. The thing for you to do is to get out and hole up until we send for you."

"I'll keep out of yore way," Webb promised. "And I'll be very grateful for anything you can do to clear me."

He spoke to John Ranger, but the daughter of the cattleman knew that he was sending her an indirect message of thanks.

Ranger took the hunted men back with him to his room. They had to get out of town before morning. After a time Uhlmann and his companions would get tired of looking for their victims and would either return to their gambling or go to bed. The best chance for a getaway would be just before daybreak. Webb's enemies of course would check up all the wagon yards and corrals in town to find the horses of Fraser and Webb. But probably they would not succeed in finding them, since Henry Mitchell had moved them to a pasture owned by his brother on the river bottom just out of town.

18 ENTER JUG PACKARD

Night still filled the sky when John Ranger walked out of the hotel to make arrangements for the escape of his friends. He stood for a moment on the sidewalk looking up and down the street. Pete McNulty moved forward from the entrance to the Legal Tender and joined the Circle J R owner.

"Ain't you up early, John?" he asked.

Ranger looked at him with disfavor. "No earlier than you are, Pete," he answered coldly.

"I'm kinda on duty," McNulty explained. "The boys think that fellow Webb is still around. We aim to cook his goose if we find him."

"Meaning just what?"

"Why, he's a murderer, escaped from the pen. You know what a desperate character he is. If he's killed resisting arrest we can't help it."

"You a deputy sheriff?"

"Not exactly. You don't have to be to collect a fellow like this with a reward on his head."

"Is there a reward offered for the arrest of Cape Sloan?"

"He's Bob Webb, that's who he is. Rhino recognized him."

"I was with Uhlmann several times in the presence of Sloan," Ranger observed. "He didn't say anything about Sloan being young Webb. If

151

you make a mistake and kill the wrong man you might find yourself in prison, Pete. Better go slow."

"We'd ought to of hanged this bird when we first saw him in the cañon," McNulty retorted bitterly. "I said so, but you and Russ Hart wouldn't have it that way."

Ranger did not think it worth while to answer that complaint. He walked up Congress Street and disappeared in the darkness. The sentry watched him go and then reported to his associates, who were playing poker in a corner of the hall.

In the east a pale promise of light was sifting into the sky when McNulty notified his companions that Ranger had returned and vanished into the hotel.

Uhlmann slammed a hamlike fist on the table and set the chips rattling. "You can't tell me he doesn't know where that wolf is holed up. Had him down to his ranch for a while, didn't he? They don't just happen to be in town at the same time."

"Don't forget there's a pot on the table that's practically mine," Cole Hawkins reminded him, and shoved in a stack of blues. "Kick 'er up five." He slid a malicious grin at the huge ungainly cattleman. "Might be they are boilin' up bad medicine for the gent whose testimony sent Webb to the pen."

"They can't do a thing to me," Uhlmann

blustered. "Webb is the one headed for trouble." He ripped out an angry oath. "If I ever get my gun on him they won't have to bother taking him back to Yuma."

"If you happened to be the lucky gent and not the one to be measured for a wooden box," Hawkins retorted. The San Simon valley man was a rustler and bad character generally, but he had, like most hardy ruffians, a sneaking fondness for cool and daring scamps. He had joined the hunt for Webb because of the excitement, yet had hoped they would not find the convict. Whatever of evil Webb might have done, he felt that the young fellow's faults were venial compared to those of Hans Uhlmann or Jug Packard.

"No if about it," the big man boasted. "I'll take that bird on any day of the week."

"Okay with me," Hawkins agreed. "Question before the house is, do you call, raise, or fold?"

Uhlmann looked at his cards again and threw them into the discard. "I'm laying down a flush. Any chump could tell you've got a full."

The San Simon rustler flipped his cards over and reached for the pot. He had two small pairs.

A man pushed through the swing doors and came back to the poker table. He was dressed in cheap and soiled clothes a sheepherder would have disdained. His unprepossessing face was seamed with wrinkles. Close-set eyes, small and shifty, slid from one to another of those at the table. The thin-lipped twisted mouth hinted at cruelty.

"'Lo, Jug," Uhlmann grunted. "I sent for you because I thought you'd like to know an old friend of yours is in town tonight."

"If Webb is here what are you all doing on yore fat behinds instead of hunting him down?" Packard demanded angrily.

The laugh of Hawkins was a taunt. "Dunno about the other boys, Jug, but I haven't lost this young fellow. Me, I kinda like his nerve. It will suit me fine if he makes a clean getaway."

Packard turned an ugly look on him. "An escaped murderer, isn't he—with a price on his head?"

Hawkins looked around the table coolly, his gaze on each of those present in turn. It came to rest at last on the mine owner. "Murder is a nasty word, Jug. I like killer better." The outlaw's voice was suave and pleasant. "Just a prejudice I have. Maybe some of these boys share it. If we took a private census of gents now here, I reckon the casualties they have caused would be found to fill quite a few graves. No blame intended, of course. The unfortunates likely asked for it. But I never heard that Giles Lemmon was any plaster saint."

"Webb had a fair trial and was convicted," Packard retorted harshly.

"The kid had bad luck. Far as I recollect none of us got as far as a court room."

Packard brushed aside any discussion of moral

values. "I'll add another two hundred dollars reward for this fellow's scalp, dead or alive."

"I'd like that four hundred dollars," Uhlmann said. "I'll hold you to that offer, Jug."

"Where was this fellow seen last?" Packard demanded. "Tell me about it."

They gave him both facts and surmises.

"You had him cornered, and you let him slip away," Jug accused.

"That's right," Hawkins agreed cheerfully. "He said 'hocus pocus open sesame' and melted into thin air."

"He's right around here somewheres," McNulty chipped in. "He couldn't of got away. We've got watchers posted in front and back."

"Ranger knows where he's at," Uhlmann supplied venomously. "I'd bet fifty plunks against a dollar Mex."

"But none of you had the guts to tell him so," Packard snarled. "You let him bluff you off."

"Nobody is holding you here, Jug," Morris said. "You go tell him."

Packard was sly and mean by nature. He preferred to use others as tools for his villainy. But there was a substratum of cold nerve in him that lay in reserve back of his caution.

"Don't think I won't," he flung back harshly. "Where's his room at?"

They told him. He turned and walked heavily out of the place.

"The little cuss is going to put it up to Ranger," Hawkins commented. He was surprised. Packard had the reputation of getting his results less directly.

The mine owner stumped up the stairs of the Tucson Hotel, walked down the corridor, and knocked at the door indicated. A voice said, "Who is it?"

Packard did not answer. He opened the door and walked into the room. The lamp was not lit, but he could see that Ranger was not alone. Two other figures bulked in the darkness. One was standing by the window, another sitting on the bed.

A bracket lamp in the corridor lit the face of the self-invited guest. "What brought you here, Packard?" asked the cattleman.

The intruder's small eyes peered at the man on the bed, then shifted to the one by the window. Coming day was beginning to lift the darkness. Packard took two or three steps toward the man by the casement.

"Hold it, Jug," warned the sitting man lightly. He was nursing a forty-five in his lap.

Packard paid no attention. He had not expected to find Bob Webb in the stockman's room. But he had recognized Fraser and had to certify his conviction that the third man present was Webb. A little near-sighted, he had almost in that dim light to push his wrinkled face against that of the suspect.

156

"You're Webb," he said after a moment. The beard, the harsh lines etched in the lean cheeks, the steely hardness of the eyes, had to be brushed aside. They had been no part of the boy he had wronged. Bitter years in prison had brought them. But the bony contour of the head could belong only to the son of the Bob Webb who had been his partner.

"Sloan is the name to you," Bob corrected.

"You'd better give up and come with me without any fuss," Packard flung out shrilly. "All I got to do is shout and—"

"No," Ranger cut in sternly. "Temporarily Mr. Sloan is my guest. You'll accept that fact."

"Or go out in smoke before yore friends arrive, Jug," Fraser added genially. "And don't think I'm loading you about that."

Packard whirled on Ranger. "You know what you're doing, don't you? Aiding and abetting the escape of a criminal wanted by the law. Do that, and you'll go join Webb at Yuma, John."

"You haven't proved that Sloan is Webb," the cattleman differed.

"You know he is. You know it doggoned well. I can bring witnesses up to swear to him. Uhlmann for one."

"But you are not going to," Fraser said gently. "You're going to sit down in a chair nice and friendly until we say 'Depart in peace,' like the Good Book has it."

"No, sir. You can't keep me. I'm going down right now to tell the boys you've got this murderer here."

Ranger confronted him as he made for the door. "Don't make a mistake," he warned. "I didn't invite you here, but since you came without being asked you'll stay. If you open your mouth to cry out I'll throttle you."

"You'll go to the pen for this," Packard gulped out.

Fraser brought a chair to the mine owner. "Sit," he ordered.

Jug glared at him. He had been top dog for so long that it came hard on him to obey. "Do you no good to bold me," he snapped sourly. "If I don't go back the boys will come looking for me."

"So they will," Fraser chuckled. "And find you tied up here nice and comfortable."

"You'll never get away," Packard prophesied spitefully. "We've got men back and front to check on you."

Fraser pushed him back into the chair. "Have to use the sheets to tie him," he said.

"We won't tie him." Webb had been watching the little plaza back of the hotel through the window. "Time to go. A friend is leaving two horses at the hitch rack for us. We'll take Packard with us and see how he likes being shot at."

Stan Fraser stared at Bob. "Take him with us?" he repeated, puzzled.

"Far as the horses. For his friends to make a target of, if they feel that way."

"Sure," cried Fraser joyfully. "Jug has a kind heart. He will protect us like we were brothers."

"I won't go a step of the way," the mine owner announced shrilly.

Sandra opened the door connecting with the next room. "Is everything all right?" she asked anxiously.

"Everything is fine," Bob answered. "We're just leaving. Sorry we barged in on you and yore father this way and forced you to hide us."

The girl knew he was trying to safeguard them against any charge Packard might make that they had aided his escape.

"Good-bye, Mr. Sloan," she said, and shook hands with him. "I hope this silly mistake about you being that man Webb will be cleared up."

Bob smiled. "We'll clear up the whole business," he said.

19   GUNS ON THE PLAZA

With Fraser's revolver prodding his back, Packard announced again doggedly that he was not going downstairs.

"Suit yoreself," the little man drawled. "You can go or stay. If you stay, it will be with a head busted by the barrel of my gun. Not such an easy tap as I gave Uhlmann. But don't let me influence you."

Packard shuffled down the corridor. "I'll fix you some day for this," he promised, his voice thick with fury.

Ranger watched them go from the door of the room. On his face was a frown of anxiety. It was his opinion that presently they would hear the roar of bullets from below. His daughter stood beside him, white to the lips. She felt a panic fear choking her throat.

Webb led the way down the stairs. He opened the back door a few inches and peered out. Several men were just emerging from the Legal Tender. One was Uhlmann. He had a revolver in his hand and was giving the others instructions where to take their posts. The two saddled horses were hitched to a rack a short distance from the hotel. A lank fellow in leather chaps and a blue shirt stood beneath a cottonwood carrying a rifle, evidently the guard posted to cover the back door.

He called to Uhlmann that the black horse with white stockings belonged to Fraser.

To make the run from the back door to the horses, with half a dozen guns trained on them, would be suicidal. Webb saw that at once. A plan jumped to his mind, one made possible by the unwilling co-operation of Packard. There was a dark closet near the entrance where buckets, brooms, and mops were kept. Given luck, it might serve the hunted men nicely.

Bob sketched in three sentences what he had in mind, explaining curtly to Packard his part in it. "You'd better make it good," he added grimly. "If you let them suspect it's a ruse you won't live long enough to enjoy tricking me. Just one suspicious move, and I'll drop you."

"You figuring on killing me?" Packard asked, gimlet orbs drilling into those of his enemy.

"If we're discovered. You'll kick off before we do."

The prisoner started to protest, looked into Webb's bleak eyes, and decided it was not worthwhile. "I'll play yore game, because I can't do anything else," he said, sullen anger in his voice.

Packard was to call his men and tell them he had discovered the hiding place of Webb. He was to head them up the stairs, bringing up the rear himself. Every foot of the way he would be covered by the guns of the two men in the closet.

"Don't get crazy and start anything," Fraser

advised. "All we'd have to do is crook our fingers."

"I'm not a fool," snarled Packard. "You've got the drop on me right now, but inside of forty-eight hours you'll both be laid out cold."

Webb spoke, in his voice the law harsh grating of steel: "You murdered my father, Packard. I'm not forgetting that. You robbed my mother and lied me into prison. Pay day is coming for you soon. I'm telling you this now so that you'll know if you lift a hand or let out a word to betray us I'd as lief shoot you in the back as I would a wolf. Better not forget that for a moment. Speak yore piece now—and make these men believe it if you want to go on living."

Bob's revolver pressed against Packard's ribs as the man put his head through the door opening and called to Uhlmann. He spoke urgently but not loud.

"Hi, Rhino, I've found Webb. He's upstairs. Bring the boys and keep 'em quiet."

"Right away, Jug." Uhlmann spoke to those with him, turned, and lumbered across from where he stood to the back door of the hotel. Three men trailed at his heels. Hawkins remained where he was, at the door of the Legal Tender. The man in chaps under the cottonwood held his ground.

"Did Ranger tell you where he was?" Uhlmann asked in a sibilant whisper.

Webb drew back to join Fraser in the darkness of the closet.

"Heard him talking with Fraser—in a room upstairs," Packard answered. "Walk soft, boys. We want to surprise them."

The old treads creaked beneath the weight of their heavy bodies. They went in single file, Uhlmann leading. Jug flung a look of bitter hate toward the closet and moved along the passage to the stairs. He knew that the revolver of his enemy covered him every foot of the way and did not feel sure that a bullet would not crash into his back. There was a bend in the staircase half-way up. If he could get past that he could shout out an alarm and send his men charging down on those below. The steps of the flight seemed interminable. Four more—three—two. He took the last at a leap and from the landing screamed at the others to come back.

"Holy Mike, what's eatin' you?" Uhlmann demanded.

Already the men hidden in the closet were bolting for the door. As they raced for the horses they heard the pounding of feet down the stairs. The cowboy beneath the cottonwood woke up and yelled, "What's going on here?" Neither Webb nor Fraser paid any heed to him. He started to run to the hitch rack, stopped, and raised his rifle.

A bullet from the door of the hotel whistled past the running men, and before the crash of the explosion had died away a second and a third shot sounded. One of them came from the gun of Hawkins. Webb pulled the slip-knot of a bridle rein and swung to the saddle of his mount. Fraser was already in motion, a few yards ahead of him. He jumped his horse to a gallop and jerked it to a sudden stop. The black had given a scream of pain and collapsed, sending its rider flying to the ground.

Bob swung round and rode back. His one idea was to pick Stan up and get away from the heavy fire centering on them. But in the second during which he faced the blazing guns his eyes took in a dozen details of the panorama in the plaza. Three or four men were strung along the wall of the hotel firing at him. Pete McNulty was drawing a bead on him from back of a drinking trough. Packard shrieked shrill orders to get him—get him. A dozen yards from the hitch rack the cowboy in chaps lay face down, his outflung hands still clinging to the rifle he would never use again.

Fraser scrambled to his feet and ran limping to his friend. He flung himself on the horse back of Bob, who whirled the cowpony in its tracks and touched it with a spur. The animal shot across the plaza like a streak of light and raced down a dusty street past the old convent. Behind them sounded the fire of the drumming weapons.

"You didn't get hit?" Bob asked.

"No. I kinda sprained my ankle when I lit after my horse went down." Fraser grinned exultantly. "We sure fooled them that time. I reckon Jug would sell himself right now for two bits."

"We'll have to pick up another horse somewhere."

"Yes, sir. On the q.t. I can see how this will make you or me out a horse thief." The little man chuckled. "I've been most everything else in my time. We're lucky to have got away whole."

"One man didn't—the man in chaps with the rifle. He was drawing a bead on me just before I reached the hitch rack. I didn't see him again till I stopped to pick you up. He was lying on the ground spraddled out, face down. Someone must have shot him by mistake for us."

Fraser could not understand that. The cowboy had not been in the line of fire. "Looks like one of Jug's warriors must of got buck fever," he hazarded. "But I'll bet my boots they lay the blame on us."

Bob thought that was very likely.

20 WHO KILLED CHUCK HOLLOWAY?

Packard tore a sunstained and shapeless hat from his head, slammed it on the ground, and stamped on it furiously. "They got away. Goddlemighty, you lunkheads had twenty cracks at them—and missed. That devil Webb rode back again, and still you couldn't hit him."

"Must be one among us who can hit the side of a barn," Hawkins jeered. "Someone killed a horse."

"Yeah, and then let Fraser climb onto Webb's horse and ride away. After you had him on the ground practically surrounded. I never saw such crazy shooting in my life."

"We'd have got them all right if you hadn't dragged us upstairs," Uhlmann grumbled. "You fixed it nice for them to reach their horses, Jug. Don't cuss us. You're the one most to blame."

Rip Morris was kneeling beside the prostrate cowboy in chaps. He looked up and called to the others. "Quit yapping, boys, and come here. They got Chuck Holloway. He's dead."

"Dead!" McNulty looked down at the man lying on the ground. "When did they kill him? Far as I could see neither of them fired a shot."

"That's right," Uhlmann agreed. "Unless it was before I got outa the hotel."

"It couldn't of been before that," Packard objected. "I saw Chuck with his rifle raised to fire. But Pete is right. Neither of these fellows fooled away any time shooting back at us. They went straight for their horses and lit out. If that's so, one of us . . ."

The mine owner did not finish the sentence. He looked round on a group of startled faces. The gaze of each shifted from one to another, and none of them liked what they saw in the eyes staring at them. Chuck must have been killed by one of their own group.

Rip Morris put into words the thought that was in the minds of all of them. "He was standing off to the right. I don't see how any of us could have done it—unless someone got jumpy and took him for a friend of Webb."

"Must have been that," Hawkins agreed. His glance went coolly round the circle. " 'Fess up, fellow, whoever it was. We'll have to stand by you."

Each denied his guilt, some profanely and some with corroborative explanation, but all explicitly and with vigor.

"Just up and shot himself, seems like," the San Simon man murmured ironically.

Morris raised another question. "Did Chuck have any enemies?"

Uhlmann stared at Rip a long time, while the meaning of the inquiry seeped into his dull mind.

"Holy Mike, you don't think one of us—on purpose—"

"Maybe it wasn't one of us," Morris suggested. "Someone could of slipped out from a house on the other side of the plaza and plugged him."

"Or Ranger from the window of his room," Packard said with acrid spite. "He was hiding Webb. Why wouldn't he help him make a getaway?"

"Might of," McNulty agreed. "But that won't go down so good with the public. John is a solid fellow, popular with all the cattlemen and well liked in town. I don't reckon we better hang it on him."

"That's right." Packard came to swift decision. "Webb did it. He had me covered with his gun when I called you fellows into the house. It was in his hand when he ran out to the plaza. When he saw Chuck in his way he cut down and let him have it. That's how it was, boys. I saw it. Who else did?"

"I did," Uhlmann assented promptly. "Just before he got on his horse. You saw him too, Pete."

McNulty showed his teeth in an ugly grin. "Sure I saw him. I remember now."

"Then that's settled," Packard concluded. "Webb has killed another man."

"Not quite settled." The words came crisp and clear from a speaker standing back of the mine owner. "If Bob Webb was carrying a gun he did

168

not have it out when he ran to the hitch rack. I was watching from the window."

Packard slewed his head round and glared at John Ranger, who had stepped out from the hotel quietly and joined them. "So it's you? Butting in again. If you're so sure Webb didn't kill this boy maybe you know who did. Maybe you had a gun out if the convict didn't."

"My daughter was standing beside me at the window," Ranger said. "She can testify I didn't fire a gun, and both of us can swear that Webb didn't."

"That goes with me, Mr. Ranger," Hawkins answered. "If you were standing at the window, perhaps you can tell us who did shoot this boy."

"No, I can't, though I saw him fall. Several guns were fired about that time within a second or two."

"It may go with you, Hawkins, but not with me," Packard cried vindictively. "Ranger was in cahoots with these scoundrels. He threatened to strangle me if I called out to you that Webb was hiding in his room. He has played in with him ever since he met the killer in the cañon. Why wouldn't he lie for him now?"

McNulty nodded vigorously in assent. "Right, Jug. I dunno what his game is, but he has taken a great shine to the jailbird."

"I like his nerve myself," Hawkins replied. "Jug hates him for some reason. That's his privilege. And I can understand why Pete doesn't like him.

But why should the rest of us get all het up to bump off the fellow or send him back to Yuma? Me, I've busted a lot of laws in my time. I've lived in the brush enough myself to favor anyone on the dodge rather than the ones hunting him."

"Is that why you were pumping lead at Webb a couple of minutes ago?" snapped McNulty.

The smile on the face of Hawkins was a little sly and mysterious. It suggested a secret source of ironic mirth.

"You got me there, Pete," he admitted. "I reckon I was some carried away by the Fourth of July you boys were pulling off."

"We'd better get poor Chuck into the Legal Tender and notify the sheriff," Morris said. "Looks to me like he's going to have a nice time finding out who did kill him."

"Carry him in, and somebody go for the sheriff," Packard ordered. He turned bitterly to Ranger. "Don't think you're going to get away with this. You aided and abetted a criminal. First you hid him, then you prevented me from getting him arrested. That's a penitentiary offense, you'll find out."

"If you can prove it." Ranger smiled blandly at the mine owner. "Your story and mine might differ. Have you any other witnesses to back the charge?"

John turned on his heel and walked back into the hotel. His daughter was waiting for him in his room. She had lit a lamp and stood tall and slender beside the table. The color had not yet washed back into her cheeks.

"Well?" she asked.

"I don't think either of them was hurt," he replied. "One poor boy who rode for Uhlmann was killed. Nobody seems to know who shot him. Probably somebody mistook him for Webb. Jug Packard was fixing to tie it to Bob when I showed up and rather spoiled his plan. Later he said very likely I did it."

"He would like to get even with you."

"Yes, but I don't see how he can prove anything against me. He has no witnesses except himself to show that we hid Webb."

"Or that we knew Cape Sloan is Bob Webb."

"No."

"The papers will be full of this," Sandra said. "You'd better see Mr. Davis again and make sure the *Star* gets the story right. Jug Packard will try to make it seem that Bob killed this boy."

"You're right," her father agreed. "Bob is the dog with a bad name. We don't want to correct a story putting the blame on him. Most of the people who read it would never see the correction."

Sandra beat a small fist despairingly into the palm of her other hand. "It's no use," she declared. "If he gets out of this he'll just get into another mix-up, and by this time everybody in the territory is on the lookout for him."

Ranger knew this was true. Yet he sympathized with the cause driving Webb to what looked like reckless folly. "You can't blame him for trying to clear his name. If he had just lit out after the jail break the stigma on his name never would have been cleared up."

"You think now it will?" the girl asked eagerly.

"Yes. We've got an investigation moving now." He added, regretfully: "But I can't promise he'll be alive when we spring our evidence on Packard, and I don't know that what we dig up will be enough to convict Jug—except in public opinion."

"If Bob Webb isn't alive, it will do him a lot of good to show he has been the victim of a conspiracy," Sandra said bitterly. "And as for the villain who sent him to prison—a lot he'll care what people think, if he escapes the law."

John put a hand gently on her shoulder. "Keep a stiff upper lip, honey," he said cheerfully. "This will work out right yet."

He wished that he believed his own prediction.

21   RETRODDEN TRAILS

When the fugitives left Tucson they did not have time to make a choice of roads. They took the one that led them most quickly out of range. It brought them to a cactus-covered mesa that extended eastward for miles. Bob turned out of the road into the thick growth of cholla, prickly pear, and greasewood. The scrub was tall, and inside of a few minutes they were in a wilderness of brush so dense that it made an ideal temporary hiding place.

To the north at the horizon's edge were the bare stark Santa Catalina mountains, to the south the Rincons. They had to decide the direction in which they had better travel, after which they must find another horse.

"They'll expect us to strike for Mexico *muy pronto*," Fraser said. "Even so, I reckon it would be the smart thing to do."

"With the border closed to us, as it will be inside of an hour? Jug isn't anybody's fool. He'll wire to Douglas, Bisbee, Nogales, and all points along the line. Soon as we show our noses officers will pounce on us. I'd say for us to get into the mountains and hole up till the chase is over. We could pass through Oracle, off to the left a bit so that we won't be seen, cross the Divide, and drop down into the San Pedro valley. Once there, we can head for the White Mountains or for the Dragoons, whichever seems the safest bet to you, Stan."

Fraser nodded agreement. "I reckon you're right. But first off, I've got to get me a horse."

"Buy one or steal one?" Bob asked.

"There are objections to both," the little man grinned, scratching his head. "If I buy one the seller is going to start talking soon as he hears about the rumpus in the plaza; if I steal a bronc I'll have officers in my hair wherever I show myself."

"Not so good," Bob admitted. "We might buy you a horse and get away with it, but soon as we talk about buying a saddle a rancher is going to get suspicious. He'll want to know where yore own saddle is. Maybe we could rope a stray mount on the range, but you can't rope a saddle too."

The eyes of Fraser lit. "You've done said it, son. We'll borrow a horse to take me as far as Oracle. I'll buy one there. McMurdo is a good friend of mine. He'll fix me up all right."

They wound in and out through the brush toward the Catalinas, one walking and the other riding. In the sunlight the mountains looked as if they were made of papier-mâché, an atmospheric effect helped by the gulches and cañons that seamed the sides of the range. From the mesa they dropped down into the valley of the Rillito and crossed its bed, a dry wash that after a cloudburst was sometimes filled with a roaring torrent of water.

Bob pointed to the sahuaro slope rising to the foothills. "A bunch of horses," he said. "You had better do the roping, Stan. I'm out of practice."

The horses were not wild, though they showed a little nervousness at the approach of Fraser. He was careful not to alarm them by any hurried movement. They were cropping alfilaria in a small draw from which it was not easy to escape without passing him. He picked a sorrel gelding, and at the first cast the loop of the rope dropped over the head of the animal. The old-timer fashioned from the rope a headstall and reins and swung to the bare back of the bronco. After a crowhop or two the horse accepted the domination of its new master.

They kept away from the road as much as possible, following the foothills until late in the afternoon. It was getting near sunset when Fraser pointed out a road winding around the side of a bluff.

"That's where yore pappy made the big mistake of his life. He and two-three of his boys came on a bunch of Pachies who had trapped a freight outfit. They drove off the Injuns. One of the mule skinners was wounded. It was Packard. If they had left him right there to die everything would have been slick. But yore pappy put him in a wagon, took the sidewinder back to Tucson, and had Mrs. Webb nurse him till he was well."

Young Webb reflected with sardonic irony that this simple act of kindness had resulted in the ruin not only of his father's life but also those of his mother and his own.

Darkness had fallen before the riders reached the live oak groves of Oracle. From a hilltop they looked down on the lights of the stage station.

"I reckon I'd better drift down and have a powwow with Jim McMurdo," Fraser said. "If it looks all right we'll wave a lantern in front of the house for you to come on in."

Bob tied the horses and sat down on a flat rock to wait. Stars flooded the sky and a big red moon was just rising over the horizon. The night was peaceful as one could imagine, but there was no serenity in the heart of this hunted man. For years he had lived like a caged beast and since his escape the life of a hunted one. The trouble was that he was at war with himself. He had built a steely wall of protective hardness around his kindly human emotions, and of late he had found them seeping through and overflowing the barrier.

A light moved to and fro in front of the house below. Bob mounted and let his horse pick a way down among the boulders, the led horse by his side.

McMurdo was a stoutly built Scot of middle age. His shrewd blue eyes, rather stern, looked steadily into those of the escaped convict.

"I knew your father," he said quietly. "A fine

man. Mr. Fraser tells me you have been wronged. I don't know about that, but I don't trust Packard. Never have. I've agreed to let Stan have a horse and saddle. My wife is making supper for you. While you eat, my son will feed your mount."

Before they went into the house Fraser released the sorrel gelding and gave it a cut with a quirt on the rump. The animal started on a trot down the road. Within twenty-four hours it would be back on its own range.

As they ate, Fraser told the story of their escape at Tucson, omitting all reference to the Rangers. Bob noticed that the manager of the stage station watched him closely. The man had something on his mind and was hesitating as to whether he had better mention it.

It was while Fraser was saddling his horse at the stable that McMurdo came out with what was troubling him.

"Know a man named String Crews?" he asked Webb.

Bob shook his head. "Don't think I do—not to remember him anyhow."

"Drove stage for me last year."

Fraser spoke up. "I knew him. Long hungry-lookin' fellow lean as a range cow after a tough winter."

"That's the man. Quit me a couple of months ago to settle on a ranch in the San Pedro valley. Long time ago he drove an ore wagon for the Johnny B."

Webb fastened his eyes on McMurdo. "In my father's time?" he asked.

"Then, and for a while afterward." The station manager turned to his son. "Bill, run up to the house and see if your mother has that package of grub packed for Mr. Fraser." After the boy had gone McMurdo said, his direct gaze on Bob: "String told me something that maybe you ought to know."

"If it is about my father's death I think I ought," Bob answered. "I've stuck around Arizona because I want to get to the bottom of this business. I think Packard murdered my father and robbed my mother. I know he lied me into prison."

"I'll give you what String told me for what it is worth, though I don't know whether he is willing to stand by it in court. He went on a spree with a man called Uhlmann about a week after your father's death. Uhlmann got very drunk and was throwing his money away. He boasted that it came easy. At first that was all he would say, but later in the night he claimed that Packard had given him five hundred dollars for a special job, a bit of dynamiting that was worth a lot to Jug."

"Did he say just what the job was?" Bob asked, his voice rough and tense.

"It was to blow up your father, but I don't know that Uhlmann admitted this in so many words. Anyhow, String understood what he meant. That wasn't the end of the story. After Uhlmann sobered up he remembered that he had talked too much, though he wasn't quite sure how far he had gone. In a roundabout way he tried to find out from String. He said he was an awful liar when he was soused and you couldn't believe a word he said. But String could see Uhlmann was worried and he began to get scared of the fellow. A few weeks later somebody shot into the cabin where String was sleeping. The bullet passed over his body so close that it ripped the bedding. String could not prove that Uhlmann had fired the shot, but he felt sure of it. That day he left his job at the Johnny B and never went back."

"Whereabouts is this ranch of his?"

"On the river. Five or six miles above Mammoth."

"I'm obliged to you, Mr. McMurdo."

"If you are innocent, I hope this will help you. Tell Crews you heard it from me."

The fugitives rode into the night up the trace which led them past the big rocks from which they could look down into the valley below, a dim gulf of space in the darkness. They made a dry camp, using their hair ropes to draw a protective circle around them against rattlesnakes. Though neither of them knew whether the rough hairs were so irritating to the belly of a rattler that the reptile would not crawl over such a rope, like a good many outdoor men of the Southwest they gave the tradition the benefit of the doubt.

By day the valley stood out in sharp detail. The silvery river wound along its floor, and here and there cottonwood groves dotted the banks. The blades of ranch windmills sparkled in the sunlight. The last time Bob had seen the San Pedro he was with his father. He remembered that it was spring, and the slope of the Galiuro Mountains which rose to hem in the opposite side of the valley had been one immense golden splash from millions of blooming poppies.

Before they reached Mammoth they left the road, cutting across the baked desert to a bend in the stream a few miles above the town. A barbed wire fence barred the way. They deflected, to follow the fence. It brought them, after two right-angle turns, to a neat whitewashed adobe house. The woman who came to the door pointed upstream.

"String lives about a mile farther up the river," she said. "On the right side."

Fraser found String as gaunt and as hungry-looking as he had been a dozen years earlier. He was directing the course of water in an alfalfa field, but he stopped to lean on his hoe while he talked. He was glad to meet Fraser and hash over old times and acquaintances. To Stan's younger friend Cape Sloan he did not pay much attention.

At Crews' insistence they stayed to eat a bachelor dinner in the unplastered adobe house of two rooms which went with the ranch. Not until they were nearly finished eating did Fraser lead the talk back to their host's freighting days at the Johnny B.

String agreed that Bob Webb had been a fine man, a good boss, always fair and reasonable. "Different from that damn fox Packard as day is from night." He pulled up and looked hard at Fraser. "I could tell you something, Stan, that would give you a jolt."

"I don't reckon you could tell me anything about that old snake in the grass that would surprise me," Fraser replied carelessly.

Crews was piqued at this cavalier indifference. "That's what *you* think, old-timer. I know better. But I reckon I'll keep my mouth shut. You're just as well off not knowing it."

That the ranchman wanted to shock his friend but did not think it would be wise to talk was clear. Bob guessed that his presence had something to do with String's reticence. When dinner was finished he strolled away to take a look at some horses in the corral.

Fraser nodded toward the retiring back of Webb. "He's all right, Sloan is, but it was smart of you to wait till he had gone to tell me about Jug." There was flattery in the wise drop of the voice, all set for the reception of confidential gossip.

It turned the scale. Crews had been telling himself he had better not tell what he knew, but now he changed his mind. He leaned forward and put his forearms on the table.

"What would you say if I told you Bob Webb wasn't killed by an accident but on purpose?" he asked.

Fraser showed the proper amazement. "Good Lord!" he gasped.

"Sure as you're a foot high."

"But—he was blown up in an explosion down in the mine."

"That's right. He was asked into the drift by a man who had set the charge and made an excuse to beat it in time."

Stan showed frank incredulity. He shook his head. "No, String. Someone must of pulled a whizzer on you. Did the fellow claim he was there and saw all this?"

The rancher hesitated. He could still stop without giving any details that might later turn out to be dynamite. But Fraser was a close-mouthed fellow, and String had an answer so pat and startling that it was not in him to suppress it.

"More than that. He told me he was the one who did it."

The old-timer felt it due his host not to discount any of the shock by reason of having heard this before. "My God!" he exclaimed. "Somebody told you he murdered Bob Webb?"

"Practically." Crews nodded his head in affirmation. "And who gave him five hundred dollars to do it."

"How came he to do it—to tell you, I mean?"

"He let it out soon after when he was dead drunk and blowing the money."

It was time, Fraser felt, to put the direction question. "Who?" he asked.

"Hans Uhlmann. Packard wanted Webb out of the way and paid him."

"To get hold of the mine."

"Yes, sir, and he got it." Crews finished the story. "Somebody shot at me one night while I was in bed. Just barely missed me. I knew it was Uhlmann. You see, he kinda remembered telling me. I lit out *prontito*. That fellow is a killer, and I knew I wouldn't last long there."

Bob watched for a sign from Fraser to rejoin the others. He did not want a premature return to interfere with what Crews had to tell.

Not till after they had left did Fraser repeat to his friend what he had just learned. They discussed whether they had better try to get Crews' sworn story down on paper or wait until they needed it. Stan favored the latter plan.

"If he has to sit around and wait after going on record he might get scared and skip. Leave him lay. He'll stay put. When we need him he'll come through."

Bob too was of the opinion that there was no need to rush him.

22   ON THE DODGE

Bob picketed his horse and lay in the brush in the shade of a clump of ocatillos while Stan rode into Mammoth and bought supplies at the little store there. It was certain that the stage had brought up news of the fight on the plaza, but unless by mischance somebody recognized Fraser he was not likely to be taken for one of the fugitives. Cowboys riding the chuck line were common as fleas in this cattle country. Work was slack, and a good many of them were drifting from one range to another.

A couple of loafers in chairs tilted back against the wall of the store watched Fraser tie at the rack and bowleg to the store. He stopped to pass the time of day with them. They gathered that he had come down from the Tonto Basin where he had been helping on a drive of stock for the Hashknife outfit. Leisurely he rolled and smoked a cigarette before going into the store to make his purchases. Thought he would cross the line into New Mexico, he said. Never had worked over there and would like to take a whirl at it.

The proprietor of the store was a scrawny little man wearing glasses. Fraser ordered flour, bacon, a package of Arbuckle's and other supplies. He bought also a coffee pot and a fry pan. While he was packing the goods in a gunny sack for easier carrying the storekeeper mentioned that the stage had been robbed yesterday five miles from Oracle.

"The hold-ups get much?" Fraser asked.

"About two hundred dollars, mostly from the passengers."

"They don't know who did it, I reckon?"

"Not for sure. Folks think it was that fellow Webb who escaped from the pen two-three months ago—him and a pal of his. They were in Tucson day before yesterday and killed a man there."

Fraser bit off the answer that was on his tongue. This was not the time to defend Bob. "Seems like Arizona has more than its share of scalawags," he said virtuously. "We'd ought to have rangers like Texas has to clear them out."

"That's right," agreed the merchant. "We got no protection. Webb and his pardner might drop in any minute, and what could I do?"

The customer looked out of the door in startled alarm. "Don't talk thataway, mister," he remonstrated. "No foolin', I don't want any truck with bad men. But shucks! we don't need to worry. Those fellows are skedaddlin' for the White Mountains or some other outlaw hole-up. They ain't stickin' around here none."

That was likely, the storekeeper agreed. He strolled outside after Fraser and watched him tie the sack behind the saddle seat.

"If you meet up with those stage hold-ups, tell 'em from me that they don't need to do any shooting any time they want what I've got," Fraser said. "I'll hand everything over cheerful."

He left the road a half a mile from Mammoth and cut into the brush. Before he reached Bob he began to sing a stanza of one of his favorite songs. He did not want his companion to make any mistake about who was approaching. Except that his voice was cracked and that he could not carry a tune, he did very well.

> "There's hard times on old Bitter Creek
> That never can be beat.
> It was root, hog, or die
> Under every wagon sheet.
> We cleared up all the Injuns,
> Drank all the alkali,
> And it's whack the cattle on, boys,
> Root, hog, or die."

"Glad you're back," Webb told him. "I got to worrying for fear you had run into trouble, and when I heard yore foghorn sounding I was afraid you had lost a rich uncle or something."

Stan dismounted and turned a severe eye on his friend. "So you been at it again soon as I let you out of my sight," he charged.

"What have I been at?" Bob inquired. He guessed that this opening was a precursor to news.

"Robbing the stage near Oracle, and right after you killed a man at Tucson."

"Was the Oracle stage held up?"

"Yes, sir. Last night. They claim you did it."

"Alone?"

"Why, no, I reckon I helped you." Fraser grinned gaily at his fellow fugitive. "That's what comes of me keeping bad company."

"I expected they would say I killed that gunman on the plaza, but it's a surprise to find I'm a road agent too."

"You might call it right coincidental that some galoots have to pick the very day we're traveling that district to rob a stage," Fraser complained cheerfully. "We have the beatingest luck—killers, horse thieves, stage robbers, all in the same day. And me in my sunset years, with my bones creakin' and aches in all my joints." It was quite evident that the old-timer was well pleased with himself.

Yet he agreed with Bob that it might be well for them to put a few more miles between them and the scenes of their crimes. They rode down the valley and camped at dusk on the river. Their intention was to hide out in the Dragoon Mountains for a few days until the first heat of the hunt for them was past.

The sun beating down on their faces woke them. For breakfast they had flapjacks, bacon, and coffee. While the shadows from the east were still long they were on their way. In the early afternoon they stopped at a water hole and rested.

"Dragoon isn't more than two-three miles from here," Fraser mentioned. "It's no great shakes of a place. But we can get tobacco at the store."

"What's that up on the hill?" Bob asked. "Looks like a mine."

"Yep. Abandoned long ago. Fellow called Frenchy worked it for a year or two."

"Let's go up and take a look at it," Bob said.

"If you like," his companion consented.

The shack was falling to pieces and the windlass had already collapsed into the shaft, but on the other side of the hill was an arroyo down which a little stream trickled and watered a small grove of live oaks.

"Why not stay right here a day or two?" Bob wanted to know. "There are water, shade, and no inhabitants. We might do worse."

"Suits me," Fraser replied.

They rode down the slope, unloaded, and unsaddled. There was a good growth of alfilaria by the stream. They picketed their mounts and relaxed.

After supper they decided to ride in to Dragoon and renew their tobacco supply. Fraser did not think it quite wise for Bob to go, but after all the chances were ten to one they would not see anybody in the drowsy village who would be any danger to them. Probably no news of the trouble on the plaza at Tucson or of the stage hold-up had reached the place.

23   WANTED—DEAD OR ALIVE

The sun was back of the western hills when Webb and Fraser rode down the dusty business street of Dragoon and pulled up at the post office, but darkness had not yet blanketed the country. The storekeeper, Mose Hersey, sat in front of the establishment and drank in the cool breeze that relieved the heat of the day. He was a soft fat man, and he felt a momentary resentment at having to get up and wait on customers so soon after supper. Unfortunately the two brown travel-stained riders tying at the rack were strangers, and he could not very well tell them to wait on themselves and pay when they came out.

Mose heaved himself out of the chair and waddled into the store after them. Apparently all they wanted was tobacco. Since he was a friendly garrulous soul, his annoyance evaporated almost at once. The shiny leather chaps, the worn boots, and the big weathered hats told him they were cowboys. He asked them for what outfit they rode.

"We're on the loose right now," Fraser told him. "Know any ranch around here that could use two top riders?"

Just at the present moment Mose did not. The Bar Double X was the biggest spread in the neighborhood, but he had heard they were laying off men.

It was darker in the store than outside but still light enough to read. Webb had stopped in front of a poster tacked to the wall close to the post office cage. It offered a reward of fifteen hundred dollars for his capture dead or alive. Two hundred of this would be paid by the state and the rest by J. Packard. The man wanted was a desperate character, a murderer escaped from the penitentiary who had just killed another man at Tucson, by name Chuck Holloway, and a few hours later had robbed the Oracle stage. There was no photograph shown of the outlaw, but a very accurate description was given of him.

Fraser stowed the tobacco in his pocket and joined Bob.

"This guy is valuable," he said. "Fifteen hundred is a lot of mazuma. More than I could make in several years chasing cows. This J. Packard, whoever he is, must be real interested."

"Probably he's just a good citizen who wants to promote law and justice," Webb suggested ironically.

"Me, I could pay off the mortgage with fifteen hundred, son," Fraser mentioned sadly. "But finding this bird would be like lookin' for a needle in a haystack, and when you find him yore troubles would be just beginning."

Mose Hersey laughed wisely. "You boys can

have him. I don't want any part of him if he is as tough as they say."

"I'll bet he's a sure enough bad man from the Brazos who would start smokin' quick," Fraser said. "The time to get him would be when he is asleep, don't you reckon?"

"Not interested, asleep or awake." Mose shook his head. "I like money well as most men, but I'd walk a mile around any desperado when he is on the prod even if the reward was ten times that big."

"Well, you ain't liable to meet him . . . You wouldn't have any mail here for Joseph K. Ward, would you?"

The postmaster knew he had not, but out of politeness he riffled through the five or six letters in the office before answering that he had not.

"I didn't hardly expect one," admitted Joseph K. Ward, alias Stanley Fraser. "My wife ran off with a traveling salesman, but I figured maybe they would be outa money by this time and she might of writ home asking me to send her some and the letter could of been forwarded."

Bob slanted a look at his companion. It said, "You blamed little son-of-a-gun. You'd rather pull a fairy tale any day than tell the truth."

Mose murmured that he was sorry Mr. Ward's home had been busted up.

"So is the city slicker sorry by this time," the alleged bereaved husband commented philosophically. "Mary Jane has the evenest bad temper

191

of anybody in Trinidad, though of course she ain't there since she lit out with the guy selling the rheumatism cure."

"Trinidad Colorado?"

"That's right. Do you think my son here favors me?"

"Quite a bit," the storekeeper fabricated, trying to say the right thing. "Course he's a whole lot bigger than you, and not so dark complected, and his eyes are different color, and his head ain't shaped the same, but outside of that he's the spittin' image of you."

"I got four more boys and two girls," Fraser went on mendaciously. "The other boys ain't so puny as this one. Bill here is the runt of the family."

"He don't look so puny to me," Mose said.

"Appearances is deceptive. Cough for the gentleman, Bill."

Bob said heartily, "You go to blazes."

"You hadn't ought to talk thataway to yore pappy," Stan reproached him mildly. To his audience of one, he explained: "Bill hates folks to know he's a mite on the sick side."

Through the door they could see that a rider had stirred up the yellow dust in the street and was heavily dismounting in front of the store. He stopped to exchange greeting with a man lounging outside, after he had glanced at the two horses already tied to the rack.

Fraser took one look at him and dropped his foolery instantly. "I reckon we better be moseyin' along, son," he drawled.

The new arrival came into the store. It was darker inside the building than out in the street, and he stood accustoming himself to the change, his bleached blue eyes squinting into the gloom.

" 'Lo, sheriff," Mose said.

" 'Lo, Hersey. My throat's dry as a lime kiln. Bust me open a can of tomatoes."

Bob had seen the man before, at the Circle J R ranch. He recognized at once the sunwrinkled face of Sheriff Norlin. The officer was wearing the same old scuffed boots, floppy Stetson hat, and corduroy trousers. If the checked shirt from which many washes had faded the color was not the same it must have been a twin.

Norlin had not identified Webb, who had wandered to the back of the store and was standing in the shadows. Fraser moved forward and stood directly between the sheriff and the convict. He bleated an enthusiastic greeting.

"Well—well, if it ain't Chad Norlin. You doggoned old vinegaroon, I ain't seen you for a month of Sundays. The last time was on the round-up at Three Cedars. Or have we met since? Sure is good to meet up with you again." Fraser caught the officer's hand and wrung it vigorously. His face beamed delight.

The sheriff was surprised at this burst of

affection. It had not occurred to him before that there was any real tie of friendship binding him. He did not know that while Fraser was firmly but unobtrusively crowding him toward the front of the store the little man was desperately hoping there was a back exit from the building by means of which Webb could escape.

"Want to show you something, Chad, though maybe you've seen it," Fraser continued eagerly. "Here's a fifteen hundred dollars reward offered for a guy escaped from the pen. Yesterday it was two hundred. Now it has jumped into big money." He put his finger on the poster just below the name of Packard. "Jug is a tight-fisted galoot. Why for is he digging up thirteen hundred bucks to get this fellow?"

Mose had been cutting open a tomato can with the heel of a hatchet. Now he brought it forward to the sheriff.

Norlin brushed the dust from the top of the can before lifting it to his mouth. "I saw that poster at Mammoth, Stan," he said. "I can tell you something you probably don't know. 'Most all of one hot day less than two weeks ago I spent in the saddle going to have a look at this fellow. I didn't know he was Webb, since he was passing as Cape Sloan. The fellow had been accused of being a rustler, and I wanted to check up on him. He was staying at the Circle J R ranch with the Rangers. I satisfied myself he couldn't be one of the waddies who ran off stock when Spillman was killed, but I had a queer feeling I was missing something. So I was. There was Webb right in my hands, and I let him go."

"That was certainly hard luck," Fraser said. "But you can't blame yoreself. You didn't know who he was."

The sheriff tilted the can and began to drink the tomato juice. Out of the corner of an eye Fraser saw that Bob was not only in the store but was coming forward quietly, evidently with the intention of passing unnoticed in the rear of Norlin while he was drinking. As Bob was brushing past, the officer glanced at him carelessly.

Norlin's eyes froze. But his right hand was holding a tomato can two feet from the butt of his revolver and the barrel of a forty-five was pressing against a rib just over his heart. His shooting iron might just as well have been in New York.

"Go right on and finish yore tomatoes," Webb advised coldly.

Chad Norlin almost strangled as the liquid went down the wrong way. When he had stopped coughing, the weapon at his side had been removed from the holster.

"Take it easy, sheriff," Bob warned. "This isn't your day."

"I won't forget this, Stan," Norlin promised. "You worked me for a sucker."

"Don't feel too bad," Fraser consoled him, with a grin. "You were took by surprise, and if I do say it I put on a good show."

"Why are you throwing in with this criminal, Fraser?" the sheriff demanded. "It means the penitentiary for you too."

"You done said it, Chad," answered Fraser chirpily. "I'm in this up to my neck. If and when Bob killed Chuck Holloway and robbed the stage I was right by his side aiding and abetting. What makes me mad is that they're offering fifteen hundred for him and not a thin dime for me. Dad-burn it, I want you to spread the word that I'm a bad man from the Guadalupe just as much as he is, and I got a right to a reasonable amount of publicity."

"This won't be so funny when you're breaking rocks with a guard over you," Norlin told him irritably.

"Change that when to if, Chad," suggested Stan. "We ain't either of us going to prison. First off, Bob never killed a man in his life, and that perjured murderer Jug Packard knows it. The same goes for his killer Uhlmann. We've declared war on those villains, and we aim to show who belongs in the pen and who doesn't."

"Shooting off yore mouth that way won't get you off," the sheriff replied angrily. "What stands out like a wooden leg is that this fellow here is an escaped convict and it's my job to arrest him. He had a fair trial, and a jury said he was guilty. That's enough for me, and it ought to be enough for you."

"Well, it ain't," the little man snapped. "Not by a jug full. There's gonna be justice done in this case."

Bob interrupted. "No use arguing, Stan. Sheriff Norlin is right. It's his job to arrest me, but this time he doesn't cut the mustard. The three of us are going to leave here together. He'll stay with us until we think it's safe to let him go."

Norlin did not attempt any protest that he knew would be futile. He walked out of the store with them and mounted as directed. When they rode into the gathering darkness his horse was between those of the others. No attempts to escape would be successful. If he tried it, they would shoot his mount. He knew they were not going to hurt him. At the first safe opportunity they would release him.

24 GOVERNOR ANDREWS ADVISES SANDRA

After telling his story Chandler Newman walked out of the governor's office to wait in the outer room. Governor Andrews ran a hand through a shock of fine white hair. He was troubled, and showed it. He shook his head slowly.

"Your evidence misses the point, John," he said. "I'll admit that Jug Packard is a crook and probably stole the Johnny B from Mrs. Webb. It looks as if he might have contrived the murder of her hus-band judging by what Fraser told you he learned from this man String Crews. I hope you get the goods on him. The scoundrel has a record as odorous as a hydrophobia skunk. He's sly as a weasel and poisonous as a sidewinder. Young Webb had plenty of provocation, but I can't go outside of the record. The prosecution made out a strong case. Witnesses swore that when he came to Packard's office he had the manner of one looking for trouble. He pushed his way in without knocking. Through the window two workingmen heard him angrily denouncing Jug and threatening to get him. Uhlmann backed Packard's story that the boy killed Giles Lemmon. I have read the testimony carefully. Webb made out a very weak case for himself."

"Uhlmann had to support Packard, since he had killed Lemmon himself while shooting at Bob Webb," Ranger pointed out.

The governor thumped a fist down on the desk. He was an honest man, doing his duty as he saw it, and unhappy at the direction in which it drove him. "Bring me some evidence to prove that," he cried. "Something more than Webb's unsupported word."

The low-pitched husky voice of Sandra took up the attack. "Bob says there was a woman in the outer office when he went in to see Packard. When he ran out of the building after the shooting he saw her in the street looking white and scared. She was Mary Gilcrest, a daughter of one of Packard's miners. What became of her? She was not a witness at the trial, though the defense tried hard to find her. She had disappeared."

The eyes of Governor Andrews softened as he looked at Sandra. He had been a cattleman himself, from the same neighborhood as the Rangers, and, even before she was born, a friend of the family. He remembered dandling her on his knee when she was less than six months old. The gallant golden youth of the girl warmed his heart. She had a provocative disturbing face, amazingly alive, and courage in her blue eyes carried like a banner.

"Never heard of her," he answered. "If this woman knew anything of importance she would have come forward at the trial, I reckon."

"Packard saw to it that she could not be reached," Sandra retorted quickly. "He sent her away until after the trial. Mr. Lansing, Bob Webb's attorney, tried to look her up. Her father pretended he did not know where she was and her mother acted as if she was afraid to talk. It was a conspiracy. I'm sure of it."

"Where is she now?" the governor asked.

"We don't know. She was married and went away, and soon afterward her father died. The mother moved. We are advertising for Mary now."

"I hope you find her. We can learn what she has to say, if anything. But I'm afraid you are depending on a frail reed. Probably she won't have anything of value to tell. And frankly, I must make it plain that I can't indorse the pardon of any man who has broken prison and is still at large."

"Not even if he is innocent?" she cried.

"If he is innocent, let him surrender. I'm willing to reopen the case."

"He won't surrender, after spending seven years in that terrible prison. He would rather be killed than be taken."

"I don't ask whether you know where he is hiding—and I don't want to know. But if you get in touch with him, try to persuade him to give himself up—or at least to get out of the country until you've worked up the case against Packard and Uhlmann."

"He won't leave," John Ranger said. "He is filled with the one thought of proving the case against Packard. I wish you knew him, Ben. Webb is not just a wild daredevil. He is fine and strong as steel—a thoroughbred."

"I have a sheepish admiration for him, even though I haven't made his acquaintance," the governor confessed, and there was a smile on his face. "Half the people in Arizona are cheering for him and laughing at the authorities. They are making a romantic Robin Hood of him. My own wife and children say they hope he won't be captured."

"Because they think he is innocent," Sandra tossed in.

"Not at all. They don't care whether he is innocent. Because of his confounded impudence."

"Was it impudence that made him ride alone against four of Pablo Lopez' killers to save me and my brother?" Sandra asked, her eyes starry with indignation.

Ben Andrews had a moment of regret for his own vanished youth. He was happily married, but the days of romance for him were gone forever. That fine rapt look in Sandra's face belonged only to lovers. It occurred to him that Bob Webb, hunted convict though he was, might have something in his life most men would never know.

"He has plenty of sand in his craw," the governor admitted. "Maybe too much. I don't suppose you can tame your wild buckaroo, Miss Sandra. He's a little too exciting for Arizona now that it claims to have passed the days of its riotous youth. Ever since he broke loose he has been in one difficulty or another. Just check up on them. To begin with, practically caught rustling."

"And proved innocent," Sandra interrupted quickly.

The governor ignored the interruption. "Kills a Mexican scoundrel the same day and wounds another." He held up a hand to ward off the protest of Ranger. "I'm merely running through a list of his activities, John. Beat up a citizen with a quirt."

"A fine citizen," Sandra flung out scornfully.

"Is accused of another murder and stage robbery. On top of that kidnaps a sheriff starting to arrest him. The fellow is making more news in the territory than Geronimo did. I'm afraid to look at my paper in the morning for fear he has committed some other outrage."

His smile robbed the indictment of much of its force. Sandra smiled back at him. "Sheriff Norlin was probably trying to win that fifteen hundred dollar reward you say ought never to have been offered."

"Well, it oughtn't," the governor admitted resentfully. "Jug had no right to print and circulate that reward poster. He did not consult me. I would never have authorized the public to bring

Webb in dead or alive, and as soon as I learned what Packard had done I called in the posters and notified the newspapers to that effect."

John Ranger nodded approval. "We know you did. That poster explains itself, Ben. You know Jug Packard is tight as the bark on a live oak. Why did he offer so much money, in an open invitation for hunters to kill rather than capture Webb? There can be only one reason. He is afraid to have Bob at large for fear he will get proof of his skulduggery."

Andrews thought that might be true. "It looks bad, John. Maybe you are right. Webb may have been framed. There is nothing I would like better than to get enough evidence to free the young fellow and to put Jug in his place at Yuma. But move carefully. And make Sandra keep out of this. If Packard thought you were working against him I wouldn't put it past him to have you dry-gulched."

"Nor I," agreed Ranger thoughtfully. "He has everything at stake that counts with him—property, power, even his life perhaps. Murder wouldn't stop him."

"But this time he must know somebody is raking up the past to get something on him." The governor put a hand on Sandra's shoulder. "Stay at home and tend to your knitting, my dear. This is war, and you must not be mixed up in it. Your young man has several good friends working for him now. Let them take care of this."

The color deepened in the girl's cheeks, but her eyes held fast to his. "He isn't my young man, but I want to see justice done," she said quietly.

Yet there was a touch of proud defiance in the poised grace of her fine lifted head. He might think what he pleased. She had enlisted in Bob Webb's cause regardless of what anybody might say. The governor read worry in John Ranger's troubled face. He too believed that Sandra was in love with this vagabond who had the brand of the criminal on him, and from such an attachment no happiness could come.

25 TWO OF A KIND

"Be reasonable, Rhino," protested Packard. "Don't get hell in your neck. All I want is for this to work out right for us both."

"All you want is for someone else to be yore catspaw," Uhlmann differed, an ugly snarl in his voice. "I'm to run the risk while you sit back not doing a frazzlin' thing that could get you into trouble, the way it has always been. By Judas priest, it won't be like that this time. If you want this fellow, you get him yoreself."

"It won't be hard," Packard continued. "He's hanging around in the brush back of the Circle J R somewheres. Locate his camp, watch your chance, and plug him in the back."

"Glad you think it's so easy, because you're going to have to nail his hide on a fence if it's done. I ain't ridin' on that kind of a job any more. My saddle is done hung up on a peg for keeps."

"Just pick your time right and there is no danger."

"Not interested," Uhlmann grunted. "You can't catch this mule with that ear of corn, Jug."

"I wouldn't wonder but what you could use a couple of hundred dollars now."

"Why, you blamed Shylock, you made a public

offer of thirteen hundred," the big ruffian cried angrily.

The mine owner thought fast for an out. "That was different. If a posse had got him they would of had to divide the dough half a dozen ways."

"Webb would be just as dead if I gunned him, wouldn't he?" The German looked at Packard with a contempt he did not take the trouble to conceal. "I never met up with a human as poisonous as you. If a skunk bit you it would die awful quick."

"No use flying off the handle and making talk like that, Rhino," Packard remonstrated with no apparent resentment. "We been friends a long time, and I don't aim to get mad because you've got a mean temper."

"Friends!" repeated Uhlmann harshly. "There never was a day you wouldn't of sold me down the river if it had paid you."

Packard did not waste breath defending himself. "We're in this together, Rhino, and up to our necks. No use loading ourselves with the idea that the past is dead and buried. This fellow Webb is dangerous as a tiger that has got loose, and he has important friends helping him. Like I told you, Ranger and his daughter called on the governor Thursday, and they took with them that fellow Newman."

"Chan Newman hasn't got a thing on me," the ranchman boasted, the small eyes in his pachydermous face gloating over his accomplice. "I didn't rob the Webbs of the Johnny B. This is your chicken coming home to roost."

"That's where you're wrong. This whole thing ties up into one ball of yarn with some loose threads sticking out. Soon as Webb begins to pull on any of those threads anything is liable to come loose." The shifty eyes of Packard's evil wrinkled face fixed fast on those of his companion. "For instance, you talked too much after this fellow's father had the accident in the mine. If this wolf got hold of that thread and raveled it out he would come right smack to you."

"And to you," Uhlmann added. "Don't forget that for a minute." Sullenly he followed this up with a question. "How is he gonna prove the accident to his old man was kinda intentional? The only talking I ever did was to String Crews, and we haven't heard of him for years. Last I knew he was figuring on drifting back to Nebraska to live."

"I don't say he can prove it," Packard replied. "I'm just pointing out that we're in the same boat and have got to pull together or sink."

"Yeah," sneered the other. "Only remember you're not a passenger in the boat and have got to do some pulling too."

"This fellow Webb is the rock on which we might founder," Packard went on, his voice oily with persuasion. "If he was out of the way we would be all right. Nobody else is going to bust a tug trying to get us in trouble. You could fix that with a crook of your finger, Rhino."

"No rheumatism in yore finger, is there?"

"You know I can't do that sort of thing, Rhino —haven't the cold nerve for it. You never saw man or devil you were afraid of. I always said you can outgame any fellow I ever met. Of course I'd be prepared to pay a reasonable sum."

Uhlmann was flattered at the praise, but not to an extent that it diverted him from an intent to get all the traffic would bear. He knew why he was being softsoaped.

"I'll not hold you up," he said. "This guy's grandstanding doesn't faze me any. I had rubbed out my first man before he was born—when I was a kid of nineteen. Any time he wants to come a-smokin' I'll be waiting at the gate."

"I know that," purred Packard. "You've got what it takes to stand up to any of them. Still, no use you running any risk."

"I won't," bragged the killer. "He won't know what's happening until it will be too late. Now about the price."

"You said it wouldn't be much, seeing as you have to get him on your own account too."

"It will be just fifteen hundred plunks, the thirteen hundred you promised and an extra two hundred as a bonus for having a crackajack gunman on the job who will do it right."

Packard let out a yelp of distress.

"Jumping creepers, Rhino, I'm no millionaire. Fact is, if I had to raise a thousand dollars right now I wouldn't know where to turn."

Uhlmann fished twenty-five cents from his pocket. "Go get yoreself a square meal, if you can find a restaurant that will let a bum dressed like you are sit down at a table," he jeered.

"I might go as high as four-five hundred," the mine owner said.

"You'll go to fifteen hundred, one third payable now."

"Have a heart, Rhino. Times are awful tight."

"You paid more than a hundred thousand spot cash for that Sinclair ranch last month."

"Somebody has misinformed you about that. It was one of those three-party deals with a lot of swapping in it and mighty little money. Tell you what I'll do—six hundred spot cash soon as the job is done."

"You're so poor I can't take yore money, Jug. To keep yore family from starving I'll pay *you* six hundred to do it." Uhlmann rose from the chair in which he had been sitting, stretched his huge arms in a deep yawn, and heavy-footed to the door. "Going to hit the hay. If you decide to take that six hundred let me know. But you're so slippery I can't let you have a nickel till I've seen Webb in his coffin."

"Wait a minute," Packard said. "Let's settle this

now. You know you're going to do this, to protect yoreself if for no other reason. What's the sense in trying to jack up the price to more than I can pay?"

"You got mighty poor all of a sudden." The ranchman's voice was heavy with sarcasm. "Must have had some losses since you got that poster out."

"When I had that printed I expect I had got jumpy. The governor called that in, so it's off." Packard moved closer to Uhlmann and dropped his voice almost to a whisper. "If anything was to happen to Webb now, the law would take it for granted he had robbed the Oracle stage *and wouldn't go looking for anybody else.* But if he lives, like as not he could prove an alibi. I wonder if you could, Rhino, if some busybody officer started to push you around."

Uhlmann glared at him angrily. "Don't threaten me, you damned Judas. I won't take it from you. For fifteen years I've known yore slimy tricks. All I have to do is open my mouth to blow you sky high."

"Now—now, don't get off on the wrong foot. I was just showing you another reason why you had better rub out this Webb. Dad-gum it, a blind man could see he's bound to have it in for us both. It's neck meat or nothing. If we don't get him, he'll get us. No two ways about that."

"Buy him off," suggested Uhlmann.

"Not the kind you can buy. He told me we had murdered his father and he meant to get us. You have seen that ad in the *Star* for Mary Gilcrest. What would she do if she saw it?"

"She would keep her mouth clamped if she knew what was good for her," Uhlmann answered brutally. "Why do you suppose I married her, except to fix it so she could not testify against me?" He showed his teeth in a savage grin.

Packard met that smile with another as evil. "I take some credit to myself for that happy marriage. Even when I bought off her pappy to send her to California until after the trial I knew she was still a danger to you. Webb's lawyer might get at her later. Seeing she was a nice plump pretty girl, I figured it would be a kindness to find her a husband who had just got him a good spread and a bunch of cows likely to have a remarkable increase on account of being close to a couple of big ranches. So I said, 'God bless you, my boy,' and sent you courting to Los Angeles. You being such a handsome buck, she couldn't resist you."

"Don't get funny at me," Uhlmann growled. "I don't like it."

"You know I wouldn't, Rhino," Packard replied, instantly dropping the sarcasm. "But about Mary. She's barred from testifying against you. But now they have started hunting for Mary Gilcrest they are sure to find out she is your wife. They'll contact her if possible, and if they get her to talking that will do a lot of harm."

"I'll have a little powwow with her," the ranchman promised, his voice harsh and grim. "After I have given her orders she wouldn't say 'Good Morning' to the Shah of Persia."

"I hope you're right," the owner of the Johnny B said doubtfully. "Sometimes she looks at you like she hates you, Rhino."

"I know I'm right. What do I care how much she hates me? A woman is like a horse. She has got to know who is master, and every so often you have to give her the whip so she won't forget it."

Packard did not comment on that. He knew how this ruffian beat his horses and he had suspected that he gave his wife the same treatment. There was a sadistic streak in the fellow that might some day get him into trouble. Horses had been known to kill cruel masters and this might be true of women driven to despair. If she was too cowed for this, she could run away and start talking. But there was nothing Jug could do about that. The German would have to keep his own household in order.

"What say we fix up the price after you've done the job?" Packard proposed. "I'll be liberal."

"The price is fixed," Uhlmann replied obstinately. "It's fifteen hundred."

"The standard price for bushwhacking a man has never been above five hundred."

"The cost of living is going up," gloated the giant. "But I'll make you an offer. We'll draw straws, and the one who loses does it for nothing."

Packard considered for a moment whether there would be any chance of gypping his co-conspirator and decided that it could not be done. Uhlmann would be too suspicious to let him get away with any sleight of hand trick. Jug might get the wrong straw.

Reluctantly he turned over to the killer five hundred dollars as a deposit for value to be received.

26 SANDRA RIDES TO VISIT A NEIGHBOR

Jim Budd brought into the parlor to meet Sandra a shuffle-footed Negro named Sam Washington. He was the cook at the Johnny B mine, and he and Jim had become close friends. Sam was as embarrassed as he would have been at a Buckingham Palace presentation, and he stood twirling his hat in two restless hands.

Sandra rose from the piano where she had been playing a Viennese waltz. She had made Jim promise to bring Sam in to see her next time he stopped at the ranch.

"I'm glad you and Jim get along so well," she said. "Make him give you a piece of that apple pie he has in the kitchen. It's delicious. But since you are a cook yourself good food may not be a treat to you. I hear you have been at the Johnny B a long time."

"Ten years come next Christmas, ma'am."

"That's a long time. I wonder if you remember a girl whose father used to work for Mr. Packard. Her name was Mary Gilcrest."

The cook twisted his face into a grimace to help his memory. "Folks they come an' go. Seem like I got a recommembrance, but I can't jest put my mind on it."

"Her father was a miner," Sandra prompted.

Sam slapped a hand on his thigh. "Pete Gilcrest. He moved away. Comes to me I done heard he was dead."

"He died in Nevada. Do you know what became of Mary?"

The Johnny B cook nodded. He had the woman placed now all right. "She up and got married."

Sandra felt a tingle of excitement run through her. The answer to the next question she asked would bring her to an impasse or would open a road for her to follow. "Did you ever hear the name of her husband?"

Sam's eyes went blank. It was as if she had drawn a curtain over them and yet left them still open. "She married a ranchman in this valley, a man who used to work for Mr. Packard. Name of Uhlmann."

"A big heavy ugly man—the one they call Rhino."

"That's him." Sam's voice had grown sullen and vindictive.

"You don't like him," the girl said quickly. "Neither do I."

"I don' want to have no truck with that man a-tall," the Negro said with finality.

"He did you a wrong some time, maybe?"

Sam hesitated. He wanted to play safe, and on the other hand he felt a desire to express to this young woman who did not like Uhlmann his

215

own bitter pent-up hatred. His fingers touched a long deep scar on his forehead.

"Once when he was drunk he did this—with a stirrup. Out of plumb meanness. Because when he came an hour late for dinner, after everybody else had eaten, I had things cleared off the table. For a month I was awful sick."

"He's a heartless brute," Sandra said, eyes flashing.

"Yes'm," Sam agreed. "Folks say he treats Mrs. Uhlmann terrible. I ain't ever seen her since she was married. Story is she don't hardly ever leave home."

Rumors about the Uhlmann family life had reached Sandra. Fortunately there were no children. There was a lot of gossip, some of which might not be true. It was said the man beat his wife with a whip.

Sandra had never met the woman, though the Uhlmanns lived only about ten miles up the valley from the Circle J R. No welcome sign for visitors was hung out at the X Bar. The girl made up her mind to ignore this, for she meant to see Mary Uhlmann and have a talk with her. Of course she must make her call at a time when the husband was not at home. Since he was notoriously absent most of the time, the chance of missing him ought to be good. She might have to try more than once before she succeeded.

That her father would not approve of such a

visit Sandra knew. He felt strongly that anything further done on behalf of Bob Webb must be undertaken by him and not by his daughter. Knowing her father, she was aware that he would think it unfair to work against a man through his wife. On both points she held a different opinion. Anything that could be done for Bob she meant to do, and she had no scruples about using Mary Uhlmann to get justice for him.

Her father left early next morning to look at a bunch of cows in the Sulphur Springs Valley that were for sale. He did not expect to get back until the evening of the second day. As soon as he was out of sight Sandra gave orders to have her horse saddled. She asked Jim Budd to put up a picnic lunch for her, since she probably would not return till sunset.

About a mile west of the ranchhouse she left the road, to follow a trail that ran up through the low hills to a rocky ridge hemming in one side of the valley for a distance of twenty miles. A gulch sown with cactus led her to the flat tops above. A fringe of bushes edged the bluff and screened her from the observation of anybody on the floor below when the path ran close to the precipice.

Now that she was in action again the girl felt happier than she had been for several days. To sit still and do nothing while Bob might be in peril had been a strain on the nerves. With the sun shining and a light cool breeze ruffling her hair as she rode, the fear of impending disaster lifted from her. In a world like this, so clean and free, the alarms knocking at her heart seemed fanciful.

Swifts ran across the path and disappeared. A road runner raced in front of her for fifty yards and then veered into the brush. Beside the trail a Gila monster lay inert and sluggish. The call of a dove sounded from an arroyo. All the familiar aspects of this desert land were reassuring.

So few traveled the rough terrain of the ridge that she was surprised to catch sight of a man on horseback. He rode toward her, and she recognized Stan Fraser. The old-timer lifted his hat and waved it, a smile of pleasure on his face.

"I'm right pleased to meet you, Miss Sandra," he said. "But aren't you off yore home range some?"

"I've heard that travel broadens one," she answered.

"And a doctor once told me that the outside of a horse is good for the inside of a man. It joggles up his liver—or something."

He shifted his seat in the saddle, resting his weight on one stirrup. "You look blooming as a pink rose. If a doc did that for you, I'd like his address."

"You've kissed the Blarney Stone, Mr. Fraser," she accused. "But I'm like all women and eat up flattery."

Stan shook his head. "I dassent say half of what I think."

Her eyes sparkled. "Go on. I won't breach-of-promise you."

"That's certainly bad news," he mourned. "You'd ought to have seen me when I first began to tail cows. But that was so long ago the Rincons were still a hole in the ground. I notice the girls' eyes pass over me and light on that young high-stepper I travel with. Outside of his being thirty years younger and full of pepper and not having a face that turns milk sour, what has that hell-a-miler got that I haven't?"

"I like mature men with sense," Sandra said demurely.

"That's me. I'll be camping on yore doorsteps soon as I am no longer on the dodge."

"How nice for me!" She put the question in her mind with obvious carelessness. "And where is the—hell-a-miler? Isn't that what you called him? I hope he hasn't gone back to Yuma yet."

Fraser waved a hand widely, to include all the territory in the hills. "Back in one of these pockets. He'll holler his head off when he learns what he missed."

"Oh," she inquired innocently. "Has he missed something?"

"Bob will think so. I'll bet he won't ever stay and clean camp again." He frowned a question at her, though his words were a statement. "Funny you came away up to this rough prong to take a ride."

"Maybe I thought I would like to visit a neighbor."

"Meaning a crazy bandit holed up here who is wanted for horse stealing, abduction, stage robbery, and murder?"

The color deepened in her cheeks. "No!" she answered sharply. "Not meaning him at all."

Fraser was puzzled. The cow trail she was taking led to no settlement, unless it might be the back boundary of Uhlmann's X Bar spread, and of course she could not be going there. In spite of her swift vigorous denial he was inclined to believe that she was riding the ridge in the hope of meeting Bob Webb.

"If you are going back now maybe I'd better ride along until you're off the steep trail," he offered. "A horse could easily break a leg in all those rocks."

"I'm not going back yet. And Beauty is very sure-footed. I won't need to trouble you."

"No trouble at all. A pleasure."

"For me too, some other day," she replied, with a smile that took away the sting of the dismissal.

But Sandra was still afraid she might have hurt the feelings of the old-timer, and she wouldn't do that for a good deal. She liked him, and he was a loyal friend of the man she loved. So she stayed to talk for a little longer in order to make sure he was not offended.

"I heard some news that will interest you and Mr. Webb," she told him. "That is, if it is news to you. This girl we are trying to find, Mary Gilcrest, is the wife of that villain Uhlmann."

It was a complete surprise to Fraser, but he picked up at once the adverse effect this was likely to have on Bob's chance of getting a pardon.

"Even if she wanted to she couldn't testify against Rhino now," he said. "Bob has the darndest luck. Of all men in the world she has to marry the one fellow she should not have."

"That would be a strange coincidence, if it is one," she replied thoughtfully. "It must have been some more of Packard's scheming. Well, I'll say '*Adios*,' Mr. Fraser."

"Don't forget to look for me on yore doorstep soon as this hunt quits getting hot," he said with a warm grin. "You saved my life the other day, and I certainly ain't going to let you throw me over now."

"Oh, I'm thinking of being an old maid," she laughed, turning away.

A little disturbed in mind, Fraser rode on. He was not sure that he ought not to stay with her until she was safely back in the valley. But she evidently wanted to be left alone.

A pass cut through the ridge. Sandra moved down into it and up a steep slope to the continuation of the ridge on the other side of the cut. In the distance, miles farther up the valley, she could see flashes of light from the sun striking the whirling blades of a windmill at the Uhlmann ranch. The X Bar was a small outfit, and as she drew nearer she saw by her field glasses that the buildings were ramshackle and the fences poorly kept up. The owner of the place paid very little attention to improving it.

As Sandra topped a small rise she came face to face with another rider. He carried a rifle, and a moment later she saw that the horseman was Uhlmann.

The rancher pulled up, surprised and disconcerted. His object in traveling along the ridge had been to escape observation. In front of her he jerked his horse roughly to a stop.

"What you doing here?" he demanded, suspicion in the look he slanted at her.

Sandra thought quickly. "I came to have a talk with you," she replied.

"Then why didn't you ride by the road?" he wanted to know.

She had an answer for that. "I thought perhaps you would rather I weren't seen going to your place, on account of the trouble at Tucson."

He digested that, before flinging a harsh question at her. "What do you want with me?"

"I want to ask you please to let Bob Webb alone. He has never harmed you, Mr. Uhlmann. Don't you think you have hurt him enough already?"

"How have I ever hurt him?" he growled.

"You testified at his trial that he killed Giles Lemmon, and you know that wasn't true," she said, looking straight into his small beady eyes.

"That so?" he jeered. "Who did?"

"Never mind that now. Why do you hate Bob so? Let the officers get him if they can. It's not your business."

"I want that reward."

"I shouldn't think you would want blood money," she said contemptuously.

"It will buy just as much." He added, with sudden anger: "And I won't be satisfied till that fellow is rubbed out or sent back."

"For seven or eight years he has been in that terrible place to serve a sentence for something he did not do. If he is a hard and bitter man now, his enemies made him that. Mr. Uhlmann, I'm only a girl, but I know you can't do a deliberate wrong to anybody without destroying yourself."

"Don't try to feed me pap," he broke out violently. "I know what I'm about, and I aim to keep right on doing it. My ideas don't change just because some fool girl has gone mushy about a killer."

She threw up a hand wearily. "If you won't listen, I can't help it."

He pushed his horse closer, so that his seamed leathery face was close to hers. "You do some listening, Miss High-and-Mighty. I'm dirt under your feet, by your way of it. The only reason you speak to me is because you are crazy about this Webb and are scared of what I'll do to him. Tell him for me I'll get him. It's gonna be him or me.

If it's the last thing I do in this world I'll be standing up pouring lead into him after he is down." He finished with a string of scabrous epithets. The savage bitterness of his pent up venom appalled her.

She turned her horse aside to pass. He caught the bridle rein.

"You've seen me now," he jeered. "And fixed up everything nice. There's nothing to keep you from headin' for home now."

"Let go that rein," Sandra ordered.

Uhlmann's eyes narrowed. "You didn't come to see me at all," he charged, "but to meet yore fancy Dan."

"Turn loose my horse," she warned, her eyes bright with anger.

"You know where he's roostin' up in these hills, and by cripes! you're gonna take me to him."

She swung her quirt, and the lash cut across the fellow's cheek. Startled by the unexpected pain, his hand dropped from the rein. Sandra was away like a frightened rabbit, her body low over the neck of her mount. Stung to fury, the man fired at her and missed. Some saving sense in him stopped the second shot. He lowered the rifle and put his horse to a gallop in pursuit. Before he had gone thirty yards he knew his lumbering sorrel could not catch her fleet-footed mount. He ground his horse viciously to a halt and poured curses at the girl disappearing into a dip.

27 BOB SADDLES

Fraser found Bob lying on his back gazing up at the thin cloud-skeins drifting across the sky.

"I'll bet you are thinking about my girl," Fraser challenged with a chuckle.

"Didn't know you had one," Bob responded cautiously, aware that there might be a catch in this. There was an air of suppressed excitement about his partner that presaged news.

"You didn't know I had a girl!" Fraser exclaimed with a show of indignation. "Shows how much you don't use yore eyes. Why, I just been out on the bluff having a nice talk with her."

Webb slanted incredulous but inquiring eyes at him. "You old roué, and I've been siding you all this time without suspecting how depraved you are."

"Nothing of the kind. I've got the most honorable intentions. I told her soon as these sheriffs quit wanting me I would be right there at the Circle J R looking for her."

The prostrate man had not moved a muscle, but his gaze still rested on Stan. "So you met Miss Ranger," he said.

"You bet I did. On one of the cow trails that run along the prong."

"Not alone?"

"Why, no, there were two of us there—Miss Sandra and me."

"She had come alone?"

"That's right."

"What for?"

Fraser abandoned his bandinage. "I don't rightly know why, boy. When I hinted it might be to find you, she put me in my place quick. There was something else in her mind."

"What could it be? Nobody lives up here."

The older man scratched his head. "She said something about going to see a neighbor."

"That doesn't make sense."

"I couldn't get it. Say, she told me something I didn't know. She has found out who married Mary Gilcrest and where she lives."

"It must have been that ad Ranger put in the papers. I suppose the woman answered it."

"I dunno about that. Give you three guesses as to who the woman married."

To get it over with and find out sooner, Bob guessed, "President Cleveland, the Czar of Russia, or John L. Sullivan."

"No, sir. A dear friend of yours. She is Mrs. Hans Uhlmann."

Bob stared at him. "You sure?"

"That's what Miss Sandra told me."

"Makes it fine for me, doesn't it? Even if she wanted to testify what she heard the law wouldn't let her. You can't make a wife give evidence against her husband. I reckon they won't allow her to go on the stand."

"Old Jug sure ties up a package nice and neat," Stan said.

His friend agreed. "The girl must have heard plenty or Packard wouldn't have thought it necessary for her to be hog-tied by marrying Uhlmann."

"By now she is good and tired of that hulking rhinoceros probably. If she knows anything and will talk there must be some way of using her. You better get you a good lawyer."

"I don't know any that lives on this street," Bob answered. "When I was in town you were hell-bent on getting me out where the neighborhood was more filled with absentees. Now you think—"

"Ranger will see one for you. I still think country air is more suitable for yore puny corporosity."

Bob did not answer that. His half-shuttered eyes were fixed on a stretch of mackerel sky. The consideration of another problem was occupying his mind. What was Sandra doing on this bare ridge ten miles from home? Had she come on the slight chance of meeting Fraser or him to tell them the news about Mary Gilcrest? It did not seem reasonable. She had no way of knowing that they were within fifty miles of the Circle J R, and if she had been aware of it the likelihood of running across the hunted men in these huddled hills slashed by gulches and ravines was not worth counting. Moreover, the information was not important, since there was nothing he could do about it.

He sat up abruptly. The answer to his question had flashed across his mind. She was going to the Uhlmann ranch. That was what she had meant when she told Fraser she was going to see a neighbor. And she meant to slip in to the X Bar by the back way. But why, instead of taking the easy road along the valley? If she wanted to see Uhlmann why make a secret of it? Above all, what could have induced her to go to see this ruffian without being accompanied by her father?

The only reason he could find was that she hoped to see not Uhlmann but his wife. Perhaps she had seen him passing the Circle J R on his way to town and knew that Mary Uhlmann would be alone. Bob did not like the idea at all. This fellow was too dangerous for Sandra to try to trick.

"I'm saddling," he said, and walked to his picketed horse.

"Going where?" Fraser asked.

"To the X Bar."

"Making a friendly call on good old Hans?"

"I'll tell you how friendly later—when I know myself."

"Think I'll mosey along to see the fireworks," Stan said.

"Hope there won't be any. Chances are that Uhlmann isn't home."

"But his wife will be—that the idea?"

"Not exactly. I think we'll find Sandra Ranger there."

Fraser slapped a hand on his chaps. "Right. That's where she was headed for when I met her. Never thought of that. That girl is bound and determined to help you whether you want her to or not."

Bob was worried for fear she might have involved herself in a perilous situation. Uhlmann would show no mercy toward a girl on account of her age and sex if she was making trouble for him.

"I wish she would mind her own affairs and keep out of mine," he blurted gruffly. "She'll get hurt if she doesn't look out."

"Funny you didn't think to tell her that the other night when she took us in and saved our lives," Fraser retorted dryly.

He understood that his friend's irritation was born of a deep concern for Sandra's safety. To some extent he shared too in Bob's apprehension.

"She's impulsive," Webb explained. "Once I helped her when she was in a jam, and she feels she has to keep on helping me."

"That must be it," Stan agreed with a grin. "All right, fellow. Let's ride."

They jogged out of the little park where they were camped and down a stiffly sloping ledge to the plateau below. It was still rough going, but Bob put his horse to a canter till they struck a cañon that led to the ridge which made a boundary for the valley. It was impossible to travel fast through the twisting boulder-strewn gulch, yet the urge driving the younger man sent him clattering and sliding along the dry bed of the stream more rapidly than was safe.

"We won't get there any sooner if we break a leg of one of our broncs," Fraser complained. "Take it easy, boy. After all, Uhlmann isn't a fool. He daren't touch a hair of that girl's head. If he did, the men in this valley would string him up so quick he wouldn't have time to get that quid of tobacco outa his cheek."

"He might figure nobody had seen her coming to his place and he could get away with rubbing her out."

"No. If it came to a showdown Sandra would tell him she had met me and told me where she was going. I was a mite scared myself at first, but there's no sense in being afraid. Sandra will be okay. You got to remember his wife is on the ranch—and maybe a rider or two. Rhino couldn't put over a thing."

This was probably true. None the less when they emerged from the cañon Bob put his horse at a gallop.

28   "I'VE MADE MY BED"

When Sandra pulled up her horse, sure that Uhlmann had given up the chase, she found herself in a huddle of low cow-backed hills all of which looked alike. If she had been a tenderfoot she would have been lost, but with the sun for a guide she knew that if she swung to the left she must strike again the barrier ridge.

Her heart was beating fast from excitement. A man had shot at her. In the race to escape she had not had time to be afraid. Now that the immediate danger was past she noticed that her knees felt weak. Fear of this big shapeless brute flooded her. John Ranger was right. She ought not to become involved in a business of this kind. Not far away, in some fold of the hills, the ruffian was probably still looking for her. They might any minute come face to face.

She had no assurance as to what direction she had better choose. He was between her and the Circle J R. There was no longer in her an urgent desire to see Mary Uhlmann at once. The thought of her own safety was uppermost. If she could reach the ridge and cut down into the valley she might hit the road that led home. This would take her through the X Bar ranch, but she was pretty sure its owner would not be there. He was a stubborn man and would likely be lying in wait for her return.

Her judgment told her to keep traveling for another mile before cutting back to the ridge and to slip down into the valley at the lower end of the ranch.

This she did and came to the ridge by a ravine that cut through the barrier wall to the floor below. Though she kept a constant alert, she saw nothing of Uhlmann. Through a poor man's gate, three strands of wire fastened to poles by staples, she passed into the pasture back of the house.

She had given up her intention of seeing Mary Uhlmann, but now she changed her mind. Her alarm was subsiding. Uhlmann could not have reached the ranchhouse yet, and there was no sign of him anywhere along the ridge. He had been riding away from the place when she met him, and she could think of no reason why meeting her might bring him back.

She skirted the yard in approaching. A saddled horse was tied to the corral fence, but it was not the one Uhlmann had been riding. As she drew nearer the house, she heard voices. By a slip-knot she tied her bridle to a rickety hitching post. Before knocking she swept the ridge again with her eyes to check on the man she was avoiding. Not a trace of life showed on its barren slope.

At her knock the voices stopped. A woman came to the door. She was tall, angular, lean as a rail. Astonishment leaped to the jet-black eyes as they took in the girl's young vital beauty.

"Who are you?" she demanded sharply.

"I'm Sandra Ranger. I want to talk with you if I may."

"You'd better get away from here." There was whipped fear on the face that turned to search the terrain. "He might come home and find you."

"I don't think he'll be here just yet. It won't take a minute for you to tell me what I want to know."

"No. Get on your horse and leave."

"Wait a minute," a drawling voice interrupted. "That's no way to treat a visitor, Mary." The owner of the voice sauntered to the door. He was a light-stepping dark man, with a face both wary and reckless. Across the left cheek, from ear to chin, a livid scar stretched. Perhaps this was what gave him the sinister and dangerous look, Sandra thought. "If Miss Ranger wants to have a little talk—why, this is a free country."

"She had better go—now. I have nothing to tell her. If she stays to talk it will only make trouble."

"Let's hear what she has to say," the man demurred. "Rhino ain't the great mogul. You shouldn't let him get you whipped, Mary."

Sandra guessed that this man was one of the lawless night riders who lived around Charleston or up in the San Simon, but she was of the opinion that there was more chance of Mary Uhlmann talking with him present than if he were away.

"It's about Bob Webb," she said. "He didn't kill that man Lemmon. You were there when he was shot. You know he didn't."

"I wasn't there," the woman cried. "I didn't see a thing."

"You were in the next room and heard everything. Hans Uhlmann shot Lemmon, by accident, while he was shooting at Bob."

"No," the woman denied violently. "You can't get me to say so. Send this girl away, Scarface."

"Don't push on the reins, Mary. I've heard it said before that this boy was railroaded to the pen. Over at Charleston the other day I met him. And I like the fellow. He got a rotten deal. Why don't you spill what you know? You don't owe Rhino a thing, the way he treats you."

"I don't know anything." The sullen lips closed tightly.

"Seven years of Bob Webb's life are buried in that prison," Sandra said. "They are hunting him to send him back. Doesn't it hurt you to know that you sent him there and that every day you keep silent is another robbed out of a life you have ruined?"

"Go away. Leave me alone. It's easy for you to talk that way, but—"

She broke off the sentence and Scarface finished it for her. "—but you don't live with that devil Rhino Uhlmann." The man put a hand on the woman's bony shoulder. "You don't have to live with him either. He treats you as no decent man would use a dog. Light out of here, Mary. You can hide where he won't find you. Long as you stay on this ranch you'll be his slave."

"I've made my bed," she answered bitterly.

"You don't have to stay in it," Sandra told her eagerly. "As long as we live we can start again. You are young and can go away and make a new life for yourself."

"I'm not young," the woman differed hopelessly. "I feel a hundred years old. I've been wrung dry, all the life squeezed out of me. It doesn't matter what becomes of me now."

"It does. It matters a lot. To feel as you do is all wrong. You can make new friends and be happy."

Mary Uhlmann's thin smile was cynical. "Happy! You don't know what you are talking about. Because you are a young girl and have not made any mistakes you think all anyone has to do to make the future rosy is to just will it so. But life isn't like that. If you take the wrong turning you can't go back."

"Oh, but I'm sure you're mistaken," Sandra cried. "Come and stay with us. Forget all this. You'd be surprised."

The girl's enthusiasm beat in vain against the woman's despair. It was too late now to turn back from this marriage she had chosen.

"Why did you marry him?" the outlaw asked.

"Because I was a fool. No use arguing. I'm here. I stay. And I'll do no talking."

"And let an innocent man suffer for what he didn't do." Sandra's voice rang out scornfully. "I don't believe it. No good woman who has to go on living with herself could be so cowardly."

A touch of red burned underneath the thin tanned cheeks of the older woman. The contempt of this spirited young thing stung her. For years she had held hidden in her heart this shameful secret, and now it had been dragged out into the open.

Round the corner of the house a man came, leading a horse. Across his cheek there was a purple weal where the lash of a quirt had fallen. He glared at Sandra, openly and evilly triumphant.

"So you lied to me," Uhlmann snarled. "You came to see her, not me. I figured it might be that way, and I slipped down by the arroyo. You don't get away from me this time, you meddler."

Sandra was afraid, but she stood stiff and straight, her gaze steadily on his fat vicious face. "Maybe if you shoot at me again you might hit me this time," she said.

"Did you shoot at Miss Ranger?" Scarface asked softly.

Uhlmann glared at him. He did not want to stop for explanations, but Scarface was a tough hardy scamp he could not ignore.

"I shot past her, just to stop the little fool," he admitted grudgingly.

The outlaw did not raise his voice. "My friend," he replied, almost in a drawl, "that don't go in this country."

The big man started to answer, but the rustler beat down his words, a sudden sharp challenge in his tone. "I always knew you were a wolf, Rhino, but I didn't know there was a broad yellow streak of coyote in you too. We don't fight women here, and we don't let low-down coyotes do it either."

Scarface waited, still leaning against the door jamb at apparent ease. His indolence was deceptive. Every muscle was set for instant action if the call came. Uhlmann's face grew purple with ugly anger. His impulse was to draw and kill, even though he too would likely be shot down. But he dared not take the risk. For if he destroyed Scarface and lived himself the girl would be a witness against him, unless he rubbed her out too. To do that would condemn him beyond a hope of escape. All this part of Arizona would turn on him and hunt him down.

"Tell you I didn't shoot at her!" he cried.

"His bullet did not miss me six inches," Sandra said. "It cut a leaf from a shrub beside the horse."

"You was too scared to tell what it hit," the ranchman charged.

"If you were just shooting into the air why

was she so scared?" demanded the other man.

"You know I wouldn't shoot at a girl, Scarface." There were tiny beads of sweat on Uhlmann's forehead. If it should be believed he had even shot at this girl his life would not be safe, regardless of the intent to hit or miss. "I was just funnin'. You know me." He ground his teeth, giving his own words the lie. "And the little devil had lashed my face with her quirt."

Scarface did not lift his steely eyes from the big leathery face. "Yes, I know you. When you come busting in here calling Miss Ranger a liar and telling her she wouldn't get away from you this time, it sounded like you were funnin'. We 'most split our sides laughing. And of course you weren't annoying her when she quirted yore ugly phiz."

"You ain't so damn lily-white yoreself, Scarface," flung out Uhlmann, searching for a defense. "Don't forget the law wants you for killing Spillman on that raid two-three weeks ago."

"All right, I'm a bad man too, even though I didn't kill Spillman. But, by God, I'm not yore kind of bad man. I don't shoot at women, and I don't rub out men for pay when they haven't a chance for their white alleys. If I was you I'd light out tonight and keep traveling till I was way deep in old Mex."

"Are you deaf, Scarface? Haven't I told you

over and over you got me wrong? I'd cut my hand off before I'd do this young lady a mite of harm. All I did was give Miss Ranger a little scare. Why, Goddlemighty, man, she's my neighbor. I've watched her grow up since she was knee-high to a duck."

Scarface laughed, not pleasantly. "If you can talk yoreself outa this you'll be good, Rhino. My guess is different. I'd say if you are here when the boys come you'll be kicking yore heels in the air under one of those cottonwoods." To Sandra he said, without lifting his eyes from the other man, "Get on yore horse, Miss, and I'll see you home safe."

He waited till she had mounted, then turned to the sullen worried ranchman. "I don't reckon you are crazy enough to pull any more gunplays. If you've got any such notion, discard it. You would only be driving more nails in yore coffin. And anyhow, I'll be on the alert long as you're in sight."

"What's the sense in talking thataway?" Uhlmann protested. "I don't aim to hurt you any." He pushed the rifle into the hands of his wife. "Here, take this gun since he's so scared."

The rustler turned to the wife of the harried man. "This fellow's ball of yarn is wound up, Mary," he said. "Rhino has reached the end of his trail here. Better fork his horse and ride with us."

"You can't talk that way to my wife," Uhlmann cried. "I won't stand for it."

"I *am* talking that way," Scarface retorted quietly. "That's the way it is. You light out, or—" He let a shrug of the shoulders finish the sentence.

The ranchman's bravado broke down. He was not afraid of this or any other man. What daunted him was the thought of the determined anger of the community moving solidly against him. He had committed the unpardonable offense of attacking a good and popular girl.

"I don't get it why you've turned against me, Scarface," he pleaded. "We been pals all these years. When you were in a tight spot I helped you out. You wouldn't throw down on me now, would you?"

"You threw down on yoreself," the outlaw told him coldly. He turned to the wife. "Are you riding with us, Mary?"

The eyes of the woman were bleak and wretched. After a moment she said in a low voice, "No, I'll stay."

Scarface walked beside Sandra's horse to the corral and swung to the saddle of his own mount. He started her down the road. Not until she was fifty yards on her way did he make a move to follow, and when he did it was with his body slewed round in the saddle to keep an eye on the killer.

The look on Uhlmann's face as he watched them

go was one of baffled hatred. The venom of fury and hate had poisoned the man for years. But a new element had been added to these, the fear of a dreadful day of judgment riding hard on his heels.

He turned with a violent malediction on his wife. "You were ready to sell me out," he cried, moving toward her.

She fell back slowly, her eyes reading hot murder in his. "No," she answered. "I didn't tell her anything. But you've hated me a long time. Maybe you had better kill me before you are hanged."

He gave a wild beast snarl, flung her furiously against the wall, and shuffled into the house. Scarface was right. He had to get away from this part of the country. What a fool he had been to let his temper trap him into this. Two hours ago he had been sitting pretty. All he had to do then was to shoot down an enemy from ambush when he found him and from that killing get safety and a big reward. Now he had brought down on him the vengeance of the whole district. But as he flung into a sack food and the few clothes he meant to carry, one resolve hardened in his tortured mind—he would get Bob Webb before he lit out for Mexico.

29 MARY UHLMANN BREAKS A LONG SILENCE

Bob cut the wires of the X Bar boundary fence and rode into the ranch of his enemy. Because he was worried about Sandra he had no time to steal up to the house Indian fashion. But he did take advantage of the contour of the land to follow the dips that would conceal them as much as possible. A draw about two hundred yards from the house offered the last chance of cover.

"Here we come, Rhino," grumbled Fraser. "A couple of easy marks. Pick us off real carefully. Take yore time."

He thought that Uhlmann probably had not got home yet, but some not too serious complaint was in order. During the past few days he had become very much attached to his companion and watched over him like a father. When let alone Bob was inclined to take too many chances. So the old-timer grumbled and followed him.

Young Webb emerged from the draw first. As he pulled up for a second to look over the cluster of buildings and the terrain around them his horse staggered and fell. The crack of a rifle had sounded. Bob flung himself out of the saddle and crouched back of the horse. The smoke puff came from the cottonwoods back of the house. A man was standing beside a saddled horse.

"Look out, Stan," Bob shouted. "Uhlmann is taking your advice." He rested his rifle barrel on the saddle and took aim.

"Missed," Fraser said, and dropped behind a clump of yucca. "Lemme have a crack at the wolf."

"Not if he can help it," Bob answered. "He's getting out of there fast."

Uhlmann had swung himself heavily astride of his mount and was riding through the grove. He had no mind to face both of them. Fraser fired twice, but they were random shots. The trees gave Uhlmann protection. He disappeared into an arroyo.

Bob examined the wound in the neck of his horse. The bullet had struck a major artery and the blood was pumping out fast.

"He's done for," Fraser told his friend.

The echo of Bob's revolver died away. He put the weapon back in its holster and looked down with a set face at the dead horse.

"I'll get the saddle later," he said, and started for the house.

Fraser offered no consolation. He knew that Bob felt he had lost a friend and that he would not want to talk about it yet.

A woman came out of the house and stood by the door. As Bob drew closer he saw fresh bruises and abrasions on her thin face. The eyes that looked at him were bitter and hopeless. She was still young in years, but the slavery of an unhappy marriage had robbed her of the joy that was her heritage.

"Is Sandra Ranger here?" Bob asked bluntly.

"No. She's gone."

"Gone where?"

"Home. Scarface Brown took her."

"Scarface—the rustler?" Bob asked.

"Yes. Don't worry. She's as safe with him as with her own pappy."

Fraser nodded. "That's right, Bob. Did yore husband tell you where he was going, ma'am?"

Her dreary laugh held no mirth. "To hell, I hope."

"We know that," Fraser replied. "I meant, where is he going right away?"

"He's on the dodge. Seems he shot at Miss Ranger up on the ridge this morning. Scarface told him he would sick the dogs on him and he lit out."

Bob felt his hackles rise. "Shot at Miss Ranger?" he repeated.

"She slashed his face with a quirt. Too bad I didn't do it long ago."

"He's headed for Mexico probably," Fraser guessed.

"Not yet." The woman's gaze rested on Bob. "Says he has a job to do first. He wants to kill another man. Is your name Webb?"

"Yes."

"I thought so. You're lucky he missed you this time."

"Miss Ranger is all right?" Bob asked. "He didn't hurt her?"

"No." She touched her face. "He took it out on me. It's nice having a wife when you have to beat somebody and nobody else is handy."

"I reckon Hans Uhlmann did you two more dirt than he ever did anybody else in the world," Fraser said. "Unless you think killing a man is worse than ruining his life."

The woman looked at Webb. "I had a share in what he did to you," she told him. "Marrying him was the craziest thing I ever did. He had me then. If I had ever told what I knew he would have killed me."

"What did you know?" Bob asked.

"I was in the outer office when Giles Lemmon was killed. It came so fast I hadn't time to get away before the shots were fired. I heard Hans cry, 'Goddlemighty, I've killed the wrong man,' and Jug Packard answered: 'Quit shooting, Rhino. I'll fix that nice.' Then I ran out of the building. Next day my father sent me to California. I didn't know anything about your trial till two months after you were in the penitentiary, and by that time I was married to Hans."

"If you'll tell that to Governor Andrews it ought

to save Bob from going back to Yuma," Fraser said.

"I'll tell him. I would have told him long ago if I hadn't been a coward." She added, as though something inside of her was forcing her to talk at last: "Hans wasn't so—so awful—in those days. He was a big bully, but he didn't look so like a hippopotamus. I was kind of pretty then, and he fooled me into thinking he was so fond of me that I could change him. His story was that you had come in to kill Packard and that when you started shooting he had to draw a gun to save the life of his boss. Afterward I knew that wasn't true, just as I knew I couldn't change him. He was bad—not bad the way Scarface or Cole Hawkins is. They are wild and reckless, and I reckon both of them have killed men in fights, but they are kindhearted and they are always gentle to me. Hans is evil. There is something about him that makes my flesh creep." Her voice broke. She was thinking, as she had done many times before, that she had been a vile creature to have lived with him so long, knowing what he was.

"You're through with him for good and all," Fraser reminded her cheerfully. "We'll take you where you will be safe—where he can't reach you."

"There's no place I can go," she said. "I don't know anybody now but riff-raff and outlaws."

"My sister would be glad to have you stay with

her at Tucson," Bob said. "But if Uhlmann found you she couldn't give protection from him."

"Miss Ranger asked me to come to their place, but I expect her father would feel differently about it," the woman said. "Anyhow, I wouldn't ask him."

"The very place for you," Fraser cried. "John Ranger is a man among a thousand. Of course he'll want you there, just as Miss Sandra does. I happen to know they were trying to get a housekeeper a week or two ago when they were in Tucson. You'd be fine for the job."

"I think I could look after a house," Mary admitted doubtfully.

"Of course you can." Fraser assumed this settled. "Rhino shot Bob's horse. We'll have to run up a couple, one for you and one for him."

"I didn't say I'd go," the woman protested.

"We'll kidnap you," Fraser laughed. "Bob and I are old hands at it. We've just turned loose a sheriff we kidnapped."

Bob brought his saddle in from the knoll where his dead horse lay. Fraser roped two other mounts in the pasture and led them to the stable. Shortly the two men and Mary Uhlmann were on their way down the valley.

Mary's life had filled her with a sense of unworthiness. The man she had married had not only abused her physically but had trampled down her spirit by his jeers and the humiliations to which he subjected her. Now she was full of fears about the reception she would meet at the Circle J R. She was the wife of a man good people despised. Her clothes were old and patched. Long ago she had lost the knack of meeting new acquaintances pleasantly, largely because of the defensive barricade she flung up, a manner dry and short even to rudeness. What would the Rangers think of her?

30   UHLMANN BORROWS FROM A FRIEND

In the darkness Uhlmann's horse picked its way through the brush up Double Fork. Until nightfall he had lain hidden in a hill pocket. He did not know whether any posse of cattlemen was out after him, but he had to keep from being seen for fear his presence in that locality would be reported. There was an open season on him now. His overbearing ways had made plenty of enemies, and any one of them could shoot him down with no risk of a penalty.

The narrow valley of the Double Fork widened into a small park. At the foot of a rocky bluff, sheltered by a few scrubby live oaks, were a corral, a stable, and a small cabin. There was a light in the house, and as Uhlmann rode forward a dog began to bark. At once the light winked out.

"You alone, Pete?" the fugitive called warily.

There was a long silence before an answer came. "I can't do a thing for you, Rhino. The boys are aimin' to tack yore hide on a fence. You better light out for the border damn fast now."

"Open that door," Uhlmann ordered.

"You hadn't ought to of come here," the man in the cabin reproached. "This is the first place they'll look for you. If you had any sense you would know that. Like as not somebody is lying back there in the brush with a rifle trained on you this very minute. When I light the lamp he would get you as you come in. Smart thing for you to do is to slip back into the live oaks and beat it hell-for-leather in the darkness."

"Yeah, you're mighty anxious for me not to get hurt," sneered Uhlmann. "If I was shot you wouldn't go down to the store and tell everybody how fine it was I had got my come-uppance at last, seeing I always had been a killer and a bad man. Not you, Pete." The voice grew suddenly harsh and imperative. "Fling open that door, damn you. And don't light the lamp. We won't need it."

McNulty's wheedling voice protested. "Now looky here, Rhino. Down at the store a couple hours ago I was warned to keep outa this if I knew what was good for me. I don't mean to let myself get drug in. Course you got my best wishes. My advice is—"

"I'll blast my way in and come a-smokin' if you don't open," the hunted man threatened savagely.

"That's no way to talk to a friend," Pete grumbled. "I'll let you in, but there's nothing I can do to help you. It's not my fault you got yore tail in a crack. You'll have to ramrod yore own way out." He drew back the bolt and opened the door.

"Have they started a posse out after me?" Uhlmann asked.

"I dunno. They were still talking when I left.

But the boys are crazy mad. They'll get you sure, if you don't pull yore freight. What in tarnation made you shoot at the girl?"

Uhlmann had not come to make explanations or to defend his case. "I'm caught short," he said bluntly. "I want money."

"I was down to the store buying supplies," McNulty answered quickly. "I ain't got but three dollars left. I'll divvy with you fifty-fifty."

"I'll take three hundred dollars. Get it outa the hiding place where you keep yore dough." In the big man's harsh voice there was an ultimatum.

"Three hundred dollars," wailed McNulty. "Why, I haven't got that much in the world. You're crazy with the heat, Rhino."

"Dig it up. I'll give you a bill of sale for enough of my stock to cover it."

"How could I use that bill of sale? The boys would know I had contacted you and they would string me up for helping you to make a getaway. They would claim I always had been in cahoots with you."

"I don't care whether you use it or not," Uhlmann growled. "It's the money I want."

"But I tell you I haven't got it." Pete pulled from his pocket a small handful of silver. "You can have all I got. Here it is."

Uhlmann's small eyes glittered like those of a cat in the darkness. "The boys are gonna hang me, you claim. Or maybe shoot me as they would a wolf. They can't do any more to me for rubbing you out too. *I want that money.*"

"If I had it, Rhino—"

"Don't talk," interrupted Uhlmann. "Get busy, or I'll let you have it in the belly and do the hunting myself."

In the pit of McNulty's stomach there was a dreadful sinking sensation. He loved the ill-gotten treasure he had piled up a little at a time. By nature he was a miser, and when he was alone he often got it out and fingered the gold pieces fondly. To give them up was far worse than letting somebody pull out his teeth. The loss of three hundred dollars would be bad enough, but he knew this ruffian well enough to be sure that he would take the whole hoard. Pete felt despairingly that he could not give up his savings, not at least without trying to talk Uhlmann out of the hold-up.

"I dunno where you got the notion that I've got money hidden away, Rhino. There's nothing to it. I hope a bolt of lightning will strike me dead if I'm lying."

"A bolt of lightning is gonna do that in about five seconds if you don't get busy," jeered Uhlmann, the barrel of his forty-five jammed into the stomach of his host. "I'll count ten. One—two—three—"

"I'll get it—the three hundred," McNulty moaned. "If you'll just step outside a minute while I find it—"

"I'm staying right here. Think I want a slug in my back?"

"Maybe I got a little more than three hundred, Rhino. You'll let me keep the rest, won't you?"

"Sure—sure. I wouldn't rob you, Pete."

McNulty's dragging feet took him to the far corner of the room. He knelt down and lifted from the puncheon floor a length of timber the face of which had been squared by a broad-ax. His fumbling fingers found a tin box and lifted it from the hole beneath. This he carried to the kitchen table. He searched for a key in the hip pocket of his jeans and brought it out reluctantly.

"I'll take that bill of sale, Rhino, though I don't reckon I can ever use it," he said.

On Uhlmann's pachydermous face was a dreadful smile. "Like you say, maybe you can't ever use it. That's yore lookout. Open the box."

The key in the trembling hand found the hole with difficulty, even after Uhlmann struck a match with his left hand. The revolver was in the right, held against Pete's backbone just below the shoulder-blades. The flame flickered out. A second lighted match showed to the robber's gleaming eyes a pile of gold coins that half filled the box.

"Good old Pete, you've been saving money for me all these years and didn't know it," he said.

McNulty slewed his head around, in time to

catch that gloating look before the match went out. "You promised me you'd only take the three hundred, Rhino," he pleaded. "God knows how many years I've scraped and slaved to get this little backlog. You wouldn't take it all from me, after we've been friends so long."

With cruel pleasure Uhlmann tasted this minute of victory after so many hours of bitter impotent anger. There was no feeling of mercy in him toward his helpless victim.

"Money is no good to you, Pete," he answered, derisive triumph in his heavy voice. "You only put it in a hole. Thinking of what a good time it is giving me will give you a kick."

McNulty made a fatal mistake. He tried to bargain. "It wouldn't be so good for you if I was to tell the boys you are holed up in this neck of the woods."

"Not so good," the hulking villain agreed.

Pete realized at once his error. He wished to heaven he had left the lamp alight. In the darkness this big devil was appalling. The only detail of the big leathery face that stood out was the dreadful shining eyes. The threat in them filled Pete with terror. A sickness ran through him. Weakness plucked all the manhood out of him.

"I wouldn't do that, Rhino—not to you," he murmured, his teeth chattering. "And us such good friends."

"Sure you wouldn't," the gunman taunted.

"You'd stay right here and not make a move—till I was out of sight."

The roar of the forty-five filled the room. Into the prone body the killer flung bullet after bullet. He snatched up the money box and ran out of the cabin. Dragging himself to the saddle, he galloped wildly into the night. He had not meant to kill Pete when he rode up Double Fork. It had been the farthest thing from his thoughts. But he saw now that it was the only way out for him. McNulty would have set the hunters on his track and they would have run him to earth. With every added mile between him and that dark cabin of death he felt easier in mind.

31 SANDRA TALKS WITH A BAD MAN AND LIKES HIM

As Sandra rode down the valley with Scarface Brown she felt an odd jubilance of spirit. The sense of danger that had been heavy on her was gone. She was safe, riding in the warm sunshine beside a man who would fight to protect her as quickly as Bob Webb had done against the raiders of Pablo Lopez. Her companion was the most notorious rustler in Arizona. Probably he had killed oftener than Uhlmann. But she knew she had no need to be afraid of him.

She slanted a smile at the long dark man riding knee to knee with her. "I've heard of you, Mr. Brown," she said demurely.

Scarface caught her mood instantly and responded to it. "Nothing but good, I hope," he replied, and flashed his fine white teeth in a grin that for the moment wiped from the brown face its sinister wariness.

"I think maybe those who told me were a little prejudiced against you," she answered.

"Some are," he admitted. "But I dare say they would allow that I have taking ways."

Sandra laughed. "Yes. They would agree to that. I'm awfully glad I met you. I don't know any bad man except by sight. Now I have one all to myself for an hour or more." Her mischievous eyes mocked him. "You *are* a bad man, aren't you? I thought I heard you tell Hans Uhlmann so."

"I don't teach in a Sunday school."

"But you stood up for me against that ruffian and made him let me go."

"That was a pleasure," he explained. "I never did like the big bully, and it seemed like a good time for a showdown."

"I was dreadfully afraid of him, but not after you spoke up." She guided her horse around a chuck hole in the road. "If you are a bad man, there must be something wrong with me. I like you."

Though he laughed, he was much pleased. His way of life did not bring him into contact with girls like this one, but he understood exactly the quality of her liking and did not intend to presume upon it. It was probable that he would never again be alone with her, since he moved outside the laws that sheltered her. Yet the memory of this meeting would always be one to remember.

"It's right funny how words are thrown at you and they stick," the scamp philosophized. "They call me a bad man, and I can't kick. I'm a pretty rough hombre, and I've ridden a lot of wild trails. Uhlmann is a bad man from where they laid the chunk. Not excusing myself or anything, he's bad in a different way from me."

"You don't need to prove that to me," Sandra agreed.

"All right. I won't start whitewashing myself. We'll take another case, this Bob Webb. He gets hot under the collar account of what Rhino and Jug Packard did to his parents, and it lands him in the pen. He breaks loose, and right away he is a bad man, a rustler, killer, stage robber, and general trouble-maker. A good citizen is beaten up by him, and a sheriff who starts to arrest him is kidnapped. I happen to know half of those things are not true, and the other half can be explained. But there he is, the dog with a bad name."

"It's very unfair," the girl protested. "People are so stupid. He isn't a bad man at all, if they would only let him alone."

"In one way he is," the rustler differed. "Sometimes when you speak of a bad man you mean one who is dangerous, a fellow not to monkey with but to ride around real careful if you want to stay healthy. Now there was old John Slaughter.* He was little, but 'Gentlemen, hush!' When those cold eyes of his blazed at you there was a funny feeling in the pit of yore stomach. He chased me

---

*Sheriff of Cochise County, Arizona, in its wild days. While he was cleaning up his territory he served notice to the rustlers, "Get out or get killed." During his term of office there was a considerable migration of night-riding gentry.

all over the White Mountains once. That was what he was paid for, and I hadn't any complaints. But to my thinking he was a bad man—dangerous back of a gun when he was after you. Don't get me wrong, Miss Ranger. He was a first-class citizen, and one of these days Arizona will likely put up a statue to him. This young fellow Webb is bad the same way. If he was an enemy of mine I'd hate to crowd him."

"He won't be your enemy," Sandra said.

"Not if I can help it," the outlaw answered dryly.

"What do you mean when you say that half of these things Bob Webb is accused of he didn't do? How do you know that? What half is false?"

Scarface took his time to reply. It was in his mind to tell her certain facts, but he did not intend to say too much. A man on the dodge as he was, a leader of the riff-raff who preyed on the property of other men, learned by the underground route the true story back of all the lawless deeds committed in his district. The obligation was on him not to divulge any of these to anybody who might carry information to the authorities. But he had his own code of right and wrong. It did not include the protection of a smug two-facer like Jug Packard or a hired assassin such as Uhlmann, who were trying to shift their crimes to the shoulders of another man.

"First off, Webb did not kill Giles Lemmon. Uhlmann did it, while he was shooting at the boy.

259

Packard fixed it up to frame the kid. Uhlmann brags too much when he is drunk. I could tell you too who shot Chuck Holloway, but I am not going to do it. I will say it was neither Fraser nor Webb."

"Father and I can testify to that. We were looking through the window watching them as they ran for their horses. Neither of them fired a shot."

"Some of the gang with Uhlmann that night give yore father credit for the shot."

"It's not true," Sandra denied indignantly.

"I know," Scarface nodded. "Holloway was a very bad character. He had been fixing to ruin the fifteen-year-old daughter of a man who was present that night. This father would not have shot him down without giving warning. I'm sure of that. Not if an emergency hadn't jumped up and kinda forced his hand. He liked Webb, and he was against this ganging-up to kill him. The man followed Uhlmann's pack of wolves out the back door of the Legal Tender. About the first thing he saw was Chuck Holloway standing not a dozen yards from Webb raising his rifle to fire at him. He couldn't miss. This man I am telling you about is a crack shot with a forty-five, one of the best I ever saw. He fired once. That was enough. Later he told me about it. Now I'm telling you. His life may be in yore hands, Miss Ranger. Some of these birds might ambush him if they knew."

"I'll be very careful," the girl promised. "The testimony of Father and me will clear Bob. We don't need to know this man's name."

"I hope you're close-mouthed. If you are not, just remember before you talk that my friend's life may hang on it." Scarface passed to another charge against Webb. "Also by the underground whisper I know that Webb and Fraser did not hold up the Oracle stage. Uhlmann and another man did it. I won't say any more about that."

When they rode into the yard of the Circle J R, Sandra was surprised to see her father dismounting from a horse.

"I thought you intended to be away two days," she said.

Ranger's eyes could not conceal their astonishment at the companion she had brought with her to the ranch. He said, "There was a letter in the mail-box that made it unnecessary for me to go."

"Father, I have done something foolish," his daughter said.

"I'm getting used to that," John Ranger replied coldly, his gaze still on the desperado. "What was it?"

"I found out that Mary Gilcrest is Uhlmann's wife, so I rode to the X Bar ranch to talk with her."

The face of the cattleman flushed angrily. "I didn't think that even you were foolish enough to do that," he told her.

Sandra had made up her mind to tell the whole story and face the consequences. "I went up along the ridge, so as not to be seen. I saw Mr. Fraser there, and after I left him I met Uhlmann." She related what had occurred there.

"He shot at you?" Ranger repeated, his face dark with anger.

"Yes." She went on to tell the rest of the story.

Once Scarface interrupted, embarrassed at the credit she gave him. "Come, Miss Ranger, all I did was to tell Rhino where to head in."

"You stood up to him and told him what he was," she cried. "You made him let me go with you and told him you would set the ranchers of the valley on him to hang him. I thought once he would shoot you."

"I knew he wouldn't," the rustler answered lightly. "I was watching him. Fact is, Mr. Ranger, I only did what any white man would do." On his face was a sarcastic smile. "If you and yore friends ever catch me with the goods there is nothing to prevent you from hanging me to a cottonwood. No obligation on yore part. I been waiting for a chance to step on that bully Uhlmann's corns."

Ranger was embarrassed. It had not been a month since he had almost caught this man driving away his stock, and if he had been captured he would certainly have been hanged on the spot. Now the man had intervened to save his daughter from the results of her folly.

He managed a smile. "Mr. Brown, you have me in a cleft stick. No matter what you say I am under a very great obligation to you. And I don't see how I can repay it. You have chosen a crooked trail to travel, and you know where it is likely to end. Unless you leave it, there is nothing I can do for you."

"Just what I've been telling you." There was a flash of teeth in the brown face as the outlaw smiled hardily. "We understand each other perfectly. I'll be saying *adios*."

"Father!" the girl murmured unhappily. She could not let the man leave on that note.

Scarface came to the rescue. "It's all right, Miss. Nothing else Mr. Ranger can say or do. He's not throwing me down. It has to be this way."

After he had mounted, Sandra impulsively walked up to him and offered her hand. "I'm not a cattleman," she said. "Whatever you are, I can't help it. I know you stood up to that villain Uhlmann and brought me back home safe. No matter what happens, I won't ever forget it."

He held her small hand in his large brown one for a moment, a smile on his face that relaxed its habitual vigilant wariness.

"That goes double, Miss. I won't forget either."

He turned his horse and rode, a lithe and graceful figure, to whatever fate destiny had in store for him.

Ranger turned to his daughter, a worried frown

on his face. "I'm glad you told him that. Though he is a scoundrel and a thief, he is a generous fellow with a clean streak in him. You put me in a nice spot, girl. He goes out of his way to help you when you are in trouble, and all I can say to him is that I hope I won't have to help hang him. Can't you stay at home and behave yourself, Sandra? Do I have to lock you in your room?"

She told him she had learned her lesson and promised to do nothing more without consulting him.

32 SANDRA FORGETS HER BRINGING UP

Mary Uhlmann need not have worried about her welcome at the Circle J R ranch. John Ranger lifted her from the saddle and gave her a smiling greeting in Spanish—"*Esta es su casa de usted.*" His daughter put strong young arms around the guest's thin shoulders and gave her a quick hug. It touched Mary deeply to be told that this was her home, to feel the warmth of the Rangers' friendliness pouring into her starved heart.

Though she did not know it, her young hostess was more emotionally disturbed than she. Sandra had given Bob Webb a very casual greeting, but her cheeks were flying signals of excitement. The man she loved was back again, unhurt, and the clouds that had hung heavy over him were breaking. She was afraid to look at him, for fear her face would tell too much.

Fraser came forward, spurs jingling. "Didn't I tell you I would be camping on yore doorstep, *compadre*, soon as the heat was off?" he asked, a twinkle in his sun-faded blue eyes.

The girl was grateful for his badinage. She knew he was giving her a chance to ease back to the normal. "Good to know there is one faithful man alive," she laughed.

"I'm him." Stan lowered his voice to a stage whisper and jerked his head toward Bob. "Course he had to drag along. Some folks never know when they are not wanted. We'll fix it to get rid of him."

Ranger was pointing out to Mrs. Uhlmann the pass over which the Apaches had crossed the Huachucas to sweep down on the valley less than twenty years before. Bob was watching Sandra and his friend, a sardonic smile on his strong-boned face.

"We mustn't hurt his feelings by hurrying him off—now he is here," Sandra pointed out.

"Oh, we'll let him stick around a little while— say about sixty years." Fraser slapped his hat against the shiny chaps and gave a small whoop of triumph at his hit.

The girl looked at him reproachfully. "You know so much! Just for that I'm going to leave you." She moved to join her father and their guest. As she passed Bob she murmured. "Want to see you alone before you go."

Webb nodded without speaking. He had something to say to her, and he preferred to say it when nobody else was present.

Sandra showed Mary to the room she was to occupy. It was the sort of bedroom the older woman had dreamed about, bright and cheerful, with chintz window curtains, a big easy-chair and soft bed, a good rag carpet. Shy embarrassment made her almost speechless. As Sandra fussed over little details that made for comfort, Mary had a feeling she ought to fight against the gratitude that was melting the protective ice so long stored in her. She was afraid to let herself be glad, for fear of the pain that would follow when she found her joy illusory.

The girl left her to wash off the dust of travel. She found Bob Webb alone on the porch. Fraser had drawn John Ranger to the barn on pretense of wanting to look at the new Hereford bull the stockman had recently bought.

"Let's go into the orchard," Sandra said. "It will be cool there."

As soon as they were among the peach trees Bob opened his attack. "Don't you know better than to go fooling around with Uhlmann?" he demanded sharply. "I've told you it isn't safe for you to try to find out anything he and Packard want kept secret. If you would only let me manage my own affairs!"

She looked at him in surprise, astonished and hurt at his brusque vehemence. "I thought that—"

"Can't you get it through yore noodle that if you learn too much about these blackhearted villains they will rub you out?" he interrupted. "They won't stop because you are a woman. That devil might have killed you today. This isn't a game they are playing with me. They mean to destroy me, just as I mean to destroy them."

Sandra knew his irritation had its genesis in his anxiety for her safety, but her anger rose at his dictatorial manner. He might make some allowance for the urge that had driven her and for the fact that her interest had uncovered the evidence that might save him.

"That's my lookout," she snapped, hot temper in her eyes. "I don't have to ask you what I can or can't do. I'll go on doing as I please."

He took her by the shoulders and shook her till her teeth chattered. When he freed her she stood staring at him in astonishment, too breathless to talk. Sandra was no more amazed than he. Until the moment that his hands were on her he had not had the remotest idea of what he was going to do. How could he explain to her that it was his dark fear for her that had boiled up in heady anger?

"Just another Uhlmann," she said. "But you haven't blacked either of my eyes yet."

He might have retorted that she had not lashed him with a quirt, but he had no spirit for contention. He had burnt out his exasperation in action. All she had done for him flooded up in his mind, not only her brave fight to save him from approaching catastrophe but of even more importance the rebirth of hope and faith in him her trust had inspired. With a little gesture of defeat he turned to go.

"Wait a minute," she ordered.

They looked steadily into each other's eyes.

Mirth began to bubble in hers. "It's not fatal to shake up a girl—when she needs it," Sandra mentioned. "Maybe it will improve her, as it does medicine in a bottle."

He was still shocked at what he had done. "I don't know how I came to lay hands on you. I must have gone crazy."

Her face had crinkled to laughter. "You're very vigorous in your punishments, sir," she said, with mock demureness, and she lifted some stray golden locks to prove it. "My hair has tumbled every which way."

All he could say was, "I don't want these villains to hurt you."

"If it has to be done, you'll do it yourself," she added with neat friendly malice.

"You wouldn't listen to me, and I thought it might make the difference between life and death for you."

"I'll listen now." A queer song of joy was singing in her breast. He would not have been so violent if it had not been for his interest in her. "And I'll promise from now on to stay at home and not lift a finger. Does that suit you?"

"It suits me fine. I'll shake hands on it."

Their hands met and clung fast. Out of that contact some magnetic force flowed that drew one irresistibly to the other. His arms went round her and their lips met in a long kiss that set the blood pounding.

He pushed her from him. "What am I doing?" he asked in a low rough voice. "There can't ever be anything between you and me. We both know that."

"But there is," she denied exultantly. "There always has been since the first moment we met."

A savage joy beat up in him, but he set himself grimly to fight it down. "No," he answered harshly. "There is the curse of the prison on me. All through your life it would rise up to destroy your happiness."

"If it is proved you are not guilty?"

"People would forget that. They would remember that I spent years in a penitentiary."

"But you are wrong," she cried. "And it wouldn't matter what they thought so long as we knew the truth."

"Not today or tomorrow maybe, but in the years to come. It would be a blot on our children's future. I've been having an impossible dream, but I've got to face facts now."

"We'll wait until you're cleared and talk of this again," she said.

"No," he flung back unhappily. "Never again. There's a wall between us we can't break down."

The girl looked at him with high spirit, her lovely young head held high. "You are wrong, Bob Webb. There's no wall except one your silly pride has built up. You can't kiss me like that and throw me over. I won't have it, for I know you love me. My future has its rights as much as yours. You can't decide this alone without consulting me."

"It's you I'm thinking of, a lovely young girl, sheltered and—"

"Fiddlesticks!" she interrupted. "I thought you had more sense. A woman doesn't sit on a pedestal, making sure her hands are lily-white and that there is no common dust on her skirts. Unless she is a fool she goes out and—and meets life. She loves and marries and has children, if she is lucky. Her hands roughen and her face wrinkles. Griefs and trouble wear her away, as they do a man. And in spite of that she is happy, given the right mate by her side."

Slender and erect, she faced him. A warm glow beat through the clear skin. Her starry eyes challenged him. She was as spirited, he thought, as a young Joan of Arc. The gospel she flung out so hotly was heresy against the traditions in which she had been brought up, that a good girl must wait demurely, eyes downcast and innocent, until the man came to seek her. She would have none of that mincing philosophy. If her happiness was at stake, she meant to fight for it.

"When I am wearing my striped uniform I am Number 4582," he reminded her gently.

"The only thing that matters about a man is what he is, not what people say about him," she retorted.

He was puzzled at her sureness. She was so young, and had gone such a little way in life, yet somehow had cut through conventions to essential truth.

"Where did you learn so much?" he asked her, a smile in his eyes.

She knew she had won. "I thought it out nights in bed when I couldn't sleep for worrying about you. I found out what was important and what wasn't." An impudent little smile wrinkled her face. "If I'm a forward hussy, I don't care."

He took her in his arms again. "I've just found out how much I like forward hussies," he told her.

33   Uhlmann Makes a Refund

Jug Packard sat behind an old scarred desk figuring a payroll. He was seated in a cheap kitchen chair. In one corner of the office were piles of old accounts tied together with strings. Dirt and disorder were everywhere.

An observer who knew Jug well would have noticed that he was expecting a visitor and had made preparations not to be surprised by him. The soiled curtains of the windows were drawn closely to prevent anybody outside from seeing into the room. A box half filled with papers had been set against the closed door so that it could not be opened without warning. The drawer of the desk was out about six inches, and in it lay a forty-five, the butt of it within six inches of Jug's fingers.

The expected caller had given Packard no advance notice of a visit. His expectation of one was due to his knowledge of a certain man's psychology. Probably the fellow had not sent word to Pete McNulty that he was coming, but Pete ought to have been ready anyhow. Jug did not intend to be taken unaware.

He had not made up his mind yet whether to kill his uninvited guest or not. It would be a popular thing to do, and just now with the cards running against him he could use some public good will. It might be the safest course, since dead men tell no tales. On the other hand it might be that he could still use Uhlmann to get rid of Webb.

The door handle turned slowly. Packard's right hand dropped into the desk. He watched the box being pushed farther into the room. His fingers came out of the drawer and rested on the desk. They were holding the revolver.

"Come in, Rhino," he invited, his voice suave and mocking. "I've been looking for you."

The box slid across the floor as the door whipped open.

Uhlmann stood on the threshold. The two men stared at each other. Packard was smiling, derisive mockery on his hatchet face.

"Nice of you to drop in on me," he jeered. "You visiting all yore old friends before you leave the country?"

"Put that gun down, Jug," growled Uhlmann. "You don't need it."

"Any more than Pete McNulty needed one," Packard reminded the other. His thin lips tightened. The foxy slyness in his face was gone, in its place a cruel implacable wariness. "Sit down in that chair, and put yore hands on its arms. Move slow. Don't forget that I can fling three-four slugs into yore belly before you drag out that gun you're thinking about."

Uhlmann glowered at him sullenly. "You gone

274

crazy with the heat, Jug? We've always been side-kicks, you and me."

"Like you and Pete were," the man behind the forty-five said, his voice low and ice-cold.

"Any man who says I killed Pete is a liar," the big man blurted out. "I ain't seen him for a week."

"I say you killed him. This whole country says it. You were seen headed up Double Fork."

"I went to get some money he owed me, but he wasn't to home."

"If he hadn't been he would have been alive today." Packard did not let his voice lift out of its low even register, but his words dripped with an imperative menace. *"Get into that chair now, or go out in smoke."*

The leaden feet of the huge killer dragged forward. He slumped down into the chair, more like a rhinoceros than ever. The small sullen eyes, the wrinkled skin of the face hanging in heavy folds, the gross body huddled into a shapeless mass, all suggested that brutal and insensitive pachyderm.

Scarcely six inches from Uhlmann's hairy hand the butt of a revolver pushed out from its holster. He knew that Packard had not forgotten this. The man was taunting him, gloating over his helplessness. There was mockery in the cruel eyes. They invited him to take a chance, to reach for his weapon and make a fighting finish. But the catch was that there was no chance. Jug was lightning-fast, and at that distance he could not miss. Before the big killer could fire a shot his great body would be crashing to the floor.

"Don't be that way, Jug," Uhlmann growled. "I came up here to figure out how I was going to get Webb. Fellow told me he and Fraser were roosting in the hills back of the Circle J R. My idea was to do the job tonight."

"Yore idea was to slip in on me and play the same trick you did on Pete," corrected Packard. "First rob me, then shoot me into a rag doll. You knew I was always here alone at night, so you figured it would be easy. That's the kind of a lunkhead you are. From the moment I heard that you were on the dodge there hasn't been a second when you could have pulled yore heavyfooted trickery on me."

"You got me wrong, Jug." Uhlmann brushed his coat sleeve across a perspiring forehead. "I wouldn't do you thataway. We've been pals a long time, you 'n' me. When you've needed help you've come to me, and I've been with you every time. Ain't that so?"

"Water over the dam. Anything you ever did for me I paid you for. And while we're talking about that, shell out the five hundred I gave you as advance on a job you didn't do."

"I aim to do it tonight, like I told you."

"Fine," answered Packard, with a titter. "I'll pay

you when you've done it. Until then I'll keep the five hundred for you. Dig it up."

Uhlmann made no motion to get the money. "You can't do that to me. I'm going through with this. I don't aim to leave until I've settled Webb's hash."

"When you do, you'll have fifteen hundred coming to you. But I reckon I'll make sure, Rhino." The man's mouth tightened. He leaned across the desk and let the end of the barrel tap gently on the wood by way of reminder. "Shell out my money, fellow."

"If I have to light out I've gotta have dough," Uhlmann pleaded. "Don't be a hog, Jug. Five hundred is nothing to you, and I aim to earn it inside of two hours."

The eyes of the mining man glittered. "When I pull this trigger there won't be any questions asked by anybody. Everybody will give me the glad hand for rubbing out a mad wolf. Don't make a mistake about this. It's the last call."

From a dry throat Uhlmann grunted surrender. It was in his mind that when he reached to open the money belt his fingers would tilt up the revolver and fling a bullet through the holster.

"Just stay where you're at," Packard ordered brusquely. "Leave yore hands on the chair arms." He rose, walked around the desk, passed back of his prisoner's chair, and drew the revolver from its case. "I wouldn't want an old pal like you to commit suicide."

The short blunt fingers of Uhlmann counted out five hundred dollars in bills and left them on the desk in front of the other man.

Packard slid the money into the open drawer and closed it. "If you really must go I won't keep you any longer," he said.

"Do I get my gun back? To fix Webb."

"You have yore rifle beside the saddle."

"I want my six-gun too," Uhlmann insisted doggedly.

The miner gave this consideration. "All right. You get it—after you are in the saddle. Let's go."

Uhlmann lumbered out of the room first, in obedience to a wave of his captor's hand. He did not feel comfortable, for he knew that though sly and cautious Jug was a man who had no regard for human life. His intention might be to destroy the trapped man before he had taken a dozen steps. The big ruffian talked, his voice not under very good control. He had to fix it in Jug's mind that he was setting out to find and kill Bob Webb.

"They're in that old Baxter cabin—the one in the foothills back of the Circle J R. I can sneak up and get Webb sure as you're a foot high, Jug. That will be fine for both of us."

"If you do, I'll send you the money, Rhino. That's a promise."

Hans Uhlmann did not believe he would keep it. Just now he was not interested in whether he would or not. The killer knew he had been a fool to come here. If he got away with his life he would be doing all right. As he flatfooted forward he half expected a bullet tearing through the muscles of his back.

"Climb up," Packard ordered, after they had reached the post to which the horse was hitched.

Uhlmann pulled himself heavily to the saddle. He still was not sure whether Jug was going to kill him. "Everything will be all right," he said hoarsely. "I'll get that fellow Webb sure."

"I'll believe it when I see him dead."

Packard broke the gun and emptied the shells into his hand. He tossed them on the ground and flung the empty revolver away.

"You can pick them up after I have gone," he said, and ran swiftly back to the office.

From a window he watched Uhlmann dismount and search the ground for the shells and the weapon. After he had apparently found them the big killer pulled himself to the back of the horse again and disappeared down the road.

Hurriedly Packard put the five hundred dollars safely away, blew out the light, and slipped out of the office. A saddled horse was waiting back of the building. A minute later he was following Uhlmann down the steep mountain trail over which ore from the mine was hauled to the plains.

34 "Till a' the Seas Gang Dry, My Dear"

After Sam Washington had washed the Packard supper dishes he carried a pail of refuse to the gulch back of the kitchen and emptied it over the precipice that fell away for a hundred feet to the floor below. It was as he was walking back to his quarters that he caught sight of a shadowy bulk which resolved itself into a man on horseback. The rider dismounted in the darkness and moved forward to the office cautiously.

Sam recognized the lumbering gait. The furtive visitor was Hans Uhlmann, who in the past forty-eight hours had become a fugitive from the vengeance of his neighbors. The cook had a large bump of curiosity tempered by caution. From an old leather trunk in his bedroom next to the kitchen he took a revolver and checked to make sure it was loaded. He did not know what Uhlmann was doing here but he meant to find out if he could. That his employer and this evil man had been accomplices in wickedness at times Sam was pretty sure. Hans might have come to plot with Packard, or he might want to destroy him as he had McNulty.

The door of the office was closed and all the curtains were drawn tight. Sam could neither see into the room nor hear anything that was said. It was impossible for him to tell whether this was a get-together meeting. He found out later, when Uhlmann slouched out of the room with a forty-five pointed at the small of his back.

By that time Sam was crouched in the brush at the edge of the gulch, a few yards from the spot where the horse of the ranchman was hitched. As Uhlmann moved through the darkness he talked, and there was something very like panic in his whinning voice. He was telling Packard that Webb was in the old Baxter cabin and he would sneak up and kill him. The answer of the mine owner made clear his position. He would pay the killer after he had done the job. But it was also plain that he did not trust his hired assassin, for he kept him covered until the man was astride his horse and left him weaponless while he backed away to safety.

Sam waited in the bushes and saw both Uhlmann and Packard ride down the road, though not together. The cook was puzzled at this set-up. It was plain that Jug meant to keep an eye on Rhino. Was it to make sure the gunman would kill Bob Webb? Or was it in his mind to rub out the villain who was doing his work?

The cook scratched his woolly thatch and talked aloud to himself. "Now looky here, Sam Washington, this plumb ain't any of yore business. Go to monkeyin' around with these two wolves and you'll ce'tainly buy yoreself a mess of trouble. What you wants to do is to include yoreself out."

He continued to grumble to himself as he saddled his old white mule and took the trail after the other two. But though he chided himself, he could not keep out of the business. He had to let Miss Sandra know about the plot to murder her friend. Very likely he would be too late. If Webb was at the Baxter cabin, and if Uhlmann rode straight there, it would take only a few seconds to call the convict to the door on some excuse and riddle him with bullets.

The road went along the rim of the cañon to the foothills. No short cut could be taken by Sam. Nor was there any chance of slipping past the men in front of him, since the trace ran along a ledge wide enough only for a wagon to pass. More than once he stopped to make sure he was not getting too close to Packard. But no sound of hoofs in front came back to him in warning.

He came out of the cañon into the roll of low hills that stretched like waves to the valley. A path that was little more than a cow trail deflected from the main road and ran toward the ridge back of the Circle J R. Sam guessed that both of the riders had taken this cut-off, but he by-passed it and headed straight for the ranchhouse.

He tied his mule to the corral fence and crossed the yard to the kitchen. Jim Budd was grinding coffee for breakfast. He slewed his head around and grinned at sight of his friend.

"What you doing here this time of night, fellow?"

"I gotta see Miss Sandra."

"Wha' for?"

Sam did not intend to let anyone else steal the credit of his news, not after having ridden twelve miles to tell his story.

"Nem' mind about that. This is impo'tant. Where is she at?"

"She's entertaining comp'ny. You cain't go bustin' in on her. You tell me what you want and I'll see—"

The mine cook turned his head to listen. From the parlor came to him the voice of a girl. She was singing, "O my luve's like a red, red rose."

"You go tell Miss Sandra quick—or her pappy, one, I don' care which—that I'm here to tell some info'mation—and there ain't no time to fool around."

"Now, Sam, you an' me is friends," Jim began, with the patient manner of one arguing a case to an unreasonable child.

Sam did not listen to him. Miss Ranger was not fifteen steps from him. Her young voice came to him clear and vibrant:

"Till a' the seas gang dry, my dear,
And the rocks melt wi' the sun,

I will luve thee still, my dear,
While the sands o' life shall run."

Jim was still talking. Sam ducked past him and through the door. He ran along the passage and into the parlor. A young man was standing at the piano beside the girl, but the colored man paid no heed to him.

"Miss Sandra," he cried, "that Uhlmann is ridin' right now to the old Baxter cabin to shoot Bob Webb."

The man leaning on the piano whirled round. "What's that?" he demanded abruptly.

If his errand had been less urgent Sam might have hesitated to tell it before this unknown visitor, but under the circumstances he blurted out details. "I done heard them talkin', Packard and Uhlmann. Jug is gonna pay him soon as he kills off Webb. I followed them down the cañon to tell you, Miss Sandra."

"Packard is with him?" the stranger demanded.

"No, sir. Jug came down after him. Rhino doesn't know it. Jug is checkin' up on him, looks like." Sam told about the miner coming out of the office on the heels of Uhlmann with a gun covering the killer.

"He doesn't trust his hired assassin."

"Not none. But both of them are out to get this Webb. If he is at the old Baxter shack they'll do it."

"This is Mr. Webb, Sam," explained Sandra. "We'll not forget that you took the trouble to warn us."

Bob looked at the Negro searchingly. This might be a plant arranged by his enemies. Sandra guessed what he was thinking.

"No, Bob," she intervened before he could speak. "Sam is our friend. Uhlmann gave him that scar on his forehead. Jim and I know he is all right."

The troubled eyes of Webb shifted to the girl. "Stan may be in the cabin. If he is—"

He did not finish the sentence. She knew what he meant.

"You said you didn't sleep in the cabin, but in a hill pocket somewhere back of it," she reminded him.

"Yes, but he was reading that Dickens story you lent me when I left. He may not have gone from the cabin yet." He added, his voice sharp with anxiety, "I'll have to hurry."

Jim Budd was in the doorway. Sandra turned to him. "Get the boys in the bunkhouse. Tell them to saddle fast." To Webb she said: "I wish father were at home. But anyhow there are five of the boys in the bunkhouse. They won't keep you waiting more than a few minutes."

"I can't wait for them." His eyes were quick with excitement. "Tell them to follow soon as they are saddled."

"It won't be more than five minutes," she pleaded.

"Five minutes is as long as five hours sometimes." He took her by the arms to move her out of the way. As he looked down at her the harshness died out of his face. "Don't worry about me. I'll be careful."

She did not trust his promise. He would be careful only if recklessness was not necessary to save his friend. His hard steely eyes had softened for the moment, but she knew that when he reached the battle zone the safety of Stan Fraser would be his first thought.

"If you all rode together," she urged, and did not get a chance to finish.

He kissed her, smiling into her troubled eyes. The assurance he gave her had nothing to do with his danger, at least not on the surface. His words came lightly, as if in jest, but she knew how much he meant them. " 'Till a' the seas gang dry, my dear,' " he said with cheerful nonchalance.

Spinning her gently out of the way, he strode from the room.

35 STAN WRITES A NOTE

Fraser grew tired of reading. This fellow Dickens was all right, but he sure was a word-slinger. The folks who read *Dombey and Son* must have had more time to burn than a sheepherder. He yawned deeply, stretched and looked at his watch. A quarter to ten. Time for all honest people, except lovers, to turn in for sleep. Since Bob was one of the exceptions, he probably would not leave the Circle J R for hours yet. When a man was with the right girl sleep was something he had no use for.

Stan grinned. That young chump was getting a break at last, after a helluva lot of lean years. Uhlmann was a fugitive. With evidence piling up against Packard as it was, looked like he might go to the pen instead of Bob. On top of that young Webb had won the nicest and best-looking girl in the county. Good going for a convict with a price on his head.

The old-timer blew out the light and sauntered from the cabin. A young moon rode a sky of scudding clouds and at the edge of these stars peeked out. Sam untied the horse he had left at a post and stood at sharp attention. He had heard the hoof of another horse strike a stone. A bullet whistled past his ear.

"Holy mackerel!" he grunted, and vaulted to the saddle.

A leaden slug purged into the adobe wall back of him. He lifted the cowpony to a canter, his body low on the animal's neck, and reined his mount sharply to the left, to put the building between him and the rifleman. At the back of the house he pulled up and reached for the Winchester in the scabbard beside the saddle.

Another gun sounded. "Two gents hunting," he said aloud, and started for an arroyo fifty yards away.

The pony staggered, lost its footing, and plunged to the ground, badly wounded by the last shot. Fraser landed on his shoulder and was for a moment stunned. He heard a triumphant yelp. It was too late now to get the rifle. He ran for the arroyo. Fortunately the moon had gone under a cloud. Though one of his attackers fired again, he reached the arroyo safely. Up this he raced to a boulder pile below the rim rock of the ridge.

Among the rocks was a scatter growth of cholla and prickly pear. Fraser realized that if he lay crouched here he would neutralize the advantage held by the attackers. Their rifles would be of no more use than revolvers at short range, and they would have to creep up close to dig him out from the rocks. Lucky for him it was a night battle. If it had been in the day-time one could have held the exit from the arroyo while the other rode up to the rim rock and picked him off from above.

What worried Stan was not his own situation but that of his friend. In thirty minutes, or an hour, or maybe two, Bob Webb would come along anticipating no danger and ride into an ambush. By a near miracle Fraser had escaped the first blast, but the killers would make sure of their victim next time.

Stan was trapped. He could not climb the sheer rock wall behind him, nor could he expose himself on either rim of the arroyo, for the clouds had been swept away and the moon shone bright over the desert. But he might be able to give Bob a warning, at a considerable risk to himself, by firing shots at intervals. If he could keep this up long enough, Bob would hear and be on the alert.

For a million years rocks had crashed down from the ridge into the small boulder field at the end of this pocket. The terrain was ideal for defense, but not so good if one every ten minutes kept calling the attention of the enemy to his position.

Fraser fired toward the mouth of the pocket and scuttled through the brush to the shelter of a boulder ten or fifteen yards distant. As he had expected, two explosions sounded so close to each other that the second seemed almost an echo of the first. He settled down in his new place, watching to make sure the enemy were not

289

stalking his cover. He was a cool customer, with nerves and muscles co-ordinated perfectly. Long habit as an outdoor Westerner had trained eyes and ears to catch the slightest stir of movement or rumor of sound. Warfare against the Apaches, terminated only in the past few years, had put a premium on still and vigilant patience.

A ruse to lessen the risk occurred to him. He picked up a bit of quartz and flung it against the face of a boulder twenty yards from his shelter. The guns of the ambushers sent bullets whistling up the draw in the direction of the sound. The old-timer chuckled. He had lured them into giving the warning without having to do it himself.

Stan knew he was in a tight spot. His assailants could not wait till morning to get him. He felt sure that they were taking advantage of the cover and of the darkness to move closer to him. But he was less distressed about this than about Bob's reaction to the warning of the shots. Webb would be alarmed at the danger of his friend and might come charging forward without taking any precautions.

A rustle in the bushes a stone's throw distant, so faint that only keen hearing could have detected it, told Stan that one of his enemies at least was working nearer through the brush. Fraser shifted his position back of the rock noiselessly. All he could do was wait until the rifleman was within range of his revolver. If the fellow stealing up on him got an open shot now he could hardly miss. Stan crouched low in the shadow of the boulder back of a clump of cholla.

His hunter was working very slowly and cautiously to the right. The moon was out again, and soon he would see his prey, a solid bulk back of the cactus, only partially protected by the embedded boulder. Fraser could not wait any longer. He had to take a chance. There was nothing for it but to dash across an open space to the refuge offered by a sunken hole back of a sandstone slab.

Stan came out on the run. From the darkness a startled voice ripped out an oath. The old-timer was in moonlight bright and clear. He was half-way to the slab when a shot rang out. A blow struck his shoulder but did not stop him. His body plunged down into the sand hole and slid along it. Though bruised and winded, he clambered to his feet and peered around the edge of the rock. A shifting shadow crossed the floor of the arroyo in front of dense shrubbery, the figure throwing the shadow concealed by the foliage. Fraser fired, guessing at the man's position. A bullet flung an answer, striking the sandstone at an angle and flying off on a ricochet.

Pain obtruded itself into Stan's consciousness. He put his hand to his shoulder and found his shirt soggy. Warm blood seeped down his back and arm. Fraser grinned wryly. This was a heck of a note. He hoped the wound was not too bad, since he was too busy just now to go see a doctor.

With divided attention he gave himself first aid. While he took the bandanna handkerchief from around his neck and tied it about the wound to stop the bleeding, he checked up intermittently on the position of his foes. If they rushed him, he wanted to be ready to give as good as they sent.

The old frontiersman was a realist. It was a three to one bet, he guessed, that he had come to the end of the trail. His hunters probably thought that the victim they had trapped was Bob Webb. They might not discover their mistake until he was dead, and if they did he would be rubbed out anyway, on the principle that a dead man could not bear witness against them.

His attackers were taking no unnecessary chances. They were huddled back of cover just as he was. The silence in the arroyo was long, broken only by the sounds of night life peculiar to the desert. In the brush were murmurs of small creeping things, almost too faint to be heard. A more strident note was the sudden clamor of a cicada. On a far-away hill a coyote lifted its mournful howl.

Still watching for the attack or for any shift in the position of his enemies, Stan put his forty-five on the ground beside him and took from a pocket an old notebook and the stub of a pencil. By the bright moonlight he wrote:

Son, they've got me trapped in the arroyo. Might be trail's end for me. There are two of the birds. Uhlmann must be one of course. Don't know who the other is. They shot Jack Pot as I was leaving the cabin and I had to skedaddle without my rifle. One of them sent a pill into my shoulder.

A bullet whistled past Stan. He put down the pencil and picked up the revolver. Very cautiously he risked a look around the edge of the sandstone slab. He could see nothing like a gunman in the dark masses of shrubbery within his vision, but he knew that one at least of his attackers lay there hugging the ground. For moral effect, to let them know he was still dangerous, he sent a shot into the chaparral.

Another stretch of silence followed. Stan wrote again.

Just swapped shots with a gent hidden in the rocks. No damage, I reckon. I'm writing you, son, to tell you—if they send me West—that I've had a good go of it since I met you that day at my corral. Unbeknownst to you, boy. I've kinda adopted the son of my old friend. I've had fun scooting over the hills and watching from a ledge now and then posses hunting us. Made me feel young again.

Got to quit. One of these Injuns is crawling around to get me on my unprotected side. So long, son. A guy can't live forever anyhow.

Stan put the note in his boot leg and picked up the forty-five.

36   SANDRA TURNS NURSE

Bob found the stirrups after he had flung himself into the saddle. He wheeled his mount and sent it galloping down the lane. Very likely Stan had left the cabin and was safely in the hills before the arrival of Uhlmann. But the old-timer's habits were not predictable. He might have decided to sit in the shack reading until Bob returned from the ranch.

There was a good deal of the Indian about Uhlmann. He liked to do his killing from ambush, and if Fraser was still at the Baxter hut the old man might never know what had hit him. For Bob had no doubt that the outlaw would not hesitate to shoot down Stan, even though the man he really wanted to get was Webb.

It was Bob's habit to ride with consideration for his horse, but tonight he plunged ahead as fast as he could drive the animal. When clear of the fence he left the road and cut across a rough uneven flat to the hills shaping shadowlike in the distance. Even when the moon sailed out from behind a cloud the pace was dangerous, for there were gopher holes into which the gelding might stumble and break a leg.

He was driven by fear that his old friend might fall at the hands of an assassin. Without a moment's hesitation Stan had joined fortunes with him, refusing to be rebuffed, cheerfully determined to make a gay adventure of their hardships. No man could have asked for a more loyal or faithful companion. He had put up with Bob's moods and diverted him with light chat when the black devil care rode on Bob's shoulders. Now the little man might be lying crumpled on the dirt floor of the adobe cabin with a bullet through his heart.

Faintly there came to him on the night breeze the faraway pop of a rifle. Bob did not slacken the pace, though his stomach muscles collapsed at the sound. A killer had fired the gun, had very likely shot down Stan without warning. A sickness ran through Bob's lithe body. If the worst had taken place, it was something he could never forget. In him burned a hot fierce rage. He would get the man who had done this, if he had to follow the trail for years. But that would not bring back to life his whimsical and warm-hearted friend.

There came a second explosion, and a third. Hope quickened in Bob. If the first bullet had destroyed Fraser there would have been no need for more. It might be that Stan was forted in the cabin—fighting back—standing off his enemies until help came.

Breathing heavily, Bob's horse pounded forward. The sound of firing came occasionally to Webb, louder as the distance lessened. He could tell now that Stan was not in the cabin. The hammering of the guns came from the arroyo south of the house. Rifles were making most of the noise, but more than once a forty-five blasted out its challenge. Stan must be penned up in the arroyo among the rocks and brush.

Bob swung to the left and crashed through the cactus. He tore up a rise to the hill crown from which a slope dipped into the arroyo. He flung himself from the saddle, slipped back of a clump of prickly pear, and lifted a yell to encourage the beleagured man.

A call, weak but undaunted, came back to him.

"Hi yi, Bob. Look out these devils don't get you."

Bob heard the rustling of somebody scuttling away through the brush. He fired a random shot then ran down the slope toward his friend, blundering among the boulders and the shinnery to find him. Stan spoke again, to localize himself.

"You all right?" Bob asked as soon as he saw Fraser.

The old man grinned up at him indomitably. "Not too all right. One of the damned wolves plugged me in the back. Up near the shoulder. Reckon a doc can fix it."

They heard a galloping horse taking off into the night, and before the sound had died away the drumming hoofs of a second.

Bob gave immediate aid as best he could and carried the light body of Fraser to the cabin. The bleeding had not stopped, and the jolting of the trip had done the wounded man no good. As soon as Bob laid him on the bed he fainted. While he was still unconscious Webb washed and dressed the torn shoulder.

Stan opened his eyes. "I must of fainted. Like a girl." His smiled derided himself. "You've sure got a pal who can take it."

"The best ever a man had." Bob escaped from emotional ground quickly. "Were there only two of them?"

"That's right—two."

"They ambushed you?"

"One of 'em took a crack at me when I came outa the house. I ducked round it, and the other fellow shot my horse. Seeing I couldn't get at my rifle, I legged it for the arroyo."

"Could you tell who either of them was?"

"I didn't see but one of the birds, and then only for a moment. That skunk Uhlmann."

"The other was Packard," Bob said.

They heard a shout and the clop-clop of horses' feet. Bob moved swiftly to the door, revolver in hand.

"Circle J R riders," a voice announced. "That you, Fraser?"

"Stan has been wounded," Bob answered. "Webb talking. Uhlmann and Packard lit out."

A slim figure slid from a saddle and came forward. "Is Stan badly hurt?" Sandra asked.

"What are you doing here?" Bob asked.

"I had to come," she replied in a low voice. "We'll talk of that later. What about Stan? If he's hurt, I can nurse him."

"Yes," Bob nodded. "I'm glad you came, though you shouldn't have. The wound is serious. I don't know how bad. Come in."

He had dressed the wound in the dark, but now he lit a lamp. With four armed Circle J R men on the scene there would be no more shots out of the darkness.

Sandra sat on the bed and put her fingers on the pulse of the wounded man. She looked up at Bob. "We can't move him now. Better send one of the boys for Doctor Logan."

In Fraser's tired eyes there was a flicker of laughter. "This is one time I put Bob's nose outa joint," he murmured. "I'll bet he's sore at me being the whitehaired boy."

"Hurry up and get well," Bob said. "Then we can talk about that."

"I don't aim to hurry a doggoned bit, if Miss Sandra is gonna be my nurse," Stan announced weakly.

"As long as you need me I'll stay with you," she promised.

Bob asked Jim Budd to ride for a doctor, and as soon as the colored man had gone drew Sandra to one side.

"I'm not sure whether the bullet went into Stan's

lung or not," he said. "But anyhow this is going to be a long sickness. If you can stay here that will be fine. I'll leave word at the ranch to relieve the boys after a while. Two guards must stay with you all the time."

"Where are you going?" she asked in quick alarm.

"I've got a job to do," he replied grimly.

She noticed how hard and stern his eyes were. "You mean—?" The question died on her lips. Sandra knew what he was going to do.

"Don't worry about me," he advised. "I'll be as safe where I am going as you will be here."

"You're going after this villain Uhlmann," she charged.

He said: "Stan has given for me these last weeks everything he had. I'm not going to let this fellow get away with this."

The girl's heart died under her ribs. "Do you have to do this, Bob? Can't you leave it to somebody who isn't already in trouble?"

"No. Stan got this wound for me, not for somebody else."

She had known what the answer would be before she put her question. When he made up his mind it was as fixed as the Rock of Gibraltar.

"I don't see how you're going to find him," she said, and could not keep out of her voice the hope that he would not. "He'll be hiding in the hills, as you were."

In his harsh bony face was the day of judgment.

"I'll find him. Right now he's riding hard to reach Mexico."

"But if he gets across the line."

"I'll go across too."

"But he'll be safe on Mexican soil. You can't touch him there."

"Can't I?"

Looking into his bleak cold eyes, Sandra shuddered. This was not the man who had promised to love her till all the seas went dry. He was as relentless as fate, and he would follow the trail until his victim was destroyed. She had to find out one thing more.

"Are you going to bring him back to Arizona for punishment?"

"That's up to him. I'll give him that chance."

"You talk as if you were God," she cried. "He may lie in wait . . . and shoot you."

"It won't be that way," he promised.

With one of the Circle J R riders he looked over the horses and picked the one with most stamina. The cowboy watched Bob fix the stirrups to the right length.

"Good luck, fellow," the ranch hand said, rage at Uhlmann surging up in him. "Blast hell out of the Dutchman."

Sandra joined them, and the cowboy slipped away into the house. Bob finished tightening the belly-band. She found no comfort in his hard and stony face.

But when he turned to her his gaze softened. He took her in his arms and held her close without speaking. She thought, despairingly, "I can't let him go—I can't." But she knew it had to be that way. How full of fear her heart was she could not let him know. She said shakily, clinging to him: "The best eating place at Nogales is Dan's Café."

"Take care of Stan," he said. "Don't let him die."

He kissed her and swung to the saddle. Without looking back he rode away. She watched him until his figure had blurred into the landscape and he was no longer even a shadow in the night.

37   WHEN ROGUES FALL OUT

On his way down from the mine Uhlmann had been in a swither of doubt. He was heading for the safety of Mexico, but he could not make up his mind whether to make a short detour and try to get Webb on the way. A man in the hills had given him a straight tip that the convict was at the Baxter cabin. He could ride across the hills below the rock rim and take a look. If he was in luck a shot in the dark would be enough.

But a new hate was simmering in his warped mind. He did not want to pull any chestnuts out of the fire for Jug Packard, who had just robbed him of five hundred dollars and sent him down the road at the point of a gun. No dependence could be put on Packard's promise to pay him for getting rid of his enemy.

The trouble was that the convict was Uhlmann's enemy too. Perhaps because he had so greatly injured young Webb he had for him a bitter malevolence, and when he came to the fork in the road that rancor tipped the scales and led him to the Baxter cabin. It would do no harm to blot out Webb if it could be done conveniently. That would be one score settled.

He drew up on the summit of a rise and looked down at a light gleaming in the darkness. The information given him had been correct. Webb and Fraser were staying there. If he had a break he could get them both.

The sound of a moving horse behind him sent a stab of fear through the man. He had been drinking a lot and his nerves were jumpy. A man had seen him on the rim rock the day before and shot at him. To be alone against the world, without friends, filled him with a dreadful loneliness.

Drawing off from the trail, he stood back of his horse with the rifle across the saddle seat. The traveler back of him did not appear. Perhaps he had imagined the sound. More than once in the long nights he had conjured up danger that did not exist.

He waited, while dragging minutes passed.

A mocking voice, from the brush behind him, put a jeering question. "On the lookout for a friend, Rhino?"

The big man swung round, incredibly fast for his size. "Where did you come from?" he demanded.

Packard gave the tittering tee-hee that passed with him for a laugh. "Thought you might need a little help."

The hunted man did not like being dogged in the darkness by the plotter whose tool he had been. Suspicions flitted through his mind, and with them ugly thoughts. He pushed them into the back-ground, to be dragged out later.

"There's a light in the cabin," he said sulkily.

"I saw it."

"Maybe we could let him have it through the window."

"And if Fraser is there too?"

"He'll have to go with the friend he's so crazy about."

"There's a back door to the cabin," Packard said. "I'll swing round and cover it from the brush. Give me ten minutes before you start the fireworks."

Neither of them trusted the other, but each knew that their desires ran together in this matter. And each villain hoped to destroy his confederate later.

The light in the cabin was blown out before Uhlmann was ready to fire, but the crack of his rifle sounded when a man came out of the cabin. Half a minute later Packard dropped their victim's horse and Fraser bolted for the arroyo. They had the fellow now, since he had lost his Winchester. It would be only a matter of time before they got him. They moved into the arroyo cautiously, wary as Indians, taking advantage of all the cover there was. But before they could finish the job that fighting fool Webb had broken their ambush and driven them away.

Packard flung himself on his horse and galloped out of the battle zone. In spite of the sly mean streak in him, the safety-first instinct in him that prompted the use of others to do his evil deeds, he was a hardy scoundrel afraid of neither God nor man. His flight was not a question of lack of courage. He had his reputation to consider, the fiction that he was a respectable and law-abiding citizen. It would be a great mistake to be recognized here as an ally of Uhlmann.

One of his worries was that Rhino knew too much about him. If the fellow was captured and not killed, he would implicate the mine owner in his crimes. Packard blamed himself for not having killed the man when he had the chance. He had been too greedy. It had been asking too much to hope that his accomplice would get rid of Webb and then let himself be trapped by Jug.

A man always cautious, he pulled up to listen. He was not expecting immediate pursuit, but it was better to make sure. On the light night breeze there came to him the beat of hoofs. A horse was traveling fast toward him. He guessed the rider of that driven animal was Uhlmann.

Under the shadow of a mesquite beside the trail he waited, revolver in hand. The huge body of Uhlmann was on the horse that came pounding down the road. Packard fired a thin split second too soon. The bullet shattered the saddle horn of the laboring animal. Uhlmann flung himself to the ground on the far side of his mount, hanging on to the bridle with his left hand.

Startled at the explosion, Packard's horse bucked violently. The rider was flung from the saddle and hit the sand hard, his weapon tossed a dozen feet from him. While one could have counted ten he lay there, jarred and breathless. It took him a long moment to scramble to his feet and another to get his fingers on the forty-five. A slug ripped into his belly. Two spat spurts of dirt from the road. A fourth struck his foot.

Packard sank down. He was through with living and knew it. But the urge to kill was still strong in him. By a tremendous effort he pushed himself up from the ground and raised the revolver weakly. The bullet went whistling into the brush.

Uhlmann did not wait to learn how desperately wounded was his foe. The man was still alive and fighting. Clumsily he pulled himself astride his horse and spurred into the chaparral. He rode up a low ridge and looked down into a swale along which men were moving at a gallop. They were headed for the Baxter cabin. Though he could not identify them in the moonlight, he had no doubt they were Circle J R men.

He knew that if he was going to get out of the country alive he had to hurry. His horse's head he pointed south. Not until he was deep in Mexico would he feel safe.

38 A Body in the Dust

Uhlmann opened cautiously the back door of the Silver Dollar saloon and looked the place over before entering. It was the slack morning hour, and there was nobody in the room except two Mexicans, a cowboy, and the bartender. He moved forward ponderously and ordered a drink. The man in the white apron put a glass and a bottle in front of him. The customer showed evidence of having traveled far. He was dusty and sweat-stained, and his little eyes were red and sunken.

"Resting yore saddle after a long ride?" the bartender asked, to make talk.

The big man glared at him sullenly. He was in a very bad humor. His horse had gone lame and added several hours to the journey. As a result he was both weary and exasperated. The bartender was bald, fat, and forty. He looked like a safe man to bully.

"That any of yore business?" Uhlmann demanded truculently.

The cowboy playing solitaire laughed. "One for you, Mike," he said. "Now will you be good?"

Mike's slaty eyes rested appraisingly on the surly giant. "No offense meant, stranger," he mentioned. "I wasn't asking where you came from or why."

A dull anger beat into Uhlmann's face, but for once he let discretion rule him. This was no time to make another enemy. *He knows who I am,* the killer thought. *I'd better drift.*

A man came through the wing doors and stopped abruptly before he reached the bar. He was Cole Hawkins from the San Simon country. His eyes fastened on the fugitive.

"So you're here," he said.

Uhlmann's ugly face broke into what was meant for a friendly smile. "Have a drink on me, Cole," he invited.

"I'll buy my own drink, you damned side-winder," Hawkins replied harshly.

The huge ruffian glared at him. "You can't talk thataway to me, Cole. I won't take it."

"You'll take it, you dirty murderer. I heard what you did last night."

Uhlmann spread his huge hands in placatory explanation. "Now looky here, Cole. I had to do it. Jug lay in wait for me. He had first shot. It was him or me, one."

"Jug?" exclaimed Hawkins in surprise. "Jug too? That's a new one on me. I was talking about Fraser."

"I didn't kill Fraser. That was Jug."

"You were there with him. You were recognized."

"Some mistake, Cole. I see now why you were sore at me. No, sir. You might know I wouldn't hurt good old Stan."

"You don't have to lie to me, Rhino. Save that talk for the man outside lookin' for you."

"What man?" Uhlmann cried.

"The man whose father you killed years ago—whose friend you shot down last night."

"You talkin' about Webb? Is he here—at Nogales?"

"He's here. To put a rope round yore neck and drag you back to be hanged."

The eyes in the leathery face of the killer betrayed him. Hawkins knew that cold despair was clutching at the man's heart. Uhlmann had not expected his enemy to be here so soon.

"Where's he at now, Cole?" the hunted man asked, his voice fallen to a hoarse whisper. "You wouldn't be joshin' me, would you? You gotta have yore little joke."

"No joke. And I'll say this. If Bob Webb didn't have first claim on you I'd drag yore big carcass back myself."

"Gimmie five minutes, Cole," Uhlmann pleaded. "I'll light a shuck across the line and never come back. You 'n' me have had good times together, old man. You wouldn't throw me down now."

The man's wheedling tone stirred contempt in the other. "You've thrown yourself down, you fool," Hawkins told him bluntly. "I never did like you even when I did business with you. Had a feeling you were rotten bad. Now I know it."

Uhlmann flared to weak passion. "I'm no more a killer than you. Think I don't know you shot Chuck Holloway that night at Tucson?"

The eyes of Hawkins narrowed and grew chill. "If I did, he had it coming—as you have." He was silent a moment, watching the harried man who had come close to the end of his crooked trail. When he spoke, his voice was low and the words spaced. "It's a show-down. Pull yore freight, wolf, right damn now, or I'll do the job the hangman is waitin' to do."

The dry lips of Uhlmann opened, but no words came from them. He wanted to fling out a defiance, to drag out his forty-five and start shooting, but he could not drive his flaccid will to obey the urge. Out of his throat came a strange animal sound of distress. His dragging feet took him through the screen doors to the narrow adobe street. Up and down the street his gaze swept. A few men were in sight, a group of three not twenty feet from him, but none of them showed any interest at his appearance.

He had made a mistake in stopping on the United States side of the line, but it might not be too late yet to get across to the Mexican side of Nogales. He would keep going, deep into Sonora, where a fugitive was safe. First, he would have to buy another horse. But not until he was in the old town.

His gross body, his flatfooted slouching gait,

made him an uncouth sight. He knew this, and usually he resented the looks that followed him. But just now all his thoughts were concerned with reaching the horse he had tied in front of a dry-goods store. As he moved down the sidewalk his eyes darted from right to left and back again. He could not believe that the avenger was so close on his heels. Probably Hawkins had been lying to frighten him. None the less when he was twenty yards from his horse he broke into a shuffling run.

Abruptly he pulled up. A slim man, coffee-brown, walked out of the dry-goods store lithely as a panther. The killer's stomach muscles tightened. An icy wave drenched him. But it was now or never. Webb was looking leisurely down the street. In a moment he would turn his head and see him.

Uhlmann fired in panic haste. Before Bob had his gun out a second bullet tore through a hanging sign above his head. He was so sure of himself that he shouted an order at the frenzied man.

"Drop that gun!"

The revolver of the killer roared again.

Bob took deliberate aim at the huge body and sent a slug crashing into it. A second one struck the desperado just below the heart, not four inches from the first. The revolver dropped from Uhlmann's fingers. He spread his two hands over his great stomach, dragging it in to ease the pain, and stumbled forward half a dozen paces. One foot caught on the other, and the giant figure pitched heavily to the sidewalk and rolled from it to the dust of the street.

Bob's harsh face, the hardness of battle still stamped on it, looked down at the inert mass of flesh and bones that had a moment earlier been quick with life. A thin trickle of smoke rose from the barrel of his forty-five. He felt no emotion, no shock. This had been a possibility he had looked forward to for years, and now that it was fulfilled he had no sense of elation. It was just something unpleasant he had been forced to do. This was no longer his enemy. It was the body of a stranger who had brought about his own destruction by his folly.

A voice said heartily. "No regrets—he's better dead."

Bob looked up, and saw Cole Hawkins. "Yes," he agreed dully.

"You're in the clear. He took three shots at you before you fired. I never saw the beat of how cool you were."

"That's right," another man spoke up. "Three-four of us saw it all. Self-defense."

"I meant to take him back to be hanged," Bob explained, his tone still lifeless. "He shot my best friend last night."

"And your worst enemy," Hawkins added.

The surprised eyes of Webb questioned him without words.

"He told me back there in the Silver Dollar," the San Simon rancher continued, "that he rubbed out Jug Packard last night."

Bob stared at him in astonishment. "Are you sure that is what he meant to tell you?"

"Dead sure. He trapped himself. I called him a murderer for what he did last night. He thought I meant Packard and said Jug tried to ambush him and was killed."

The convict made no comment. This was not the way he had planned his vengeance, but he could see that it might be better for Packard to fall at other hands than his.

He drew a long breath. "I reckon if there are no objections I'll ride back to the Circle J R and see how Stan is making it."

"Nobody will stop you, Mr. Sloan," Hawkins said, stressing the name. "We'd better see the sheriff and explain how this happened."

Webb took the advice of the ranchman and gave the sheriff the name of Cape Sloan, which meant nothing to the officer. He told Bob that since the killing had been clearly self-defense no arrest would be made.

Hawkins said, "I'm going north, and if you have no objections I'll ride part way with you."

When they came to the parting of the ways, a few miles south of the Circle J R, Bob made a remark that surprised the other.

"I've been told you saved my life once."

The cattleman glanced at him quickly. "News to me," he answered.

"On the plaza back of the Tucson Hotel not long ago."

"Funny how news gets around," Hawkins commented dryly. "One man saw me fire that shot. He wasn't going to tell anybody. Now two people inside of an hour accuse me of it—you and Uhlmann."

"I'm not accusing you," Bob replied. "I'm thanking you."

"No need of that. I had an axe of my own to grind. When I saw his rifle aimed at you I let him have it. Understand, I'll deny this if anybody else puts it up to me."

Bob assured him that nobody would ever hear of this through anything he would say.

Hawkins nodded. "That's all right. I'll be saying *adios*, Mr. Webb. Good luck."

They took different trails. The one Bob followed led him to the Circle J R.

39 "While the Sands o' Life Shall Run"

Sandra walked out of the cabin with the doctor and looked an anxious question at him.

"Fraser is a tough old *hombre*," he said. "Barring unexpected bad luck he's going to make it. What he needs is good nursing more than a doctor—and I can see he's going to get it."

"I'm glad," the girl said, deeply pleased. "When his friend, Bob Webb, comes back he will be so happy."

The doctor slanted a smile at her. "I should think he might be." He had heard stories of Sandra's eager interest in Webb.

She replied, with a sigh, "I wish he hadn't felt he had to go and bring that villain back. You don't think—?"

Doctor Logan finished her uncompleted query. "I think your young man will come back sound as a dollar. He's too hard a nut for Uhlmann to crack."

Sandra's attention had strayed. A rider was coming over the hill. She watched him, in her eyes a queer look, a suspended hope. The man on horseback waved a hand at her. He put his horse to a canter, and she broke into a run. Doctor

Logan smiled again. Her young man had flung himself from the saddle and taken her into his arms.

"By golly, I was right," the doctor said aloud, and walked into the house.

Bob's first word was, "Stan?"

"Doctor Logan says he's going to be all right."

"Glory hallelujah!" he cried. "I've been worrying all day about him."

"You didn't find Uhlmann." she said.

His voice and manner changed. "Yes, I found him."

"Did—did you leave him at the ranch?"

"No." He added, gravely: "I left him at Nogales."

Back of the words she read futility. An anxious excitement set the blood pounding through her heart. "You killed him." It was a statement, not a question.

"Yes."

"Tell me."

"I came out of a store and he fired. He had the first three shots and missed. Several men saw it. The sheriff said I was free to go."

She held him close in her strong young arms. "I've been so frightened. I kept seeing you—trapped. And now he's gone. And Jug Packard too. Did you know that Uhlmann killed him near here after the fight in the arroyo?"

"I heard so."

"All your enemies are gone. We can forget the

long nightmare of the dreadful years that have passed. We'll be together—always."

He laughed, happily. " 'While the sands o' life shall run.' "

It was surprising what a change the laughter made in his harsh bony face. The years and all they had done to him were lifted from it. She thought. *I'm going to make him laugh often. I'm going to make him forget all he has been through.*

She said: "Governor Andrews will pardon you now. He's been waiting for a chance. We have plenty of evidence now. And you'll be a hero for ridding Arizona of that bad man."

He did not like that. The thought of public acclaim for what he had done disgusted him.

Yet the papers were full of the story. Editorials demanded that he be pardoned. Almost unanimously the people of the territory agreed that a great injustice had been done him. No act of the administration of Governor Andrews was more generally approved than the pardoning of Robert Webb.

One unexpected result was the attitude of the Packard heirs. The family of the mine owner had been alienated from him for years. He was the skeleton in the closet of their lives. They had lived in Tucson and had seen him only at rare intervals. Even before the pardon his son had come to Bob with an offer of restitution. He suggested turning over to Webb a majority of the Johnny B stock.

Bob wanted no part of the mine. He hoped never to see it again. But since he wished to get hold of a cattle ranch he made it clear he would accept a fair monetary compensation. Young Packard suggested he take the Sinclair ranch with all the cattle and equipment on it. This was a fine spread, recently bought by Jug for close to a hundred thousand dollars. Bob looked the place over and accepted the offer.

The young couple moved to it. On it a large family of Webbs were born and brought up. Among her noisy and turbulent brood Sandra moved happily, ruling lightly and wisely. With the passing years she retained the loveliness that had distinguished her youth. When her husband looks at her today, grey-haired, the toll the decades have taken stamped on her face, he still thinks her the paragon of women.

Center Point Large Print
600 Brooks Road / PO Box 1
Thorndike, ME 04986-0001 USA

(207) 568-3717

US & Canada:
1 800 929-9108
www.centerpointlargeprint.com